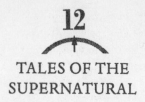

12

TALES OF THE
SUPERNATURAL

MICHAEL COX is a senior commissioning editor with Oxford
University Press. He has edited *The Oxford Book of English Ghost
Stories* (1986), *Victorian Ghost Stories* (1991) (both with R. A.
Gilbert), *Victorian Detective Stories* (1992), *The Oxford Book of
Historical Stories* (with Jack Adrian, 1994), *The Oxford Book of Spy
Stories* (1996), *The Oxford Book of Twentieth-Century Ghost Stories*
(1996), and *Twelve Victorian Ghost Stories* (1997).

D1353786

www.online-literature.com.

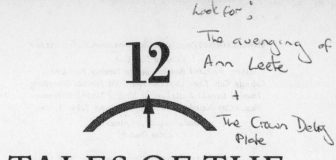

Look for;
The avenging of
Ann Leete
+
The Crown Derby
Plate

12

TALES OF THE
SUPERNATURAL

Selected and introduced by
MICHAEL COX

Oxford   New York

OXFORD UNIVERSITY PRESS

1997

Oxford University Press, Great Clarendon Street, Oxford OX2 6DP

Oxford New York
Athens Auckland Bangkok Bogota Bombay Buenos Aires
Calcutta Cape Town Dar es Salaam Delhi Florence Hong Kong
Istanbul Karachi Kuala Lumpur Madras Madrid Melbourne
Mexico City Nairobi Paris Singapore Taipei Tokyo Toronto
and associated companies in
Berlin Ibadan

Oxford is a trade mark of Oxford University Press

Introduction and selection ©
Michael Cox 1997

First published as an Oxford University Press paperback 1997

British Library Cataloguing in Publication Data
Data available

Library of Congress Cataloging in Publication Data
Data available

ISBN 0–19–288027–6

1 3 5 7 9 10 8 6 4 2

Typeset by Jayvee, Trivandrum, India
Printed in Great Britain by
Caledonian International Book Manufacturing Ltd.
Glasgow

CONTENTS

Contents

INTRODUCTION

One of the most intriguing questions one can ask about supernatural fiction is also the most obvious: why do people read it? Those for whom this type of fiction holds no appeal might argue that a taste for fiction based on the frankly impossible is an immature one; for isn't it more profitable, more adult, to read novels or stories that reflect life as it is, rather than as it can never be? Tales of the supernatural, however, have demonstrated by their resilience, as well as by their attraction to writers of all persuasions, that there lies at their very heart something irreducibly compelling, something that speaks unwaveringly to readers in every generation, even in the final years of the twentieth century. As Dr Johnson observed, when it comes to the existence of ghosts, 'All argument is against it, but all belief is for it'.

Ghost stories, for instance, being probably the dominant category amongst the various types of imaginative literature we call supernatural fiction, are constantly being reinvented, and yet they remain anchored to immemorial beliefs. We know, of course, like Dr Johnson, that the dead cannot return; but we may often feel the temptation to believe otherwise. Our ancestors were clearer on this point. For them, knowledge and belief were intertwined. Medieval authors, on what they often felt to be unimpeachable authority, told stories not only of corpses animated by the devil, but also of the undead—revenants—who displayed an interest in the living for their own, usually malevolent, purposes. Several anecdotes in Walter Map's *De Nugis Curialium* (twelfth century), for instance, tell of predatory corpses preying on the living. But though such things were widely accepted as fact, there was a great deal less certainty about why they happened. Theology could offer no comforting explanation as to the mechanisms of these outrages, typified by the following story dating from about 1400 and translated, appropriately, by the scholar and ghost-story writer M. R. James:

Concerning the spirit of Robert, the son of Robert de Boltebo of Killebourne, who was caught in the cemetery. The younger Robert died and was buried in the cemetery, but he used to go out from his grave at night and terrify and disturb the townspeople, and the dogs of the town used to follow him and howl mightily. . . . Finally, some young men decided to catch him somehow if they could, and they met at the cemetery. But when he appeared, they all fled except two, one of whom was named Robert Foxton. He seized him as he was going out from the cemetery and put him on the church-stile, while the other shouted bravely, 'Hold him fast until I can get there!' But the other one answered, 'Go quickly to the parish priest so that he can be conjured!' . . . The parish priest came quickly and conjured him in the name of the Holy Trinity, . . . Having been conjured in this way, he answered from the depths of his entrails; not with his tongue but as if from an empty jar, and he confessed various trespasses.

What is important here, in relation to supernatural fiction in general and to ghost stories in particular, is the juxtaposition of corroborative detail—both circumstantial ('one of whom was named Robert Foxton') and physical ('He seized him . . .')—with an event that is outside the natural order of things. The supernatural appears, at the moment of crisis, to be entangled with the natural; the tangible is intermixed with the intangible in a way that is utterly inexplicable. The palpability of the revenant is also striking: this is no incorporeal spirit, but a hideously transformed human body. But why will this corpse not lie still? Why is the settled order of nature being violated in this way? By what agency do the dead continue to walk the earth?

The medieval chroniclers had no answers to such questions. Their sense of bafflement is, I think, exactly the response that the best writers of supernatural stories have sought to create in their fictions. A story that is completely worked out, with neat successions of cause and effect, rarely succeeds in unsettling us. It is true that the revenants of fiction often act according to a deadly and terrible logic; but it is *their* logic, not ours. The most disturbing tales of the supernatural are those in which our human reason is disabled by the unknowable otherness of such aberrations. Only questions remain. ' "But why did you come?" ' asks the bewildered Silbermeister at the end of Perceval Landon's 'Railhead', included in this collection. ' "Why did you come?" His eyes turned in his head: "I sent no message"; and then he fell on the floor in a dead faint.'

Part of the appeal of supernatural fiction, therefore, is that it arouses those primitive fears and apprehensions that we fondly thought had been bred out of us by civilization and the march of reason. But they are there still, lurking silently in the shadows of our bright, materialistic civilization; and in supernatural fiction we find ourselves once more in a world we can neither know nor, because knowledge is power, control. Yet knowing that what we are reading is fiction, not a transcript of reality, makes the experience of fear a vicarious one. Being afraid is not pleasurable; but being afraid knowing that we are in no kind of danger certainly can generate what M. R. James called 'pleasure of a certain sort'.

The stories in this collection all, to some degree or other, provide such pleasure, and taken together form a pretty representative sample of what supernatural fiction, as a literary genre, has to offer readers. In the first place, they are all complete, self-contained narratives, rather than extracts from longer works, emphasizing that the short story has been supernatural fiction's dominant mode since the late eighteenth century. They also show the ways in which writers have used everyday settings and situations to heighten the impact of the supernatural violation when it comes—another primary characteristic of the genre. Above all, they show us ordinary men and women confronted by mysteries that are beyond both nature and reason. Ever since supernatural fiction began to mature into a distinct literary genre in the early nineteenth century, Western culture has prided itself on its power to explain what to past ages had been unknowable. But, as these twelve stories suggest, it is salutary from time to time to remind ourselves that all knowledge is relative; that there will always be ultimate mysteries that impose a limit on human abilities; that the fabric of our lives is but a thin and fragile bridge across an abyss, out of which, at any moment, can come the thing we fear most.

Michael Cox
October 1996

1

J. S. LE FANU

Wicked Captain Walshawe, of Wauling

I

PEG O'NEILL PAYS THE CAPTAIN'S DEBTS

A very odd thing happened to my uncle, Mr Watson, of Haddlestone; and to enable you to understand it, I must begin at the beginning.

In the year 1822, Mr James Walshawe, more commonly known as Captain Walshawe, died at the age of eighty-one years. The Captain in his early days, and so long as health and strength permitted, was a scamp of the active, intriguing sort; and spent his days and nights in sowing his wild oats, of which he seemed to have an inexhaustible stock. The harvest of this tillage was plentifully interspersed with thorns, nettles, and thistles, which stung the husbandman unpleasantly, and did not enrich him.

Captain Walshawe was very well known in the neighbourhood of Wauling, and very generally avoided there. A 'captain' by courtesy, for he had never reached that rank in the army list. He had quitted the service in 1766, at the age of twenty-five; immediately previous to which period his debts had grown so troublesome, that he was induced to extricate himself by running away with and marrying an heiress.

Though not so wealthy quite as he had imagined, she proved a very comfortable investment for what remained of his shattered affections; and he lived and enjoyed himself very much in his old way, upon her income, getting into no end of scrapes and scandals, and a good deal of debt and money trouble.

When he married his wife, he was quartered in Ireland, at Clonmel, where was a nunnery, in which, as pensioner, resided Miss O'Neill, or as she was called in the country, Peg O'Neill—the heiress of whom I have spoken.

Her situation was the only ingredient of romance in the affair, for the young lady was decidedly plain, though good-humoured looking, with that style of features which is termed *potato*; and in figure she was a little too plump, and rather short. But she was impressible; and the handsome young English Lieutenant was too much for her monastic tendencies, and she eloped.

In England there are traditions of Irish fortune-hunters, and in Ireland of English. The fact is, it was the vagrant class of each country that chiefly visited the other in old times; and a handsome vagabond, whether at home or abroad, I suppose, made the most of his face, which was also his fortune.

At all events, he carried off the fair one from the sanctuary; and for some sufficient reason, I suppose, they took up their abode at Wauling, in Lancashire.

Here the gallant captain amused himself after his fashion, sometimes running up, of course on business, to London. I believe few wives have ever cried more in a given time than did that poor, dumpy, potato-faced heiress, who got over the nunnery garden wall, and jumped into the handsome Captain's arms, for love.

He spent her income, frightened her out of her wits with oaths and threats, and broke her heart.

Latterly she shut herself up pretty nearly altogether in her room. She had an old, rather grim, Irish servant-woman in attendance upon her. This domestic was tall, lean, and religious, and the Captain knew instinctively she hated him; and he hated her in return, and often threatened to put her out of the house, and sometimes even to kick her out of the window. And whenever a wet day confined him to the house, or the stable, and he grew tired of smoking, he would begin to swear and curse at her for a *diddled* old mischief-maker, that could never be easy, and was always troubling the house with her cursed stories, and so forth.

But years passed away, and old Molly Doyle remained still in her original position. Perhaps he thought that there must be somebody there, and that he was not, after all, very likely to change for the better.

II
THE BLESSED CANDLE

He tolerated another intrusion, too, and thought himself a paragon of patience and easy good-nature for so doing. A Roman Catholic clergyman, in a long black frock, with a low standing collar, and a little white muslin fillet round his neck—tall, sallow, with blue chin, and dark steady eyes—used to glide up and down the stairs, and through the passages; and the Captain sometimes met him in one place and sometimes in another. But by a caprice incident to such tempers he treated this cleric exceptionally, and even with a surly sort of courtesy, though he grumbled about his visits behind his back.

I do not know that he had a great deal of moral courage, and the ecclesiastic looked severe and self-possessed; and somehow he thought he had no good opinion of him, and if a natural occasion were offered, might say extremely unpleasant things, and hard to be answered.

Well the time came at last, when poor Peg O'Neill—in an evil hour Mrs James Walshawe—must cry, and quake, and pray her last. The doctor came from Penlynden, and was just as vague as usual, but more gloomy, and for about a week came and went oftener. The cleric in the long black frock was also daily there. And at last came that last sacrament in the gates of death, when the sinner is traversing those dread steps that never can be retraced; when the face is turned for ever from life, and we see a receding shape, and hear a voice already irrevocably in the land of spirits.

So the poor lady died; and some people said the Captain 'felt it very much'. I don't think he did. But he was not very well just then, and looked the part of mourner and penitent to admiration—being seedy and sick. He drank a great deal of brandy and water that night, and called in Farmer Dobbs, for want of better company, to drink with him; and told him all his grievances, and how happy he and 'the poor lady up-stairs' might have been, had it not been for liars, and pick-thanks, and tale-bearers, and the like, who came between them—meaning Molly Doyle—whom, as he waxed eloquent over his liquor, he came at last to curse and rail at by name, with more than his accustomed freedom. And he described his own natural character and amiability in such moving terms, that he wept maudlin tears of sensibility over his theme; and when Dobbs was gone, drank some more grog, and took to railing and cursing again by himself; and then mounted the stairs unsteadily, to see 'what the devil Doyle and the other —— old witches were about in poor Peg's room'.

When he pushed open the door, he found some half-dozen crones, chiefly Irish, from the neighbouring town of Hackleton, sitting over tea and snuff, etc., with candles lighted round the corpse, which was arrayed in a strangely cut robe of brown serge. She had secretly belonged to some order—I think the Carmelite, but I am not certain—and wore the habit in her coffin.

'What the d—— are you doing with my wife?' cried the Captain, rather thickly. 'How dare you dress her up in this —— trumpery, you—you cheating old witch; and what's that candle doing in her hand?'

I think he was a little startled, for the spectacle was grisly enough. The dead lady was arrayed in this strange brown robe, and in her rigid fingers, as in a socket, with the large wooden beads and cross wound round it, burned a wax candle, shedding its white light over the sharp features of the corpse. Moll Doyle was not to be put down by the Captain, whom she hated, and accordingly, in her phrase, 'he got as good as he gave'. And the Captain's wrath waxed fiercer, and he chucked the wax taper from the dead hand, and was on the point of flinging it at the old serving-woman's head.

'The holy candle, you sinner!' cried she.

'I've a mind to make you eat it, you beast,' cried the Captain.

But I think he had not known before what it was, for he subsided a little sulkily, and he stuffed his hand with the candle (quite extinct by this time) into his pocket, and said he—

'You know devilish well you had no business going on with y-y-your d—— *witch*-craft about my poor wife, without my leave—you do— and you'll please to take off that d—— brown pinafore, and get her decently into her coffin, and I'll pitch your devil's waxlight into the sink.'

And the Captain stalked out of the room.

'An' now her poor sowl's in prison, you wretch, be the mains

4

o' ye; an' may yer own be shut into the wick o' that same candle, till it's burned out, ye savage.'

'I'd have you ducked for a witch, for two-pence,' roared the Captain up the staircase, with his hand on the banisters, standing on the lobby. But the door of the chamber of death clapped angrily, and he ·went down to the parlour, where he examined the holy candle for a while, with a tipsy gravity, and then with something of that reverential feeling for the symbolic, which is not uncommon in rakes and scamps, he thoughtfully locked it up in a press, where were accumulated all sorts of obsolete rubbish—soiled packs of cards, disused tobacco-pipes, broken powder-flasks, his military sword, and a dusky bundle of the 'Flash Songster', and other questionable literature.

He did not trouble the dead lady's room any more. Being a volatile man it is probable that more cheerful plans and occupations began to entertain his fancy.

III

MY UNCLE WATSON VISITS WAULING

So the poor lady was buried decently, and Captain Walshawe reigned alone for many years at Wauling. He was too shrewd and too experienced by this time to run violently down the steep hill that leads to ruin. So there was a method in his madness; and after a widowed career of more than forty years, he, too, died at last with some guineas in his purse.

Forty years and upwards is a great *edax rerum*, and a wonderful chemical power. It acted forcibly upon the gay Captain Walshawe. Gout supervened, and was no more conducive to temper than to enjoyment, and made his elegant hands lumpy at all the small joints, and turned them slowly into crippled claws. He grew stout when his exercise was interfered with, and ultimately almost corpulent. He suffered from what Mr Holloway calls 'bad legs', and was wheeled about in a great leathern-backed chair, and his infirmities went on accumulating with his years.

I am sorry to say, I never heard that he repented, or turned his thoughts seriously to the future. On the contrary, his talk grew fouler, and his fun ran upon his favourite sins, and his temper waxed more truculent. But he did not sink into dotage. Considering his bodily infirmities, his energies and his malignities, which were many and active, were marvellously little abated by time. So he went on to the close. When his temper was stirred, he cursed and swore in a way that made decent people tremble. It was a word and a blow with him; the latter, luckily, not very sure now. But he would seize his crutch and make a swoop or a pound at the offender, or shy his medicine-bottle, or his tumbler, at his head.

It was a peculiarity of Captain Walshawe, that he, by this time, hated nearly everybody. My Uncle, Mr Watson, of Haddlestone, was cousin to the Captain, and his heir-at-law. But my Uncle had lent him money on mortgage of his estates, and there had been a treaty to sell, and terms and a price were agreed upon, in 'articles' which the lawyers said were still in force.

I think the ill-conditioned Captain bore him a grudge for being richer than he, and would have liked to do him an ill turn. But it did not lie in his way; at least while he was living.

My Uncle Watson was a Methodist, and what they call a 'class-leader'; and, on the whole, a very good man. He was now near fifty—grave, as beseemed his profession—somewhat dry—and a little severe, perhaps—but a just man.

A letter from the Penlynden doctor reached him at Haddlestone, announcing the death of the wicked old Captain; and suggesting his attendance at the funeral, and the expediency of his being on the spot to look after things at Wauling. The reasonableness of this striking my good Uncle, he made his journey to the old house in Lancashire incontinently, and reached it in time for the funeral.

My Uncle, whose traditions of the Captain were derived from his mother, who remembered him in his slim, handsome youth—in shorts, cocked-hat and lace, was amazed at the bulk of the coffin which contained his mortal remains; but the lid being already screwed down, he did not see the face of the bloated old sinner.

IV
IN THE PARLOUR

What I relate, I had from the lips of my uncle, who was a truthful man, and not prone to fancies.

The day turning out awfully rainy and tempestuous, he persuaded the doctor and the attorney to remain for the night at Wauling.

There was no will—the attorney was sure of that; for the Captain's enmities were perpetually shifting, and he could never quite make up his mind, as to how best to give effect to a malignity whose direction was being constantly modified. He had had instructions for drawing a will a dozen times over. But the process had always been arrested by the intending testator.

Search being made, no will was found. The papers, indeed were all right, with one important exception: the leases were nowhere to be seen. There were special circumstances connected with several of the principal tenancies on the estate—unnecessary here to detail—which rendered the loss of these documents one of very serious moment, and even of very obvious danger.

My uncle, therefore, searched strenuously. The attorney was at his elbow, and the doctor helped with a suggestion now and then. The old serving-man seemed an honest deaf creature, and really knew nothing.

My Uncle Watson was very much perturbed. He fancied—but this possibly was only fancy—that he had detected for a moment a queer look in the attorney's face; and from that instant it became fixed in his mind that he knew all about the leases. Mr Watson expounded that evening in the parlour to the doctor, the attorney, and the deaf servant. Ananias and Sapphira figured in the foreground; and the awful nature of fraud and theft, or tampering in anywise with the plain rule of honesty in matters pertaining to estates, etc., were point-edly dwelt upon; and then came a long and strenuous prayer, in which he entreated with fervour and aplomb that the hard heart of the sinner who had abstracted the leases might be softened or broken in such a way as to lead to their restitution; or that, if he continued reserved and contumacious, it might at least be the will of Heaven to bring him to public justice and the documents to light. The fact is, that he was praying all this time at the attorney.

When these religious exercises were over, the visitors retired to their rooms, and my Uncle Watson wrote two or three pressing letters by the fire. When his task was done, it had grown late; the candles were flaring in their sockets, and all in bed, and, I suppose, asleep, but he.

The fire was nearly out, he chilly, and the flame of the candles throbbing strangely in their sockets shed alternate glare and shadow round the old wainscoted room and its quaint furniture. Outside were the wild thunder and piping of the storm; and the rattling of distant windows sounded through the passages, and down the stairs, like angry people astir in the house.

My Uncle Watson belonged to a sect who by no means reject the supernatural, and whose founder, on the contrary, has sanctioned ghosts in the most emphatic way. He was glad therefore to remember, that in prosecuting his search that day, he had seen some six inches of wax candle in the press in the parlour; for he had no fancy to be over-taken by darkness in his present situation. He had no time to lose; and taking the bunch of keys—of which he was now master—he soon fit-ted the lock, and secured the candle—a treasure in his circumstances; and lighting it, he stuffed it into the socket of one of the expiring can-dles, and extinguishing the other, he looked round the room in the steady light reassured. At the same moment, an unusually violent gust of the storm blew a handful of gravel against the parlour window, with a sharp rattle that startled him in the midst of the roar and hub-bub; and the flame of the candle itself was agitated by the air.

V
THE BED-CHAMBER

My Uncle walked up to bed, guarding his candle with his hand, for the lobby windows were rattling furiously, and he disliked the idea of being left in the dark more than ever.

His bedroom was comfortable, though old-fashioned. He shut and bolted the door. There was a tall looking-glass opposite the foot of his four-poster, on the dressing-table between the windows. He tried to make the curtains meet, but they would not draw; and like many a gentleman in a like perplexity, he did not possess a pin, nor was there one in the huge pincushion beneath the glass.

He turned the face of the mirror away therefore, so that its back was presented to the bed, pulled the curtains together, and placed a chair against them, to prevent their falling open again. There was a good fire, and a reinforcement of round coal and wood inside the fender. So he piled it up to ensure a cheerful blaze through the night, and placing a little black mahogany table, with the legs of a Satyr, beside the bed, and his candle upon it, he got between the sheets, and laid his red night-capped head upon his pillow, and disposed himself to sleep.

The first thing that made him uncomfortable was a sound at the foot of his bed, quite distinct in a momentary lull of the storm. It was only the gentle rustle and rush of the curtains, which fell open again; and as his eyes opened, he saw them resuming their perpendicular dependence, and sat up in his bed almost expecting to see something uncanny in the aperture.

There was nothing, however, but the dressing-table, and other dark furniture, and the window-curtains faintly undulating in the violence of the storm. He did not care to get up, therefore—the fire being bright and cheery—to replace the curtains by a chair, in the position in which he had left them, anticipating possibly a new recurrence of the relapse which had startled him from his incipient doze.

So he got to sleep in a little while again, but he was disturbed by a sound, as he fancied, at the table on which stood the candle. He could not say what it was, only that he wakened with a start, and lying so in some amaze, he did distinctly hear a sound which startled him a good deal, though there was nothing necessarily supernatural in it. He described it as resembling what would occur if you fancied a thinnish table-leaf, with a convex warp in it, depressed the reverse way, and suddenly with a spring recovering its natural convexity. It was a loud, sudden thump, which made the heavy candlestick jump, and there was an end, except that my uncle did not get again into a doze for ten minutes at least.

The next time he awoke, it was in that odd, serene way that sometimes occurs. We open our eyes, we know not why, quite placidly, and are on the instant wide awake. He had had a nap of some duration this time, for his candle-flame was fluttering and flaring, *in articulo*, in the silver socket. But the fire was still bright and cheery; so he popped the extinguisher on the socket, and almost at the same time there came a tap at his door, and a sort of crescendo 'hush-sh-sh!' Once more my Uncle was sitting up, sacred and perturbed, in his bed. He recollected, however, that he had bolted his door; and such inveterate materialists are we in the midst of our spiritualism, that this reassured him, and he breathed a deep sigh, and began to grow tranquil. But after a rest of a minute or two, there came a louder and sharper knock at his door; so that instinctively he called out, 'Who's there?' in a loud, stern key. There was no sort of response, however. The nervous effect of the start subsided; and I think my Uncle must have remembered how constantly, especially on a stormy night, these creaks or cracks which simulate all manner of goblin noises, make themselves naturally audible.

VI
THE EXTINGUISHER IS LIFTED

After a while, then, he lay down with his back turned toward that side of the bed at which was the door, and his face toward the table on which stood the massive old candlestick, capped with its extinguisher, and in that position he closed his eyes. But sleep would not revisit them. All kinds of queer fancies began to trouble him—some of them I remember.

He felt the point of a finger, he averred, pressed most distinctly on the tip of his great toe, as if a living hand were between his sheets, and making a sort of signal of attention or silence. Then again he felt something as large as a rat make a sudden bounce in the middle of his bolster, just under his head. Then a voice said 'Oh!' very gently, close at the back of his head. All these things he felt certain of, and yet investigation led to nothing. He felt odd little cramps stealing now and then about him; and then, on a sudden, the middle finger of his right hand was plucked backwards, with a light playful jerk that frightened him awfully.

Meanwhile the storm kept singing, and howling, and ha-ha-hooing hoarsely among the limbs of the old trees and the chimney-pots; and my Uncle Watson, although he prayed and meditated as was his wont when he lay awake, felt his heart throb excitedly, and sometimes thought he was beset with evil spirits, and at others that he was in the early stage of a fever.

He resolutely kept his eyes closed, however, and, like St Paul's shipwrecked companions, wished for the day. At last another little doze seems to have stolen upon his senses, for he awoke quietly and completely as before—opening his eyes all at once, and seeing everything as if he had not slept for a moment.

The fire was still blazing redly—nothing uncertain in the light—the massive silver candlestick, topped with its tall extinguisher, stood on the centre of the black mahogany table as before; and, looking by what seemed a sort of accident to the apex of this, he beheld something which made him quite misdoubt the evidence of his eyes.

He saw the extinguisher lifted by a tiny hand, from beneath, and a small human face, no bigger than a thumbnail, with nicely proportioned features peep from beneath it. In this Lilliputian countenance was such a ghastly consternation as horrified my Uncle unspeakably. Out came a little foot then and there, and a pair of wee legs, in short silk stockings and buckled shoes, then the rest of the figure; and, with the arms holding about the socket, the little legs stretched and stretched, hanging about the stem of the candlestick till the feet reached the base, and so down the Satyr-like leg of the table, till they reached the floor, extending elastically, and strangely enlarging in all proportions as they approached the ground, where the feet and buckles were those of a well-shaped, full grown man, and the figure tapering upward until it dwindled to its original fairy dimensions at the top, like an object seen in some strangely curved mirror.

Standing upon the floor he expanded, my amazed Uncle could not tell how, into his proper proportions; and stood pretty nearly in profile at the bedside, a handsome and elegantly shaped young man, in a bygone military costume, with a small laced, three-cocked hat and plume on his head, but looking like a man going to be hanged—in unspeakable despair.

He stepped lightly to the hearth, and turned for a few seconds very dejectedly with his back toward the bed and the mantelpiece, and he saw the hilt of his rapier glittering in the firelight; and then walking across the room he placed himself at the dressing-table, visible through the divided curtains at the foot of the bed. The fire was blazing still so brightly that my uncle saw him as distinctly as if half a dozen candles were burning.

VII
THE VISITATION CULMINATES

The looking-glass was an old-fashioned piece of furniture, and had a drawer beneath it. My Uncle had searched it carefully for the papers in the daytime; but the silent figure pulled the drawer quite out, pressed a spring at the side, disclosing a false receptacle behind it, and from this he drew a parcel of papers tied together with pink tape.

All this time my Uncle was staring at him in a horrified state, neither winking nor breathing, and the apparition had not once given the smallest intimation of consciousness that a living person was in the same room. But now, for the first time, it turned its livid stare full upon my Uncle with a hateful smile of significance, lifting up the little parcel of papers between his slender finger and thumb. Then he made a long, cunning wink at him, and seemed to blow out one of his cheeks in a burlesque grimace, which, but for the horrific circumstances, would have been ludicrous. My Uncle could not tell whether this was really an intentional distortion or only one of those horrid ripples and deflections which were constantly disturbing the proportions of the figure, as if it were seen through some unequal and perverting medium.

The figure now approached the bed, seeming to grow exhausted and malignant as it did so. My Uncle's terror nearly culminated at this point, for he believed it was drawing near him with an evil purpose. But it was not so; for the soldier, over whom twenty years seemed to have passed in his brief transit to the dressing-table and back again, threw himself into a great high-backed armchair of stuffed leather at the far side of the fire, and placed his heels on the fender. His feet and legs seemed indistinctly to swell, and swathings showed themselves round them, and they grew into something enormous, and the upper figure swayed and shaped itself into corresponding proportions, a great mass of corpulence, with a cadaverous and malignant face, and the furrows of a great old age, and colourless glassy eyes; and with these changes, which came indefinitely but rapidly as those of a sunset cloud, the fine regimentals faded away, and a loose, grey, woollen drapery, somehow, was there in its stead; and all seemed to be stained and rotten, for swarms of worms seemed creeping in and out, while the figure grew paler and paler, till my Uncle, who liked his pipe, and employed the simile naturally, said the whole effigy grew to the colour of tobacco ashes, and the clusters of worms into little wriggling knots of sparks such as we see running over the residuum of a burnt sheet of paper. And so with the strong draught caused by the fire, and the current of air from the window, which was rattling in the storm, the feet seemed to be drawn into the fireplace, and the whole figure, light as ashes, floated away with them, and disappeared with a whisk up the capacious old chimney.

It seemed to my Uncle that the fire suddenly darkened and the air grew icy cold, and there came an awful roar and riot of tempest, which shook the old house from top to base, and sounded like the yelling of a bloodthirsty mob on receiving a new and long-expected victim.

Good Uncle Watson used to say, 'I have been in many situations of fear and danger in the course of my life, but never did I pray with so much agony before or since; for then, as now, it was clear beyond a cavil that I had actually beheld the phantom of an evil spirit.'

CONCLUSION

Now there are two curious circumstances to be observed in this relation of my Uncle's, who was, as I have said, a perfectly veracious man.

First—The wax candle which he took from the press in the parlour and burnt at his bedside on that horrible night was unquestionably, according to the testimony of the old deaf servant, who had been fifty years at Wauling, that identical piece of 'holy candle' which had stood in the fingers of the poor lady's corpse, and concerning which the old Irish crone, long since dead, had delivered the curious curse I have mentioned against the Captain.

Secondly—Behind the drawer under the looking-glass, he did actually discover a second but secret drawer, in which were concealed the identical papers which he had suspected the attorney of having made away with. There were circumstances, too, afterwards disclosed which convinced my Uncle that the old man had deposited them there preparatory to burning them, which he had nearly made up his mind to do.

Now, a very remarkable ingredient in this tale of my Uncle Watson was this, that so far as my father, who had never seen Captain Walshawe in the course of his life, could gather, the phantom had exhibited a horrible and grotesque, but unmistakable resemblance to that defunct scamp in the various stages of his long life.

Wauling was sold in the year 1837, and the old house shortly after pulled down, and a new one built nearer to the river. I often wonder whether it was rumoured to be haunted, and, if so, what stories were current about it. It was a commodious and stanch old house, and withal rather handsome; and its demolition was certainly suspicious.

2

MRS J. H. RIDDELL

A Terrible Vengeance

I
VERY STRANGE

Round Dockett Point and over Dumsey Deep the water-lilies were blooming as luxuriantly as though the silver Thames had been the blue Mummel Lake.

It was the time for them. The hawthorn had long ceased to scent the air; the wild roses had shed their delicate leaves; the buttercups and cardamoms and dog-daisies that had dotted the meadows were garnered into hay. The world in early August needed a fresh and special beauty, and here it was floating in its matchless green bark on the bosom of the waters.

If those fair flowers, like their German sisters, ever at nightfall assumed mortal form, who was there to tell of such vagaries? Even when the moon is at her full there are few who care to cross Chertsey Mead, or face the lonely Stabbery.

Hard would it be, indeed, so near life, railways, civilization, and London, to find a more lonely stretch of country, when twilight visits the landscape and darkness comes brooding down over the Surrey and Middlesex shores, than the path which winds along the river from Shepperton Lock to Chertsey Bridge. At high noon for months together it is desolate beyond description—silent, save for the rippling and sobbing of the currents, the wash of the stream, the swaying of the osiers, the trembling of an aspen, the rustle of the withies, or the noise made by a bird, or rat, or stoat, startled by the sound of unwonted footsteps. In the warm summer nights also, when tired holiday-makers are sleeping soundly, when men stretched on the green sward outside their white tents are smoking, and talking, and planning

15

excursions for the morrow; when in country houses young people are playing and singing, dancing or walking up and down terraces over-looking well-kept lawns, where the evening air is laden with delicious perfumes—there falls on that almost uninhabited mile or two of river-side a stillness which may be felt, which the belated traveller is loth to disturb even by the dip of his oars as he drifts down with the current past objects that seem to him unreal as fragments of a dream.

It had been a wet summer—a bad summer for the hotels. There had been some fine days, but not many together. The weather could not be depended upon. It was not a season in which young ladies were to be met about the reaches of the Upper Thames, disporting themselves in marvellous dresses, and more marvellous headgear, unfurling brilliant parasols, canoeing in appropriate attire, giving life and colour to the streets of old-world villages, and causing many of their inhabitants to consider what a very strange sort of town it must be in which such extraordinarily robed persons habitually reside.

Nothing of the sort was to be seen that summer, even as high as Hampton. Excursions were limited to one day; there were few tents, few people camping-out, not many staying at the hotels; yet it was, perhaps for that reason, an enjoyable summer to those who were not afraid of a little, or rather a great deal, of rain, who liked a village inn all the better for not being crowded, and who were not heartbroken because their womenfolk for once found it impossible to accompany them.

Unless a man boldly decides to outrage the proprieties and decen-cies of life, and go off by himself to take his pleasure selfishly alone, there is in a fine summer no door of escape open to him. There was a time—a happy time—when a husband was not expected to sign away his holidays in the marriage articles. But what boots it to talk of that remote past now? Everything is against the father of a family at pre-sent. Unless the weather help him, what friend has he? and the weather does not often in these latter days prove a friend.

In that summer, however, with which this story deals, the stars in their courses fought for many an oppressed paterfamilias. Any curi-ous enquirer might then have walked ankle-deep in mud from Penton Hook to East Molesey, and not met a man, harnessed like a beast of burden, towing all his belongings upstream, or beheld him rowing against wind and tide as though he were a galley-slave chained to the oar, striving all the while to look as though enjoying the fun.

Materfamilias found it too wet to patronize the Thames. Her dear little children also were conspicuous by their absence. Charming young ladies were rarely to be seen—indeed, the skies were so treacherous that it would have been a mere tempting of Providence to risk a pretty dress on the water; for which sufficient reasons furnished houses remained unlet, and lodgings were left empty; taverns and hotels welcomed visitors instead of treating them scurvily; and the river, with its green banks and its leafy aits, its white swans, its water-lilies, its purple loosestrife, its reeds, its rushes, its weeping willows, its quiet backwaters, was delightful.

One evening two men stood just outside the door of the Ship, Lower Halliford, looking idly at the water, as it flowed by more rapidly than is usually the case in August. Both were dressed in suits of serviceable dark grey tweed; both wore round hats; both evidently belonged to that class which resembles the flowers of the field but in the one respect that it toils not, neither does it spin; both looked intensely bored; both were of rather a good appearance.

The elder, who was about thirty, had dark hair, sleepy brown eyes, and a straight capable nose; a heavy moustache almost concealed his mouth, but his chin was firm and well cut. About him there was an indescribable something calculated to excite attention, but nothing in his expression to attract or repel. No one looking at him could have said offhand, 'I think that is a pleasant fellow,' or 'I am sure that man could make himself confoundedly disagreeable.'

His face revealed as little as the covers of a book. It might contain interesting matter, or there might be nothing underneath save the merest commonplace. So far as it conveyed an idea at all, it was that of indolence. Every movement of his body suggested laziness; but it would have been extremely hard to say how far that laziness went. Mental energy and physical inactivity walk oftener hand in hand than the world suspects, and mental energy can on occasion make an indolent man active, while mere brute strength can never confer intellect on one who lacks brains.

In every respect the younger stranger was the opposite of his companion. Fair, blue-eyed, light-haired, with soft moustache and tenderly cared-for whiskers, he looked exactly what he was—a very shallow, kindly, good fellow, who did not trouble himself with searching into the depths of things, who took the world as it was, who did not go out to meet trouble, who loved his species, women included, in an honest way; who liked amusement, athletic sports of all sorts—dancing, riding, rowing, shooting; who had not one regret, save that hours in a Government office were so confoundedly long, 'eating the best part out of a day, by Jove'; no cause for discontent, save that he had very little money, and into whose mind it had on the afternoon in question been forcibly borne that his friend was a trifle heavy—'carries too many guns,' he considered—'and not exactly the man to enjoy a modest dinner at Lower Halliford'.

For which cause, perhaps, he felt rather relieved when his friend refused to partake of any meal.

'I wish you could have stayed,' said the younger, with that earnest and not quite insincere hospitality people always assume when they feel a departing guest is not to be overpersuaded to stay.

'So do I,' replied the other. 'I should have liked to stop with *you*, and I should have liked to stay here. There is a sleepy dullness about the place which exactly suits my present mood, but I must get back to town. I promised Travers to look in at his chambers this evening, and tomorrow as I told you, I am due in Norfolk.'

'What will you do, then, till train-time? There is nothing up from here till nearly seven. Come on the river for an hour with me.'

'Thank you, no. I think I will walk over to Staines.'

'Staines! Why Staines in heaven's name?'

'Because I am in the humour for a walk—a long, lonely walk; because a demon has taken possession of me I wish to exorcize; because there are plenty of trains from Staines; because I am weary of the Thames Valley line, and any other reason you like. I can give you none better than I have done.'

'At least let me row you part of the way.'

'Again thank you, no. The eccentricities of the Thames are not new to me. With the best intentions, you would land me at Laleham when I should be on my (rail) way to London. My dear Dick, step into that boat your soul has been hankering after for the past half-hour, and leave me to return to town according to my own fancy.'

'I don't half like this,' said genial Dick. 'Ah! here comes a pretty girl—look.'

Thus entreated, the elder man turned his head and saw a young girl, accompanied by a young man, coming along the road, which leads from Walton Lane to Shepperton.

She was very pretty, of the sparkling order of beauty, with dark eyes, rather heavy eyebrows, dark thick hair, a ravishing fringe, a delicious hat, a coquettish dress, and shoes which by pretty gestures she seemed to be explaining to her companion were many—very many—sizes too large for her. Spite of her beauty, spite of her dress, spite of her shoes so much too large for her, it needed but a glance from one conversant with subtle social distinctions to tell that she was not quite her 'young man's' equal.

For, in the parlance of Betsy Jane, as her 'young man' she evidently regarded him, and as her young man he regarded himself. There could be no doubt about the matter. He was over head and ears in love with her; he was ready to quarrel—indeed, had quarrelled with father, mother, sister, brother on her account. He loved her unreasonably—he loved her miserably, distractedly; except at odd intervals, he was not in the least happy with her. She flouted, she tormented, she maddened him; but then, after having nearly driven him to the verge of distraction, she would repent sweetly, and make up for all previous shortcomings by a few brief minutes of tender affection. If quarrelling be really the renewal of love, theirs had been renewed once a day at all events, and frequently much oftener.

Yes, she was a pretty girl, a bewitching girl, and arrant flirt, a scarcely well-behaved coquette; for as she passed the two friends she threw a glance at them, one arch, piquant, inviting glance, of which many would instantly have availed themselves, venturing the consequences certain to be dealt out by her companion, who, catching the look, drew closer to her side, not too well pleased, apparently. Spite of a little opposition, he drew her hand through his arm, and walked on with an air of possession infinitely amusing to onlookers, and plainly distasteful to his lady-love.

'A clear case of spoons,' remarked the younger of the two visitors, looking after the pair.

'Poor devil!' said the other compassionately.

His friend laughed, and observed mockingly paraphrasing a very different speech,—

'But for the grace of God, there goes Paul Murray.'

'You may strike out the "but"', replied the person so addressed, 'for that is the very road Paul Murray is going, and soon.'

'You are not serious!' asked the other doubtfully.

'Am I not? I am though, though not with such a vixen as I dare swear that little baggage is. I told you I was due tomorrow in Norfolk. But see, they are turning back; let us go inside.'

'All right,' agreed the other, following his companion into the hall. 'This is a great surprise to me, Murray: I never imagined you were engaged.'

'I am not engaged yet, though no doubt I shall soon be,' answered the reluctant lover. 'My grandmother and the lady's father have arranged the match. The lady does not object, I believe, and who am I, Savill, that I should refuse good looks, a good fortune, and a good temper?'

'You do not speak as though you liked the proposed bride, nevertheless,' said Mr Savill dubiously.

'I do not dislike her, I only hate having to marry her. Can't you understand that a man wants to pick a wife for himself—that the one girl he fancies seems worth ten thousand of a girl anybody else fancies? But I am so situated—Hang it, Dick! what are you staring at that dark-eyed witch for?'

'Because it is so funny. She is making him take a boat at the steps, and he does not want to do it. Kindly observe his face.'

'What is his face to me?' retorted Mr Murray savagely.

'Not much, I daresay, but it is a good deal to him. It is black as thunder, and hers is not much lighter. What a neat ankle, and how you like to show it, my dear. Well, there is no harm in a pretty ankle or a pretty foot either, and you have both. One would not wish one's wife to have a hoof like an elephant. What sort of feet has your destined maiden, Paul?'

'I never noticed.'

'That looks deucedly bad,' said the younger man, shaking his head.

'I know, however, she has a pure, sweet face,' observed Mr Murray gloomily.

'No one could truthfully make the same statement about our young friend's little lady,' remarked Mr Savill, still gazing at the girl, who was seating herself in the stern. 'A termagant, I'll be bound, if ever there was one. Wishes to go up stream, no doubt because he wishes to go down. Any caprice about the Norfolk "fair"?'

'Not much, I think. She is good, Dick—too good for me,' replied the other, sauntering out again.

'That is what we always say about the things we do not know. And so your grandmother has made up the match?'

'Yes: there is money, and the old lady loves money. She says she wants to see me settled—talks of buying me an estate. She will have to do something, because I am sure the stern parent on the other side would not allow his daughter to marry on expectations. The one drop of comfort in the arrangement is that my aged relative will have to come down, and pretty smartly too. I would wed Hecate, to end this state of bondage, which I have not courage to flee from myself. Dick, how I envy you who have no dead person's shoes to wait for!'

'You need not envy me,' returned Dick, with conviction, 'a poor unlucky devil chained to a desk. There is scarce a day of my life I fail to curse the service, the office, and Fate—'

'Curse no more, then,' said the other; 'rather go down on your knees and thank Heaven you have, without any merit of your own, a provision for life. I wish Fate or anybody had coached me into the Civil Service—apprenticed me to a trade—sent me to sea—made me enlist, instead of leaving me at the mercy of an old lady who knows neither justice nor reason—who won't let me do anything for myself, and won't do anything for me—who ought to have been dead long ago, but who never means to die—'

'And who often gives you in one cheque as much as the whole of my annual salary,' added the other quietly.

'But you know you will have your yearly salary as long as you live. I never know whether I shall have another cheque.'

'It won't do, my friend,' answered Dick Savill; 'you feel quite certain you can get money when you want it.'

'I feel certain of no such thing,' was the reply. 'If I once offended her—' he stopped, and then went on: 'And perhaps when I have spent

21

twenty years in trying to humour such caprices as surely woman never had before, I shall wake one morning to find she has left every penny to the Asylum for Idiots.'

'Why do you not pluck up courage, and strike out some line for yourself?'

'Too late, Dick, too late. Ten years ago I might have tried to make a fortune for myself, but I can't do that now. As I have waited so long, I must wait a little longer. At thirty a man can't take pick in hand and try to clear a road to fortune.'

'Then you had better marry the Norfolk young lady.'

'I am steadily determined to do so. I am going down with the firm intention of asking her.'

'And do you think she will have you?'

'I think so. I feel sure she will. And she is a nice girl—the sort I would like for a wife, if she had not been thrust upon me.'

Mr Savill stood silent for a moment, with his hands plunged deep in his pockets.

'Then when I see you next?' he said tentatively.

'I shall be engaged, most likely—possibly even married,' finished the other, with as much hurry as his manner was capable of. 'And now jump into your boat, and I will go on my way to—Staines—'

'I wish you would change your mind, and have some dinner.'

'I can't; it is impossible. You see I have so many things to do and to think of. Goodbye, Dick. Don't upset yourself—go downstream, and don't get into mischief with those dark eyes you admired so much just now.'

'Make your mind easy about that,' returned the other, colouring, however, a little as he spoke. 'Goodbye, Murray. I wish you well through the campaign.' And so, after a hearty handshake, they parted, one to walk away from Halliford, and past Shepperton Church, and across Shepperton Range, and the other, of course, to row upstream, through Shepperton Lock, and on past Dockett Point.

In the grey of the summer's dawn, Mr Murray awoke next morning from a terrible dream. He had kept his appointment with Mr Travers and a select party, played heavily, drank deeply, and reached home between one and two, not much the better for his trip to Lower Halliford, his walk, and his carouse.

Champagne, followed by neat brandy, is not perhaps the best thing to ensure a quiet night's rest; but Mr Murray had often enjoyed sound repose after similar libations; and it was, therefore, all the more unpleasant that in the grey dawn he should wake suddenly from a dream, in which he thought someone was trying to crush his head with a heavy weight.

Even when he had struggled from sleep, it seemed to him that a wet dead hand lay across his eyes, and pressed them so hard he could not move the lids. Under the weight he lay powerless, while a damp, ice-cold hand felt burning into his brain, if such a contradictory expression may be permitted.

The perspiration was pouring from him; he felt the drops falling on his throat, and trickling down his neck; he might have been lying in a bath, instead of on his own bed, and it was with a cry of horror he at last flung the hand aside, and, sitting up, looked around the room, into which the twilight of morning was mysteriously stealing.

Then, trembling in every limb, he lay down again, and fell into another sleep, from which he did not awake till aroused by broad daylight and his valet.

'You told me to call you in good time, sir,' said the man.

'Ah, yes, so I did,' yawned Mr Murray. 'What a bore! I will get up directly. You can go, Davis. I will ring if I want you.'

Davis was standing, as his master spoke, looking down at the floor. 'Yes, sir.' he answered, after the fashion of a man who has something on his mind—and went.

He had not, however, got to the bottom of the first flight when peal after peal summoned him back.

Mr Murray was out of bed, and in the middle of the room, the ghastly pallor of his face brought into full prominence by the crimson dressing-gown he had thrown round him on rising.

'What is that?' he asked. 'What in the world is that, Davis?' and he pointed to the carpet, which was covered, Mrs Murray being an old-fashioned lady, with strips of white drugget.

'I am sure I do not know, sir,' answered Davis. 'I noticed it the moment I came into the room. Looks as if someone with wet feet had been walking round and round the bed.'

It certainly did. Round and round, to and fro, backwards and forwards, the feet seemed to have gone and come, leaving a distinct mark wherever they pressed.

'The print is that of a rare small foot, too,' observed Davis, who really seemed half stupefied with astonishment.

'But who would have dared—' began Mr Murray.

'No one in this house,' declared Davis stoutly. 'It is not the mark of a boy or woman inside these doors'; and then the master and the man looked at each other for an instant with grave suspicion.

But for that second they kept their eyes thus occupied; then, as by common consent, they dropped their glances to the floor. 'My God!' exclaimed Davis. 'Where have the footprints gone?'

He might well ask. The drugget, but a moment before wet and stained by the passage and repassage of those small restless feet, was now smooth and white, as when first sent forth from the bleach-green. On its polished surface there could not be discerned a speck or mark.

II
WHERE IS LUCY?

In the valley of the Thames early hours are the rule. There the days have an unaccountable way of lengthening themselves out which makes it prudent, as well as pleasant, to utilize all the night in preparing for a longer morrow.

For this reason, when eleven o'clock p.m. strikes, it usually finds Church Street, Walton, as quiet as its adjacent graveyard, which lies still and solemn under the shadow of the old grey tower hard by that ancient vicarage which contains so beautiful a staircase.

About the time when Mr Travers' friends were beginning their evening, when talk had abated and play was suggested, the silence of Church Street was broken and many a sleeper aroused by a continuous knocking at the door of a house as venerable as any in that part of Walton. Rap—rap—rap—rap awoke the echoes of the old-world village street, and at length brought to the window a young man, who, flinging up the sash, enquired—

'Who is there?'

'Where is Lucy? What have you done with my girl?' answered a strained woman's voice from out the darkness of that summer night.

'Lucy?' repeated the young man; 'is not she at home?'

'No; I have never set eyes on her since you went out together.'

'Why, we parted hours ago. Wait a moment, Mrs Heath; I will be down directly.'

No need to tell the poor woman to 'wait'. She stood on the step, crying softly and wringing her hands till the door opened, and the same young fellow who with the pretty girl had taken boat opposite the Ship Hotel bade her 'Come in'.

Awakened from some pleasant dream, spite of all the trouble and hurry of that unexpected summons, there still shone the light of a reflected sunshine in his eyes and the flush of happy sleep on his cheek. He scarcely understood yet what had happened, but when he saw Mrs Heath's tear-stained face, comprehension came to him, and he said abruptly—

'Do you mean that she has never returned home?'

'Never!'

They were in the parlour by this time, and looking at each other by the light of one poor candle which he had set down on the table.

'Why, I left her,' he said, 'I left her long before seven.'

'Where?'

'Just beyond Dockett Point. She would not let me row her back. I do not know what was the matter with her, but nothing I did seemed right.'

'Had you any quarrel?' asked Mrs Heath anxiously.

'Yes, we had; we were quarrelling all the time—at least she was with me; and at last she made me put her ashore, which I did sorely against my will.'

'What had you done to my girl, then?'

'I prayed of her to marry me—no great insult, surely, but she took it as one. I would rather not talk of what she answered. Where can she be? Do you think she can have gone to her aunt's?'

'If so, she will be back by the last train. Let us get home as fast as possible. I never thought of that. Poor child! she will go out of her mind if she finds nobody to let her in. You will come with me. O, if she is not there, what shall I do—what ever shall I do?'

The young man had taken his hat, and was holding the door open for Mrs Heath to pass out.

'You must try not to fret yourself,' he said gently, yet with a strange repression in his voice. 'Very likely she may stay at her aunt's all night.'

'And leave me in misery, not knowing where she is? Oh, Mr Grantley, I could never believe that.'

Mr Grantley's heart was very hot within him; but he could not tell the poor mother he believed that when Lucy's temper was up she would think of no human being but herself.

'Won't you take my arm, Mrs Heath?' he asked with tender pity. After all, though everything was over between him and Lucy, her mother could not be held accountable for their quarrel; and he had loved the girl with all the romantic fervour of love's young dream.

'I can walk faster without it, thank you,' Mrs Heath answered. 'But Mr Grantley, whatever you and Lucy fell out over, you'll forget it, won't you? It isn't in you to be hard on anybody, and she's only a spoiled child. I never had but the one, and I humoured her too much; and if she is wayward, it is all my own fault—all my own.'

'In case she does not return by this train,' said the young man, wisely ignoring Mrs Heath's enquiry, 'had I not better telegraph to her aunt directly the office opens?'

'I will be on my way to London long before that,' was the reply. 'But what makes you think she won't come? Surely you don't imagine she has done anything rash?'

'What do you mean by rash?' he asked evasively.

'Made away with herself.'

'*That!*' he exclaimed. 'No, I feel very sure she has done nothing of the sort.'

'But she might have felt sorry when you left her—vexed for having angered you—heartbroken when she saw you leave her.'

'Believe me, she was not vexed or sorry or heartbroken; she was only glad to know she had done with me,' he answered bitterly.

'What has come to you, Mr Grantley?' said Mrs Heath, in wonder. 'I never heard you speak the same before.'

'Perhaps not; I never felt the same before. It is best to be plain with you,' he went on. 'All is at an end between us; and that is what your daughter has long been trying for.'

'How can you say that, and she so fond of you?'

'She has not been fond of me for many a day. The man she wants to marry is not a poor fellow like myself, but one who can give her carriages and horses, and a fine house, and as much dress as she cares to buy.'

'But where could she ever find a husband able to do that?'

'I do not know, Mrs Heath. All I do know is that she considers I am no match for her; and now my eyes are opened, I see she was not a wife for me. We should never have known a day's happiness.'

It was too dark to see his face, but his changed voice and words and manner told Lucy's mother the kindly lad, who a couple of years before came courting her pretty daughter, and offended all his friends for her sake, was gone away for ever. It was a man who walked by her side—who had eaten of the fruit of the tree, and had learned to be as a god, knowing good from evil.

'Well, well,' she said brokenly, 'you are the best judge, I suppose; but O, my child, my child!'

She was so blinded with tears she stumbled, and must have fallen had he not caught and prevented her. Then he drew her hand within his arm, and said—

'I am so grieved for you. I never received anything but kindness from you.'

'And indeed,' she sobbed, 'you never were anything except good to me. I always knew we couldn't be considered your equals, and I often had my doubts whether it was right to let you come backwards and forwards as I did, parting you from all belonging to you. But I thought, when your mother saw Lucy's pretty face—for it is pretty, Mr Grantley—'

'There never was a prettier,' assented the young man, though, now his eyes were opened, he knew Lucy's beauty would scarcely have recommended her to any sensible woman.

'I hoped she might take to her, and I'd never have intruded. And I was so proud and happy, and fond of you—I was indeed; and I used to consider how, when you came down, I could have some little thing you fancied. But that's all over now. And I don't blame you; only my heart is sore and troubled about my foolish girl.'

They were on Walton Bridge by this time, and the night air blew cold and raw down the river, and made Mrs Heath shiver.

'I wonder where Lucy is,' she murmured, 'and what she'd think if she knew her mother was walking through the night in an agony about her? Where was it you said you left her?'

'Between Dockett Point and Chertsey. I shouldn't have left her had she not insisted on my doing so.'

'Isn't that the train?' asked Mrs Heath, stopping suddenly short and listening intently.

'Yes; it is just leaving Sunbury Station. Do not hurry; we have plenty of time.'

They had: they were at Lucy's home, one of the small houses situated between Battlecreese Hill and the Red Lion in Lower Halliford before a single passenger came along The Green, or out of Nannygoat Lane.

'My heart misgives me that she has not come down,' said Mrs Heath.

'Shall I go up to meet her?' asked the young man; and almost before the mother feverishly assented, he was striding through the summer night to Shepperton Station, where he found the lights extinguished and every door closed.

III

POOR MRS HEATH

By noon the next day every one in Shepperton and Lower Halliford knew Lucy Heath was 'missing'.

Her mother had been up to Putney, but Lucy was not with her aunt, who lived not very far from the Bridge on the Fulham side, and who, having married a fruiterer and worked up a very good business, was inclined to take such bustling and practical views of life and its concerns as rather dismayed her sister-in-law, who had spent so many years in the remote country, and then so many other years in quiet Shepperton, that Mrs Pointer's talk flurried her almost as much as the noise of London, which often maddens middle-aged and elderly folk happily unaccustomed to its roar.

Girt about with a checked apron which lovingly enfolded a goodly portion of her comfortable figure, Mrs Pointer received her early visitor with the sportive remark, 'Why, it's never Martha Heath! Come along in; a sight of you is good for sore eyes.'

But Mrs Heath repelled all such humorous observations, and chilled those suggestions of hospitality the Pointers were never backward in making by asking in a low choked voice—

'Is Lucy here?'

'Lor! whatever put such a funny notion into your head?'

'Ah! I see she is,' trying to smile. 'After all, she spent the night with you.'

'Did what?' exclaimed Mrs Pointer. 'Spent the night—was that what you said? No, nor the day either, for this year nearly. Why, for the last four months she hasn't set foot across that doorstep, unless it might be to buy some cherries, or pears, or apples, or grapes, or suchlike, and then she came in with more air than any lady; and after paying her money and getting her goods went out again, just as if I hadn't been her father's sister and Pointer my husband. But there! for any sake, woman, don't look like that! Come into the parlour and tell me what is wrong. You never mean she has gone away and left you?'

Poor Mrs Heath was perfectly incapable at that moment of saying what she did mean. Seated on a stool, and holding fast by the edge of the counter for fear of falling, the shop and its contents, the early busses, the people going along the pavement, the tradesmen's carts, the private carriages, were, as in some terrible nightmare, gyrating before her eyes. She could not speak, she could scarcely think, until that wild whirligig came to a stand. For a minute or two even Mrs Pointer seemed multiplied by fifty; while her checked apron, the bananas suspended from hooks, the baskets of fruit, the pineapples, the melons, the tomatoes, and the cob-nuts appeared and disappeared, only to reappear and disappear like the riders in a maddening giddy-go-round.

'Give me a drop of water,' she said at last; and when the water was brought she drank a little and poured some on her handkerchief and dabbed her face, and finally suffered herself to be escorted into the parlour, where she told her tale, interrupted by many sobs. It would have been unchristian in Mrs Pointer to exult; but it was only human to remember she had remarked to Pointer, in that terrible spirit of prophecy bestowed for some inscrutable reason on dear friends and close relations, she knew some such trouble must befall her sister-in-law.

'You made an idol of that girl, Martha,' she went on, 'and now it is coming home to you. I am sure it was only last August as ever was that Pointer—But here he is, and he will talk to you himself.'

Which Mr Pointer did, being very fond of the sound of his own foolish voice. He stated how bad a thing it was for people to be above their station or to bring children up above that rank of life in which it had pleased God to place them. He quoted many pleasing saws uttered by his father and grandfather; remarked that as folks sowed they were bound to reap; reminded Mrs Heath they had the word of Scripture for the fact—than, which, parenthetically, no fact could be truer, as he knew—that a man might not gather grapes from thorns or even figs from thistles. Further he went on to observe generally—the observation having a particular reference to Lucy—that it did not do to judge things by their looks. Over and over again salesmen had tried to 'shove off a lot of foreign fruit on him, but he wasn't a young bird to be taken in by that chaff'. No; what he looked to was quality; it was what his customers expected from him, and what he could honestly declare his customers got. He was a plain man, and he thought honesty was the best policy. So as Mrs Heath had seen fit to come to them in her trouble he would tell her what he thought, without beating about the bush. He believed Lucy had 'gone off'.

'But where?' asked poor Mrs Heath.

'That I am not wise enough to say; but you'll find she's gone off. Girls in her station don't sport chains and bracelets and brooches for nothing—'

'But they did not cost many shillings,' interposed the mother.

'She might tell you that,' observed Mrs Pointer, with a world of meaning.

'To say nothing,' went on Mr Pointer, 'of grey gloves she could not abear to be touched. One day she walked in when I was behind the counter, and, not knowing she had been raised to the peerage, I shook hands with her as a matter of course; but when I saw the young lady look at her glove as if I had dirtied it, I said "O, I beg your pardon, miss"—jocularly, you know. "They soil so easily," she lisped.'

'I haven't patience with such ways!' interpolated Mrs Pointer, without any lisp at all. 'Yes, it's hard for you, Martha, but you may depend Pointer's right. Indeed, I expected how it would be long ago. Young women who are walking in the straight road don't dress as Lucy dressed, or dare their innocent little cousins to call them by their Christian names in the street. Since the Spring, and long before, Pointer and me has been sure Lucy was up to no good.'

'And you held your tongues and never said a word to me!' retorted Mrs Heath, goaded and driven to desperation.

'Much use it would have been saying any word to you,' answered Mrs Pointer. 'When you told me about young Grantley, and I bid you be careful, how did you take my advice? Why, you blared out at me, went on as if I knew nothing and had never been anywhere. What I told you then, though, I tell you now: young Grantleys, the sons of rectors and the grandsons of colonels, don't come after farmer's daughters with any honest purpose.'

'Yet young Grantley asked her last evening to fix a day for their marriage,' said Mrs Heath, with a little triumph.

'O, I daresay!' scoffed Mrs Pointer.

'Talk is cheap,' observed Mr Pointer.

'Some folks have more of it than money,' supplemented his wife.

'They have been, as I understand, keeping company for some time now,' said the fruiterer, with what he deemed a telling and judicial calmness. 'So if he asked her to name the day, why did she not name it?'

'I do not know. I have never seen her since.'

'O, then you had only his word about the matter,' summed up Mr Pointer. 'Just as I thought—just as I thought.'

'What did you think?' enquired the poor troubled mother.

'Why, that she has gone off with this Mr Grantley.'

'Ah, you don't know Mr Grantley, or you wouldn't say such a thing.'

'It is true,' observed Mr Pointer, 'that I do not know the gentleman, and, I may add, I do not want to know him; but speaking as a person acquainted with the world—'

'I'll be getting home,' interrupted Mrs Heath. 'Most likely my girl is there waiting for me, and a fine laugh she will have against her poor old mother for being in such a taking. Yes, Lucy will have the breakfast ready. No, thank you; I'll not wait to take anything. There will be a train back presently; and besides, to tell you the truth, food would choke me till I sit down again with my girl, and then I won't be able to eat for joy.'

Husband and wife looked at each other as Mrs Heath spoke, and for the moment a deep pity pierced the hard crust of their worldly egotism.

'Wait a minute,' cried Mrs Pointer, 'and I'll put on my bonnet and go with you.'

'No,' interrupted Mr Pointer, instantly seizing his wife's idea, and appropriating it as his own. 'I am the proper person to see this affair out. There is not much doing, and if there were, I would leave everything to obtain justice for your niece. After all, however wrong she may have gone, she is your niece, Maria.'

With which exceedingly nasty remark, which held a whole volume of unpleasant meaning as to what Mrs Pointer might expect from that relationship in the future, Mr Pointer took Mrs Heath by the arm, and piloted her out into the street, and finally to Lower Halliford, where the missing Lucy was not, and where no tidings of her had come.

IV
MR GAGE ON PORTENTS

About the time when poor distraught Mrs Heath, having managed to elude the vigilance of that cleverest of men, Maria Pointer's husband, had run out of her small house, and was enlisting the sympathies of gossip-loving Shepperton in Lucy's disappearance, Mr Paul Murray arrived at Liverpool Street Station, where his luggage and his valet awaited him.

'Get tickets, Davis,' he said; 'I have run it rather close'; and he walked towards Smith's stall, while his man went into the booking-office.

As he was about to descend the stairs, Davis became aware of a very singular fact. Looking down the steps, he saw precisely the same marks that had amazed him so short a time previously, being printed hurriedly off by a pair of invisible feet, which ran to the bottom and then flew as if in the wildest haste to the spot where Mr Murray stood.

'I am not dreaming, am I?' thought the man; and he shut his eyes and opened them again.

The footprints were all gone!

At that moment his master turned from the bookstall and

proceeded towards the train. A porter opened the door of a smoking carriage, but Murray shook his head and passed on. Mr Davis, once more looking to the ground, saw that those feet belonging to no mortal body were still following. There were not very many passengers, and it was quite plain to him that wherever his master went, the quick, wet prints went too. Even on the step of the compartment Mr Murray eventually selected the man beheld a mark, as though some one had sprung in after him. He secured the door, and then walked away, to find a place for himself, marvelling in a dazed state of mind what it all meant; indeed, he felt so much dazed that, after he had found a seat to his mind, he did not immediately notice an old acquaintance in the opposite corner, who affably enquired—

'And how is Mr Davis?'

Thus addressed, Mr Davis started from his reverie, and exclaimed, 'Why, bless my soul, Gage, who'd have thought of seeing you here?' after which exchange of courtesies the pair shook hands gravely and settled down to converse.

Mr Davis explained that he was going down with his governor to Norwich; and Mr Gage stated that he and the old general had been staying at Thorpe, and were on their way to Lowestoft. Mr Gage and his old general had also just returned from paying a round of visits in the West of England. 'Pleasant enough, but slow,' finished the gentleman's gentleman. 'After all, in the season or out of it, there is no place like London.'

With this opinion Mr Davis quite agreed, and said he only wished he had never to leave it, adding—

'We have not been away before for a long time; and we should not be going where we are now bound if we had not to humour some fancy of our grandmother's.'

'Deuced rough on a man having to humour a grandmother's fancy,' remarked Mr Gage.

'No female ought to be left the control of money,' said Mr Davis with conviction. 'See what the consequences have been in this case— Mrs Murray outlived her son, who had to ask her for every shilling he wanted, and she is so tough she may see the last of her grandson.'

'That is very likely,' agreed the other. 'He looks awfully bad.'

'You saw him just now, I suppose?'

'No; but I saw him last night at Chertsey Station, and I could but notice the change in his appearance.'

For a minute Mr Davis remained silent. 'Chertsey Station!' What could his master have been doing at Chertsey? That was a question he would have to put to himself again, and answer for himself at some convenient time; meanwhile he only answered—

'Yes, I observe an alteration in him myself. Anything fresh in the paper?'

'No,' answered Mr Gage, handing his friend over the *Daily News*— the print he affected: 'everything is as dull as ditchwater.'

For many a mile Davis read or affected to read; then he laid the paper aside, and after passing his case, well filled with a tithe levied on Mr Murray's finest cigars, to Gage, began solemnly—

'I am going to ask you a curious question, Robert, as from man to man.'

'Ask on,' said Mr Gage, striking a match.

'Do you believe in warnings?'

The old General's gentleman burst out laughing. He was so tickled that he let his match drop from his fingers unapplied.

'I am afraid most of us have to believe in them, whether we like it or not,' he answered, when he could speak. 'Has there been some little difference between you and your governor, then?'

'You mistake,' was the reply. 'I did not mean warnings in the sense of notice, but warnings as warnings, you understand.'

'Bother me if I do! Yes, now I take you. Do I believe in "coming events casting shadows before," as some one puts it? Has any shadow of a coming event been cast across you?'

'No, nor across anybody, so far as I know; but I've been thinking the matter over lately, and wondering if there can be any truth in such notions.'

'What notions?'

'Why, that there are signs and suchlike sent when trouble is coming to anyone.'

'You may depend it is right enough that signs and tokens are sent. Almost every good family has its special warning: one has its mouse, another its black dog, a third its white bird, a fourth its drummer-boy, and so on. There is no getting over facts, even if you don't understand them.'

34

'Well, it is very hard to believe.'

'There wouldn't be much merit in believing if everything were as plain as a pikestaff. You know what the Scotch minister said to his boy: "The very devils believe and tremble." You wouldn't be worse than a devil, would you?'

'Has any sign ever appeared to you?' asked Davis.

'Not exactly; but lots of people have told me they have to them; for instance, old Seal, who drove the Dowager Countess of Ongar till the day of her death, used to make our hair stand on end talking about phantom carriages that drove away one after another from the door of Hainault House, and wakened every soul on the premises, night after night till the old Earl died. It took twelve clergymen to lay the spirit.'

'I wonder one wasn't enough!' ejaculated Davis.

'There may have been twelve spirits, for all I know,' returned Gage, rather puzzled by this view of the question; 'but anyhow, there were twelve clergymen, with the bishop in his lawn sleeves chief among them. And I once lived with a young lady's-maid, who told me when she was a girl she made her home with her father's parents. On a win- ter's night, after everybody else had gone to bed, she sat up to make some girdle-bread—that is a sort of bread the people in Ireland, where she came from, bake over the fire on a round iron plate; with plenty of butter it is not bad eating. Well, as I was saying, she was quite alone; she had taken all the bread off, and was setting it up on edge to cool, supporting one piece against the other, two and two, when on the table where she was putting the cakes she saw one drop of blood fall, and then another, and then another, like the beginning of a shower.

'She looked to the ceiling, but could see nothing, and still the drops kept on falling slowly, slowly; and then she knew something had gone wrong with one dear to her; and she put a shawl over her head, and without saying a word to anybody, went through the loneliness and darkness of night all by herself to her father's.'

'She must have been a courageous girl,' remarked Mr Davis.

'She was, and I liked her well. But to the point. When she reached her destination she found her youngest brother dead. Now what do you make of that?'

'It's strange, but I suppose he would have died all the same if she had not seen the blood-drops, and I can't see any good seeing them did her. If she had reached her father's in time to bid brother goodbye, there would have been some sense in such a sign. As it is, it seems to me a lot of trouble thrown away.'

Mr Gage shook his head.

'What a sceptic you are, Davis! But there! London makes sceptics of the best of us. If you had spent a winter, as I did once, in the Highlands of Scotland, or heard the Banshee wailing for the General's nephew in the county of Mayo, you wouldn't have asked what was the use of second sight or Banshees. You would just have stood and trembled as I did many and many a time.'

'I might,' said Davis doubtfully, wondering what his friend would have thought of those wet little footprints. 'Hillo, here's Peterborough! Hadn't we better stretch our legs? and a glass of something would be acceptable.'

Of that glass, however, Mr Davis was not destined to partake.

'If one of you is Murray's man,' said the guard as they jumped out, 'he wants you.'

'I'll be back in a minute,' observed Mr Murray's man to his friend, and hastened off.

But he was not back in a minute; on the contrary, he never returned at all.

V

KISS ME

The first glance in his master's face filled Davis with a vague alarm. Gage's talk had produced an effect quite out of proportion to its merit, and a cold terror struck to the valet's heart as he thought there might, spite of his lofty scepticism, be something after all in the mouse, and the bird, and the drummer-boy, in the black dog, and the phantom carriages, and the spirits it required the united exertions of twelve clergymen (with the bishop in lawn sleeves among them) to lay; in Highland second sight and Irish Banshees; and in little feet paddling round and about a man's bed and following wherever he went. What awful disaster could those footprints portend? Would the train be smashed up? Did any river lie before them? and if so, was the sign vouchsafed as a warning that they were likely to die by drowning? All these thoughts, and many more, passed through Davis' mind as he stood looking at his master's pallid face and waiting for him to speak.

'I wish you to come in here,' said Mr Murray after a pause, and with a manifest effort. 'I am not quite well.'

'Can I get you anything, sir?' asked the valet. 'Will you not wait and go by another train?'

'No; I shall be better presently; only I do not like being alone.'

Davis opened the door and entered the compartment. As he did so, he could not refrain from glancing at the floor, to see if those strange footsteps had been running races there.

'What are you looking for?' asked Mr Murray irritably. 'Have you dropped anything?'

'No, sir; O, no! I was only considering where I should be most out of the way.'

'There,' answered his master, indicating a seat next the window, and at the same time moving to one on the further side of the carriage.

'Let no one get in; say I am ill—mad; that I have scarlet fever—the plague—what you please.' And with this wide permission Mr Murray laid his legs across the opposite cushion, wrapped one rug round his shoulders and another round his body, turned his head aside, and went to sleep or seemed to do so.

'If he is going to die, I hope it will be considered in my wages, but I am afraid it won't. Perhaps it is the old lady; but that would be too good fortune,' reflected Davis; and then he fell 'a-thinkynge, a-thinkynge,' principally of Gage's many suggestions and those mysterious footprints, for which he kept at intervals furtively looking. But they did not appear; and at last the valet, worn out with vain conjections, dropped into a pleasant doze, from which he did not awake till they were nearing Norwich.

'We will go to an hotel till I find out what Mrs Murray's plans are,' said that lady's grandson when he found himself on the platform; and as if they had been only waiting this piece of information, two small invisible feet instantly skipped out of the compartment they had just vacated, and walked after Mr Murray, leaving visible marks at every step.

'Great heavens! what is the meaning of this?' mentally asked Davis, surprised by fright after twenty prayerless and scheming years into an exclamation which almost did duty for a prayer. For a moment he felt sick with terror; then clutching his courage with the energy of desperation, he remembered that though wet footprints might mean death and destruction to the Murrays, his own ancestral annals held no record of such a portent.

Neither did the Murrays', so far as he was aware, but then he was aware of very little about that family. If the Irish girl Gage spoke of was informed by drops of blood that her brother lay dead, why should not Mr Murray be made aware, through the token of these pattering footsteps, that he would very soon succeed to a large fortune?

Then any little extra attention Mr Davis showed his master *now* would be remembered in his wages.

It was certainly unpleasant to know these damp feet had come down from London, and were going to the hotel with them; but 'needs must' with a certain driver, and if portents and signs and warnings were made worth his while, Mr Davis conceived there might be advantages connected with them.

Accordingly, when addressing Mr Murray, his valet's voice assumed a more deferential tone than ever, and his manner became so respectfully tender, that onlookers rashly imagined the ideal master and the faithful servant of fiction had at last come in the flesh to Norwich. Davis' conduct was, indeed, perfect: devoted without being intrusive, he smoothed away all obstacles which could be smoothed, and even, by dint of a judicious two minutes alone with the doctor for whom he sent, managed the introduction of a useful sedative in some medicine, which the label stated was to be taken every four hours.

He saw to Mr Murray's rooms and Mr Murray's light repast, and then he waited on Mr Murray's grandmother, and managed that lady so adroitly, she at length forgave the offender for having caught a chill.

'Your master is always doing foolish things,' she said. 'It would have been much better had he remained even for a day or two in London rather than risk being laid up. However, you must nurse him carefully, and try to get him well enough to dine at Losdale Court on Monday. Fortunately tomorrow is Sunday, and he can take complete rest. Now Davis, remember I trust to you.'

'I will do my best, ma'am,' Davis said humbly, and went back to tell his master the interview had gone off without any disaster.

Then, after partaking of some mild refreshment, he repaired to bed in a dressing-room opening off Mr Murray's apartment, so that he might be within call and close at hand to administer those doses which were to be taken at intervals of four hours.

'I feel better tonight,' said Mr Murray last thing.

'It is this beautiful air, sir,' answered Davis, who knew it was the sedative. 'I hope you will be quite well in the morning.'

But spite of the air, in the grey dawn Mr Murray had again a dreadful dream—a worse dream than that which laid its heavy hand on him in London. He thought he was by the riverside beyond Dockett Point—beyond where the water-lilies grow. To his right was a little grove of old and twisted willows guarding a dell strewed in dry seasons with the leaves of many autumns, but, in his dream, wet and sodden by reason of heavy rain. There in June wild roses bloomed; there in winter hips and haws shone ruddy against the snow. To his left flowed a turbid river—turbid with floods that had troubled its peace. On the other bank lay a stagnant length of Surrey, while close at hand the Middlesex portion of Chertsey Mead stretched in a hopeless flat on to the bridge, just visible in the early twilight of a summer's evening that had followed after a dull lowering day.

From out of the gathering gloom there advanced walking perilously near to Dumsey Deep, a solitary female figure, who, when they met, said, 'So you've come at last'; after which night seemed to close around him, silence for a space to lay its hands upon him.

About the same time Davis was seeing visions also. He had lain long awake, trying to evolve order out of the day's chaos, but in vain. The stillness fretted him; the idea that even then those mysterious feet might in the darkness be printing their impress about his master's bed irritated his brain. Twice he got up to give that medicine ordered to be taken every four hours, but finding on each occasion Mr Murray sleeping quietly, he forbore to arouse him.

He heard hour after hour chime, and it was not till the first hint of dawn that he fell into a deep slumber. Then he dreamt about the subject nearest his heart—a public house.

He thought he had saved or gained enough to buy a roadside inn on which he had long cast eyes of affectionate regard—not in London, but not too far out: a delightful inn, where holidaymakers always stopped for refreshment, and sometimes for the day; an inn with a pretty old-fashioned garden filled with fruit trees and vegetables, with a grass-plot around which were erected little arbours, where people could have tea or stronger stimulants; a skittle-ground, where men could soon make themselves very thirsty; and many other advantages tedious to mention. He had the purchase-money in his pocket, and, having paid a deposit, was proceeding to settle the affair, merely diverging from his way to call on a young widow he meant to make Mrs Davis—a charming woman, who, having stood behind a bar before, seemed the very person to make the Wheatsheaf a triumphant success. He was talking to her sensibly, when suddenly she amazed him by saying, in a sharp, hurried voice. 'Kiss me, kiss me, kiss me!' three times over.

The request seemed so strange that he stood astounded, and then awoke to hear the same words repeated.

'Kiss me, kiss me, kiss me!' some one said distinctly in Mr Murray's room, the door of which stood open, and then all was quiet.

Only half awake, Davis sprang from his bed and walked across the floor, conceiving, so far as his brain was in a state to conceive anything, that his senses were playing him some trick.

'You won't?' said the voice again, in a tone which rooted him to the spot where he stood; 'and yet, as we are never to meet again, you might *Kiss me once,*' the voice added caressingly, '*only once more.*'

'Who the deuce has he got with him now?' thought Davis; but almost before the question was shaped in his mind there came a choked, gasping cry of 'Unloose me, tigress, devil!' followed by a sound of desperate wrestling for life.

In a second, Davis was in the room. Through the white blinds light enough penetrated to show Mr Murray in the grip apparently of some invisible antagonist, who seemed to be strangling him.

To and fro from side to side the man and the unseen phantom went swaying in that awful struggle. Short and fast came Mr Murray's breath, while, making one supreme effort, he flung his opponent from him and sank back across the bed exhausted.

Wiping the moisture from his forehead, Davis, trembling in every limb, advanced to where his master lay, and found *he was fast asleep!*

Mr Murray's eyes were wide open, and he did not stir hand or foot while the man covered him up as well as he was able, and then looked timidly around, dreading to see the second actor in the scene just ended.

'I can't stand much more of this,' Davis exclaimed, and the sound of his own voice made him start.

There was brandy in the room which had been left overnight, and the man poured himself out and swallowed a glass of the liquor. He ventured to lift the blind and look at the floor, which was wet, as though buckets of water had been thrown over it, while the prints of little feet were everywhere.

Mr Davis took another glass of brandy. *That* had not been watered.

'Well, this is a start!' he said in his own simple phraseology. 'I wonder what the governor has been up to?'

For it was now borne in upon the valet's understanding that this warning was no shadow of any event to come, but the tell-tale ghost of some tragedy which could never be undone.

VI
FOUND DROWNED

After such a dreadful experience it might have been imagined that Mr Murray would be very ill indeed; but what we expect rarely comes to pass, and though during the whole of Sunday and Monday Davis felt, as he expressed the matter, 'awfully shaky', his master appeared well and in fair spirits.

He went to the Cathedral, and no attendant footsteps dogged him. On Monday he accompanied his grandmother to Losdale Court, where he behaved so admirably as to please even the lady on whose favour his income depended. He removed to a furnished house Mrs Murray had taken, and prepared to carry out her wishes. Day succeeded day and night to night, but neither by day nor night did Davis hear the sound of any ghostly voices or trace the print of any phantom foot.

Could it be that nothing more was to come of it—that the mystery was never to be elucidated but fade away as the marks of dainty feet had vanished from floor, pavement, steps, and platform?

The valet did not believe it; behind those signs made by nothing human lay some secret well worth knowing, but it had never been possible to know much about Mr Murray.

'He was so little of a gentleman' that he had no pleasant, careless ways. He did not leave his letters lying loose for all the world to read. He did not tear up papers, and toss them into a waste-paper basket. He had the nastiest practice of locking up and burning; and though it was Mr Davis's commendable custom to collect and preserve unconsidered odds and ends as his master occasionally left in his pockets, these, after all, were trifles light as air.

Nevertheless, as a straw shows how the wind blows, so that chance remark anent Chertsey Station made by Gage promised to provide a string on which to thread various little beads in Davis' possession.

The man took them out and looked at them: a woman's fall—white tulle, with black spots, smelling strongly of tobacco-smoke and musk; a receipt for a bracelet, purchased from an obscure jeweller; a Chertsey Lock ticket; and the return half of a first-class ticket from Shepperton to Waterloo, stamped with the date of the day before they left London.

At these treasures Davis looked long and earnestly.

'We shall see,' he remarked as he put them up again; 'there I think the scent lies hot.'

It could not escape the notice of so astute a servant that his master was unduly anxious for a sight of the London papers, and that he glanced through them eagerly for something he apparently failed to find—more, that he always laid the print aside with a sigh of relief. Politics did not seem to trouble him, or any public burning question.

'He has some burning question of his own,' thought the valet, though he mentally phrased his notion in different words.

Matters went on thus for a whole week. The doctor came and went and wrote prescriptions, for Mr Murray either was still ailing or chose to appear so. Davis caught a word or two which had reference to the patient's heart, and some shock. Then he considered that awful night, and wondered how he, who 'was in his sober senses, and wide awake, and staring', had lived through it.

'My heart, and a good many other things, will have to be considered,' he said to himself. No wages could pay for what has been put upon me this week past. I wonder whether I ought to speak to Mr Murray now?'

Undecided on this point, he was still considering it when he called his master on the following Sunday morning. The first glance at the stained and polished floor decided him. Literally it was interlaced with footprints. The man's hand shook as he drew up the blind, but he kept his eyes turned on Mr Murray while he waited for orders, and walked out of the room when dismissed as though such marks had been matters of customary occurrence in a nineteenth-century bedroom.

No bell summoned him back on this occasion. Instead of asking for information, Mr Murray dropped into a chair and nerved himself to defy the inevitable.

Once again there came a pause. For three days nothing occurred; but on the fourth a newspaper and a letter arrived, both of which Davis inspected curiously. They were addressed in Mr Savill's hand-writing, and they bore the postmark 'SHEPPERTON'.

The newspaper was enclosed in an ungummed wrapper, tied round with a piece of string. After a moment's reflection Davis cut that string, spread out the print, and beheld a column marked at top with three blue crosses, containing the account of an inquest held at the King's Head on a body found on the previous Sunday morning, close by the 'Tumbling Bay'.

It was that of a young lady who had been missing since the previous Friday week, and could only be identified by the clothes.

Her mother, who, in giving evidence, frequently broke down, told how her daughter on the evening in question went out for a walk and never returned. She did not wish to go, because her boots were being mended, and her shoes were too large. No doubt they had dropped off. She had very small feet, and it was not always possible to get shoes to fit them. She was engaged to be married to the gentleman with whom she went out. He told her they had quarrelled. She did not believe he could have anything to do with her child's death; but she did not know what to think. It had been said her girl was keeping company with somebody else, but that could not be true. Her girl was a good girl.

Yes; she had found a bracelet hidden away among her girl's clothes, and she could not say how she got the seven golden sovereigns that were in the purse, or the locket taken off the body; but her girl was a good girl, and she did not know whatever she would do without her, for Lucy was all she had.

Walter Grantley was next examined, after being warned that anything he said might be used against him.

Though evidently much affected, he gave his evidence in a clear and straightforward manner. He was a clerk in the War Office. He had, against the wishes of all his friends, engaged himself to the deceased, who, after having some time professed much affection, had latterly treated him with great coldness. On the evening in question she reluctantly came out with him for a walk; but after they passed the Ship she insisted he should take a boat. They turned and got into a boat. He wanted to go down the river, because there was no lock before Sunbury. She declared if he would not row her up the river, she would go home.

They went up the river, quarrelling all the way. There had been so much of this sort of thing that after they passed through Shepperton Lock he tried to bring matters to a conclusion, and asked her to name a day for their marriage. She scoffed at him and asked if he thought she meant to marry a man on such a trumpery salary. Then she insisted he should land her; and after a good deal of argument he did land her; and rowed back alone to Halliford. He knew no more.

Richard Savill deposed he took a boat at Lower Halliford directly after the last witness, with whom he was not acquainted, and rowed up towards Chertsey, passing Mr Grantley and Miss Heath, who were evidently quarrelling. He went as far as Dumsey Deep, where, finding the stream most heavily against him, he turned, and on his way back saw the young lady walking slowly along the bank. At Shepperton Lock he and Mr Grantley exchanged a few words, and rowed down to Halliford almost side by side. They bade each other good-evening, and Mr Grantley walked off in the direction of Walton where it was proved by other witnesses he arrived at eight o'clock, and did not go out again till ten, when he went to bed.

All efforts to trace what had become of the unfortunate girl proved unavailing, till a young man named Lemson discovered the body on the previous Sunday morning close by the Tumbling Bay. The coroner wished to adjourn the inquest, in hopes some further light might be thrown on such a mysterious occurrence; but the jury protested so strongly against any proceeding of the sort, that they were directed to return an open verdict.

No one could dispute that the girl had been 'found drowned', or that there was 'no evidence to explain how she came to be drowned'.

At the close of the proceedings, said the local paper, an affecting incident occurred. The mother wished the seven pounds to be given to the man 'who brought her child home', but the man refused to accept a penny. The mother said she would never touch it, when a relation stepped forward and offered to take charge of it for her.

The local paper contained also a leader on the tragedy, in the course of which it remarked how exceedingly fortunate it was that Mr Savill chanced to be staying at the Ship Hotel, so well known to boating-men, and that he happened to go up the river and see the poor young lady after Mr Grantley left her, as otherwise the latter gentleman might have found himself in a most unpleasant position. He was much to be pitied, and the leader-writer felt confident that every one who read the evidence would sympathize with him. It was evident the inquiry had failed to solve the mystery connected with Miss Heath's untimely fate, but it was still competent to pursue the matter if any fresh facts transpired.

'I must get to know more about all this,' thought Davis as he refolded and tied up the paper.

VII
DAVIS SPEAKS

If there be any truth in old saws, Mr Murray's wooing was a very happy one. Certainly it was very speedy. By the end of October he and Miss Ketterick were engaged, and before Christmas the family lawyers had their hands full drawing settlements and preparing deeds. Mrs Murray disliked letting any money slip out of her own control, but she had gone too far to recede, and Mr Ketterick was not a man who would have tolerated any proceeding of the sort.

Perfectly straightforward himself, he compelled straightforwardness in others, and Mrs Murray was obliged to adhere to the terms proposed when nothing seemed to her less probable than that the marriage she wished ever would take place. As for the bridegroom, he won golden opinions from Mr Ketterick. Beyond the income to be ensured to his wife and himself, he asked for nothing. Further he objected to nothing. Never before, surely, had man been so easily satisfied.

'All I have ever wanted,' he said, 'was some settled income, so that I might not feel completely dependent on my grandmother. That will now be secured, and I am quite satisfied.'

He deferred to Mr Ketterick's opinions and wishes. He made no stipulations.

'You are giving me a great prize,' he told the delighted father, 'of which I am not worthy, but I will try to make her happy.'

And the gentle girl was happy: no tenderer or more devoted lover could the proudest beauty have desired. With truth he told her he 'counted the days till she should be his'. For he felt secure when by her side. The footsteps had never followed him to Losdale Court. Just in the place that of all others he would have expected them to come, he failed to see that tiny print. There were times when he even forgot it for a season; when he did remember it, he believed, with the faith born of hope, that he should never see it again.

'I wonder he has the conscience,' muttered Mr Davis one morning, as he looked after the engaged pair. The valet had the strictest ideas concerning the rule conscience should hold over the doings of other folks, and some pleasingly lax notions about the sacrifices conscience had a right to demand from himself. 'I suppose he thinks he is safe now that those feet are snugly tucked up in holy ground,' proceeded Davis, who, being superstitious, faithfully subscribed to all the old formulæ. 'Ah! he doesn't know what I know—yet'; which last word, uttered with much gusto, indicated a most unpleasant quarter of an hour in store at some future period for Mr Murray.

It came one evening a week before his marriage. He was in London, in his grandmother's house, writing to the girl he had grown to love with the great, entire, remorseful love of his life, when Davis, respectful as ever, appeared, and asked if he might speak a word. Mr Murray involuntarily put his letter beneath some blotting-paper, and, folding his hands over both, answered, unconscious of what was to follow, 'Certainly'.

Davis had come up with his statement at full-cock, and fired at once.

'I have been a faithful servant to you, sir.'

Mr Murray lifted his eyes and looked at him. Then he knew what was coming. 'I have never found fault with you, Davis,' he said, after an almost imperceptible pause.

'No, sir, you have been a good master—a master I am sure no servant who knew his place could find a fault with.'

If he had owned an easy mind and the smallest sense of humour—neither of which possessions then belonged to Mr Murray—he might have felt enchanted with such a complete turning of the tables; but as matters stood, he could only answer, 'Good master as I have been, I suppose you wish to leave my service. Am I right, Davis?'

'Well, sir, you are right and you are wrong. I do not want to leave your service just yet. It may not be quite convenient to you for me to go now; only I want to come to an understanding.'

'About what?' Mr Murray asked, quite calmly, though he could feel his heart thumping hard against his ribs, and that peculiar choking sensation which is the warning of what in such cases must come some day.

'Will you cast your mind back, sir, to a morning in last August, when you called my attention to some extraordinary footprints on the floor of your room?'

'I remember the morning,' said Mr Murray, that choking sensation seeming to suffocate him. 'Pray go on.'

If Davis had not been master of the position, this indifference would have daunted him; as it was, he again touched the trigger, and fired this: '*I know all!*'

Mr Murray's answer did not come so quick this time. The waters had gone over his head, and for a minute he felt as a man might if suddenly flung into a raging sea, and battling for his life. He was battling for his life with a wildly leaping heart. The noise of a hundred billows seemed dashing on his brain. Then the tempest lulled, the roaring torrent was stayed, and then he said interrogatively, 'Yes?'

The prints of those phantom feet had not amazed Davis more than did his master's coolness.

'You might ha' knocked me down with a feather,' he stated, when subsequently relating this interview. 'I always knew he was a queer customer, but I never knew how queer till then.'

'Yes?' said Mr Murray, which reply quite disconcerted his valet.

'I wouldn't have seen what I have seen, sir,' he remarked, 'not for a king's ransom.'

'No?'

'No, sir, and that is the truth. What we both saw has been with me at bed and at board, as the saying is, ever since. When I shut my eyes I still feel those wet feet dabbling about the room; and in the bright sunshine I can't help shuddering, because there seems to be a cold mist creeping over me.'

'Are you not a little imaginative, Davis?' asked his master, himself repressing a shudder.

'No, sir, I am not; no man can be that about which his own eyes have seen and his own ears have heard; and I have heard and seen what I can never forget, and what nothing could pay me for going through.'

'Nevertheless?' suggested Mr Murray.

'I don't know whether I am doing right in holding my tongue, in being so faithful, sir; but I can't help it. I took to you from the first, and I wouldn't bring harm on you if any act of mine could keep it from you. When one made the remark to me awhile ago it was a strange thing to see a gentleman attended by a pair of wet footprints, I said they were a sign in your family that some great event was about to happen.'

'Did you say so?'

'I did, sir, Lord forgive me!' answered Davis, with unblushing mendacity. 'I have gone through more than will ever be known over this affair, which has shook me, Mr Murray. I am not the man I was before ghosts took to following me, and getting into trains without paying any fare, and waking me in the middle of the night, and rousing me out of my warm bed to see sights I would not have believed I could have seen if anybody had sworn it to me. I have aged twenty-five years since last August—my nerves are destroyed; and so, sir, before you got married, I thought I would make bold to ask what I am to do with a constitution broken in your service and hardly a penny put by'; and, almost out of breath with his pathetic statement, Davis stopped and waited for an answer.

With a curiously hunted expression in them, Mr Murray raised his eyes and looked at Davis.

'You have thought over all this,' he said. 'How much do you assess them at?'

'I scarcely comprehend, sir—assess what at?'

'Your broken constitution and the five-and-twenty years you say you have aged.'

His master's face was so gravely serious that Davis could take the question neither as a jest nor a sneer. It was a request to fix a price, and he did so.

'Well, sir,' he answered, 'I have thought it all over. In the night-watches, when I could get no rest, I lay and reflected what I ought to do. I want to act fair. I have no wish to drive a hard bargain with you, and, on the other hand, I don't think I would be doing justice by a man that has worked hard if I let myself be sold for nothing. So, sir, to cut a long story short, I am willing to take two thousand pounds.'

'And where do you imagine I am to get two thousand pounds?'

Mr Davis modestly intimated he knew his place better than to presume to have any notion, but no doubt Mr Murray could raise that sum easily enough.

'If I could raise such a sum for you, do you not think I should have raised it for myself long ago?'

Davis answered that he did; but, if he might make free to say so, times were changed.

'They are, they are indeed,' said Mr Murray bitterly; and then there was silence.

Davis knocked the conversational ball the next time.

'I am in no particular hurry, sir,' he said. 'So, long as we understand one another I can wait till you come back from Italy, and have got the handling of some cash of your own. I daresay even then you won't be able to pay me off all at once; but if you would insure your life—'

'I can't insure my life: I have tried, and been refused.'

Again there ensued a silence, which Davis broke once more.

'Well, sir,' he began, 'I'll chance that. If you will give me a line of writing about what you owe me, and make a sort of a will, saying I am to get two thousand, I'll hold my tongue about what's gone and past. And I would not be fretting, sir, if I was you: things are quiet now, and, please God, you might never have any more trouble.'

Mr Davis, in view of his two thousand pounds, his widow, and his wayside public, felt disposed to take an optimistic view of even his master's position; but Mr Murray's thoughts were of a different hue. 'If I do have any more,' he considered, 'I shall go mad'; a conclusion which seemed likely enough to follow upon even the memory of those phantom feet coming dabbling out of an unseen world to follow him with their accursed print in this.

Davis was not going abroad with the happy pair. For sufficient reason Mr Murray had decided to leave him behind, and Mrs Murray, ever alive to her own convenience, instantly engaged him to stay on with her as butler, her own being under notice to leave.

Thus, in a semi-official capacity, Davis witnessed the wedding, which people considered a splendid affair.

What Davis thought of it can never be known, because when he left Losdale Church his face was whiter than the bride's dress; and after the newly wedded couple started on the first stage of their life-journey he went to his room, and stayed in it till his services were required.

'There is no money would pay me for what I've seen,' he remarked to himself. 'I went too cheap. But when once I handle the cash I'll try never to come anigh him or them again.'

What was he referring to? Just this. As the bridal group moved to the vestry he saw, if no one else did, those wet, wet feet softly and swiftly threading their way round the bridesmaids and the grooms-man, in front of the relations, before Mrs Murray herself, and hurry on to keep step with the just wed pair.

For the last time the young wife signed her maiden name. Friends crowded around, uttering congratulations, and still through the throng those unnoticed feet kept walking in and out, round and round, backward and forward, as a dog threads its way through the people at a fair. Down the aisle, under the sweeping dresses of the ladies, past courtly gentlemen, Davis saw those awful feet running gleefully till they came up with bride and bridegroom.

'She is going abroad with them,' thought the man; and then for a moment he felt as if he could endure the ghastly vision no longer, but must faint dead away. 'It is a vile shame,' he reflected, 'to drag an innocent girl into such a whirlpool'; and all the time over the church step the feet were dancing merrily.

The clerk and the verger noticed them at last.

'I wonder who has been here with wet feet?' said the clerk; and the verger wonderingly answered he did not know.

Davis could have told him, had he been willing to speak or capable of speech.

VIII

HE'D HAVE SEEN ME RIGHTED

It was August once again—August, fine, warm, and sunshiny—just one year after that damp afternoon on which Paul Murray and his friend stood in front of the Ship at Lower Halliford. No lack of visitors that season. Hotels were full, and furnished houses at a premium. The hearts of lodging-house keepers were glad. Ladies arrayed in rainbow hues flashed about the quiet village streets; boatmen reaped a golden harvest; all sorts of crafts swarmed on the river. Men in flannels gallantly towed their feminine belongings up against a languidly flowing stream. Pater and materfamilias, and all the olive branches, big and little, were to be met on the Thames, and on the banks of Thames, from Richmond to Staines, and even higher still. The lilies growing around Dockett Point floated with their pure cups wide open to the sun; no close folding of the white wax-leaves around the golden centre that season. Beside the water purple loosestrife grew in great clumps of brilliant colour dazzling to the sight. It was, in fact, a glorious August, in which pleasure-seekers could idle and sun themselves and get tanned to an almost perfect brown without the slightest trouble.

During the past twelvemonth local tradition had tried hard to add another ghost at Dumsey Deep to that already established in the adjoining Stabbery; but the unshrinking brightness of that glorious summer checked belief in it for the time. No doubt when the dull autumn days came again, and the long winter nights, full of awful possibilities, folded water and land in fog and darkness, a figure dressed in grey silk and black velvet fichu, with a natty grey hat trimmed with black and white feathers on its phantom head, with small feet covered by the thinnest of openwork stockings, from which the shoes, so much too large, had dropped long ago, would reappear once more, to the terror of all who heard, but for the time being, snugly tucked up in holy ground the girl whose heart had rejoiced in her beauty, her youth, her admirers, and her finery, was lying quite still and quiet, with closed eyes, and ears that heard neither the church bells nor the splash of oars nor the murmur of human voices.

Others, too, were missing from—though not missed by—Shepperton (the Thames villages miss no human being so long as other human beings, with plenty of money, come down by rail, boat, or carriage to supply his place). Paul Murray, Dick Savill, and Walter Grantley were absent. Mrs Heath, too, had gone, a tottering, heartbroken woman, to Mr Pointer's, where she was most miserable, but where she and her small possessions were taken remarkably good care of.

'Only a year agone,' she said one day, 'my girl was with me. In the morning she wore her pretty cambric with pink spots; and in the afternoon, that grey silk in which she was buried—for we durst not change a thread, but just wrapped a winding-sheet round what was left. O! Lucy, Lucy, Lucy! to think I bore you for that!' and then she wept softly, and nobody heeded or tried to console her, for 'what', as Mrs Pointer wisely said, 'was the use of fretting over a daughter dead a twelvemonth, and never much of a comfort neither?'

Mr Richard Savill was still 'grinding away', to quote his expression. Walter Grantley had departed, so reported his friends, for the diamond-fields; his enemies improved on this by carelessly answering—

'Grantley! O, he's gone to the devil'; which latter statement could not have been quite true, since he has been back in England for a long time, and is now quite well to do and reconciled to his family.

As for Paul Murray, there had been all sorts of rumours floating about concerning him.

The honeymoon had been unduly protracted; from place to place the married pair wandered—never resting, never staying; alas! for him there was no rest—there could be none here.

It mattered not where he went—east, west, south, or north—those noiseless wet feet followed; no train was swift enough to outstrip them; no boat could cut the water fast enough to leave them behind; they tracked him with dogged persistence; they were with him sleeping, walking, eating, drinking, praying—for Paul Murray in those days often prayed after a desperate heathenish fashion—and yet the plague was not stayed; the accursed thing still dogged him like a Fate.

After a while people began to be shy of him, because the footsteps were no more intermittent; they were always where he was. Did he enter a cathedral, they accompanied him; did he walk solitary through the woods or pace the lakeside, or wander by the sea, they were ever and always with the unhappy man.

They were worse than any evil conscience, because conscience often sleeps, and they from the day of his marriage never did. They had waited for that—waited till he should raise the cup of happiness to his lips, in order to fill it with gall—waited till his wife's dream of bliss was perfect, and then wake her to the knowledge of some horror more agonizing than death.

There were times when he left his young wife for days and days, and went, like those possessed of old, into the wilderness, seeking rest and finding none; for no legion of demons could have cursed a man's life more than those wet feet, which printed marks on Paul Murray's heart that might have been branded by red-hot irons.

All that had gone before was as nothing to the trouble of having involved another in the horrible mystery of his own life—and that other a gentle, innocent, loving creature he might just as well have killed as married.

He did not know what to do. His brain was on fire; he had lost all hold upon himself, all grip over his mind. On the sea of life he tossed like a ship without a rudder, one minute taking a resolve to shoot himself, the next turning his steps to seek some priest, and confess the whole matter fully and freely, and, before he had walked a dozen yards, determining to go away into some savage and desolate land, where those horrible feet might, if they pleased, follow him to his grave.

By degrees this was the plan which took firm root in his dazed brain; and accordingly one morning he started for England, leaving a note in which he asked his wife to follow him. He never meant to see her sweet face again, and he never did. He had determined to go to his father-in-law and confess to him; and accordingly, on the anniversary of Lucy's death, he found himself at Losdale Court, where vague rumours of some unaccountable trouble had preceded him.

Mr Ketterick was brooding over these rumours in his library, when, as if in answer to his thoughts, the servant announced Mr Murray.

'Good God!' exclaimed the older man, shocked by the white, haggard face before him, 'what is wrong?'

'I have been ill,' was the reply.

'Where is your wife?'

'She is following me. She will be here in a day or so.'

'Why did you not travel together?'

'That is what I have come to tell you.'

Then he suddenly stopped and put his hand to his heart. He had voluntarily come up for execution, and now his courage failed him. His manhood was gone, his nerves unstrung. He was but a poor, weak, wasted creature, worn out by the ceaseless torment of those haunting feet, which, however, since he turned his steps to England had never followed him. Why had he travelled to Losdale Court? Might he not have crossed the ocean and effaced himself in the Far West, without telling his story at all?

Just as he had laid down the revolver, just as he had turned from the priest's door, so now he felt he could not say that which he had come determined to say.

'I have walked too far,' he said, after a pause. 'I cannot talk just yet. Will you leave me for half an hour? No; I don't want anything, thank you—except to be quiet.' Quiet!—ah, heavens!

After a little he rose and passed out on to the terrace. Around there was beauty and peace and sunshine. He—he—was the only jarring element, and even on him there seemed falling a numbed sensation which for the time being stimulated rest.

He left the terrace and crossed the lawn till he came to a great cedar tree, under which there was a seat, where he could sit a short time before leaving the Court.

Yes, he would go away and make no sign. Dreamily he thought of the wild lone lands beyond the sea, where there would be none to ask whence he came or marvel about the curse which followed him. Over the boundless prairie, up the mountain heights, let those feet pursue him if they would. Away from his fellows he could bear his burden. He would confess to no man—only to God, who knew his sin and sorrow; only to his Maker, who might have pity on the work of his hands, and some day bid that relentless avenger be still.

No, he would take no man into his confidence; and even as he so decided, the brightness of the day seemed to be clouded over, warmth was exchanged for a deadly chill, a horror of darkness seemed thrown like a pall over him, and a rushing sound as of many waters filled his ears.

An hour later, when Mr Ketterick sought his son-in-law, he found him lying on the ground, which was wet and trampled, as though by hundreds of little feet.

His shouts brought help, and Paul Murray was carried into the house, where they laid him on a couch and piled rugs and blankets over his shivering body.

'Fetch a doctor at once,' said Mr Ketterick.

'And a clergyman,' added the housekeeper.

'No, a magistrate,' cried the sick man, in a loud voice.

They had thought him insensible, and, startled, looked at each other. After that he spoke no more, but turned his head away from them and lay quiet.

The doctor was the first to arrive. With quick alertness he stepped across the room, pulled aside the coverings, and took the patient's hand; then after gently moving the averted face, he said solemnly, like a man whose occupation has gone—

'I can do nothing here; he is dead.'

It was true. Whatever his secret, Paul Murray carried it with him to a country further distant than the lone land where he had thought to hide his misery.

'It is of no use talking to me,' said Mr Davis, when subsequently telling his story. 'If Mr Murray had been a gentleman as was a gentleman, he'd have seen me righted, dead or not. *She* was able to come back— at least, her feet were; and he could have done the same if he'd liked. It was as bad as swindling not making a fresh will after he was married.

How was I to know that will would turn out so much waste paper? And then when I asked for my own, Mrs Murray dismissed me without a character, and Mr Ketterick's lawyers won't give me anything either; so a lot I've made by being a faithful servant, and I'd have all servants take warning by me.'

Mr Davis is his own servant now, and a very bad master he finds himself.

3

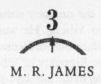

M. R. JAMES

Number 13

Among the towns of Jutland, Viborg justly holds a high place. It is the seat of a bishopric; it has a handsome but almost entirely new cathedral, a charming garden, a lake of great beauty, and many storks. Near it is Hald, accounted one of the prettiest things in Denmark; and hard by is Finderup, where Marsk Stig murdered King Erik Glipping on St Cecilia's Day, in the year 1286. Fifty-six blows of square-headed iron maces were traced on Erik's skull when his tomb was opened in the seventeenth century. But I am not writing a guidebook.

There are good hotels in Viborg—Preisler's and the Phoenix are all that can be desired. But my cousin, whose experiences I have to tell you now, went to the Golden Lion the first time that he visited Viborg. He has not been there since, and the following pages will, perhaps, explain the reason of his abstention.

The Golden Lion is one of the very few houses in the town that were not destroyed in the great fire of 1726, which practically demolished the cathedral, the Sognekirke, the Raadhuus, and so much else that was old and interesting. It is a great red-brick house—that is, the front is of brick, with corbie steps on the gables and a text over the door; but the courtyard into which the omnibus drives is of black and white wood and plaster.

The sun was declining in the heavens when my cousin walked up to the door, and the light smote full upon the imposing façade of the house. He was delighted with the old-fashioned aspect of the place, and promised himself a thoroughly satisfactory and amusing stay in an inn so typical of old Jutland.

It was not business in the ordinary sense of the word that had brought Mr Anderson to Viborg. He was engaged upon some researches into the Church history of Denmark, and it had come to his knowledge that in the Rigsarkiv of Viborg there were papers, saved from the fire, relating to the last days of Roman Catholicism in the country. He proposed, therefore, to spend a considerable time—perhaps as much as a fortnight or three weeks—in examining and copying these, and he hoped that the Golden Lion would be able to give him a room of sufficient size to serve alike as a bedroom and a study. His wishes were explained to the landlord, and, after a certain amount of thought, the latter suggested that perhaps it might be the best way for the gentleman to look at one or two of the larger rooms and pick one for himself. It seemed a good idea.

The top floor was soon rejected as entailing too much getting upstairs after the day's work; the second floor contained no room of exactly the dimensions required; but on the first floor there was a choice of two or three rooms which would, so far as size went, suit admirably.

The landlord was strongly in favour of Number 17, but Mr Anderson pointed out that its windows commanded only the blank wall of the next house, and that it would be very dark in the afternoon. Either Number 12 or Number 14 would be better, for both of them looked on the street, and the bright evening light and the pretty view would more than compensate him for the additional amount of noise.

Eventually Number 12 was selected. Like its neighbours, it had three windows, all on one side of the room; it was fairly high and unusually long. There was, of course, no fireplace, but the stove was handsome and rather old—a cast-iron erection, on the side of which was a representation of Abraham sacrificing Isaac, and the inscription, 'I Bog Mose, Cap. 22,' above. Nothing else in the room was remarkable; the only interesting picture was an old coloured print of the town, date about 1820.

Suppertime was approaching, but when Anderson, refreshed by the ordinary ablutions, descended the staircase, there were still a few minutes before the bell rang. He devoted them to examining the list of his fellow-lodgers. As is usual in Denmark, their names were displayed on a large blackboard, divided into columns and lines, the numbers of the rooms being painted in at the beginning of each line. The list was not exciting. There was an advocate, or Sagförer, a German, and some bagmen from Copenhagen. The one and only point which suggested any food for thought was the absence of any Number 13 from the tale of the rooms, and even this was a thing which Anderson had already noticed half a dozen times in his experience of Danish hotels. He could not help wondering whether the objection to that particular number, common as it is, was so widespread and so strong as to make it difficult to let a room so ticketed, and he resolved to ask the landlord if he and his colleagues in the profession had actually met with many clients who refused to be accommodated in the thirteenth room.

He had nothing to tell me (I am giving the story as I heard it from him) about what passed at supper, and the evening, which was spent in unpacking and arranging his clothes, books, and papers, was not more eventful. Towards eleven o'clock he resolved to go to bed, but with him, as with a good many other people nowadays, an almost necessary preliminary to bed, if he meant to sleep, was the reading of a few pages of print, and he now remembered that the particular book which he had been reading in the train, and which alone would satisfy him at that present moment, was in the pocket of his greatcoat, then hanging on a peg outside the dining-room.

To run down and secure it was the work of a moment, and, as the passages were by no means dark, it was not difficult for him to find his way back to his own door. So, at least, he thought; but when he arrived there, and turned the handle, the door entirely refused to open, and he caught the sound of a hasty movement towards it from within. He had tried the wrong door, of course. Was his own room to the right or to the left? He glanced at the number: it was 13. His room would be on the left; and so it was. And not before he had been in bed for some minutes, had read his wonted three or four pages of his book, blown out his light, and turned over to go to sleep, did it occur to him that, whereas on the blackboard of the hotel there had been no Number 13, there was undoubtedly a room numbered 13 in the hotel. He felt rather sorry he had not chosen it for his own. Perhaps he might have done the landlord a little service by occupying it, and given him the chance of saying that a well-born English gentleman had lived in it for three weeks and liked it very much. But probably it was used as a servant's room or something of the kind. After all, it was most likely not so large or good a room as his own. And he looked drowsily about the room, which was fairly perceptible in the half-light from the street-lamp. It was a curious effect, he thought. Rooms usually look larger in a dim light than a full one, but this seemed to have contracted in length and grown proportionately higher. Well, well! sleep was more important than these vague ruminations—and to sleep he went.

On the day after his arrival Anderson attacked the Rigsarkiv of Viborg. He was, as one might expect in Denmark, kindly received, and access to all that he wished to see was made as easy for him as possible. The documents laid before him were far more numerous and interesting than he had at all anticipated. Besides official papers, there was a large bundle of correspondence relating to Bishop Jörgen Friis, the last Roman Catholic who held the see, and in these there cropped up many amusing and what are called 'intimate' details of private life and individual character. There was much talk of a house owned by the Bishop, but not inhabited by him, in the town. Its tenant was apparently somewhat of a scandal and a stumbling-block to the reforming party. He was a disgrace, they wrote, to the city; he practised secret and wicked arts, and had sold his soul to the enemy. It was of a piece with the gross corruption and superstition of the Babylonish Church that such a viper and blood-sucking *Troldmand* should be patronized and harboured by the Bishop. The Bishop met these reproaches boldly; he protested his own abhorrence of all such things as secret arts, and required his antagonists to bring the matter before the proper court—of course, the spiritual court—and sift it to the bottom. No one could be more ready and willing than himself to condemn Mag Nicolas Francken if the evidence showed him to have been guilty of any of the crimes informally alleged against him.

Anderson had not time to do more than glance at the next letter of the Protestant leader, Rasmus Nielsen, before the record office was closed for the day, but he gathered its general tenor, which was to the effect that Christian men were now no longer bound by the decisions of Bishops of Rome, and that the Bishop's Court was not, and could not be, a fit or competent tribunal to judge so grave and weighty a cause.

On leaving the office, Mr Anderson was accompanied by the old gentleman who presided over it, and, as they walked, the conversation very naturally turned to the papers of which I have just been speaking.

Herr Scavenius, the Archivist of Viborg, though very well informed as to the general run of the documents under his charge, was not a specialist in those of the Reformation period. He was much interested in what Anderson had to tell him about them. He looked forward with great pleasure, he said, to seeing the publication in which Mr Anderson spoke of embodying their contents. 'This house of the Bishop Friis,' he added, 'it is a great puzzle to me where it can have stood. I have studied carefully the topography of old Viborg, but it is most unlucky—of the old terrier of the Bishop's property which was made in 1560, and of which we have the greater part in the Arkiv—just the piece which had the list of the town property is missing. Never mind. Perhaps I shall some day succeed to find him.'

After taking some exercise—I forget exactly how or where—Anderson went back to the Golden Lion, his supper, his game of patience, and his bed. On the way to his room it occurred to him that he had forgotten to talk to the landlord about the omission of Number 13 from the hotel board, and also that he might as well make sure that Number 13 did actually exist before he made any reference to the matter.

The decision was not difficult to arrive at. There was the door with its number as plain as could be, and work of some kind was evidently going on inside it, for as he neared the door he could hear footsteps and voices, or a voice, within. During the few seconds in which he halted to make sure of the number, the footsteps ceased, seemingly very near the door, and he was a little startled at hearing a quick hissing breathing as of a person in strong excitement. He went on to his own room, and again he was surprised to find how much smaller it seemed now than it had when he selected it. It was a slight disappointment, but only slight. If he found it really not large enough, he could very easily shift to another. In the meantime he wanted something—as far as I remember it was a pocket-handkerchief—out of his portmanteau, which had been placed by the porter on a very inadequate trestle or stool against the wall at the farthest end of the room from his bed. Here was a very curious thing: the portmanteau was not to be seen. It had been moved by officious servants; doubtless the contents had been put in the wardrobe. No, none of them were there. This was vexatious. The idea of a theft he dismissed at once. Such things rarely happen in Denmark, but some piece of stupidity had certainly been performed (which is not so uncommon), and the *stuepige* must be severely spoken to. Whatever it was that he wanted, it was not so necessary to his comfort that he could not wait till the morning for it, and he therefore settled not to ring the bell and disturb the servants. He went to the window—the right-hand window it was—and looked out on the quiet street. There was a tall building opposite, with large spaces of dead wall; no passers-by; a dark night; and very little to be seen of any kind.

The light was behind him, and he could see his own shadow clearly cast on the wall opposite. Also the shadow of the bearded man in Number 11 on the left, who passed to and fro in shirtsleeves once or twice, and was seen first brushing his hair, and later on in a nightgown. Also the shadow of the occupant of Number 13 on the right. This might be more interesting. Number 13 was, like himself, leaning on his elbows on the window-sill looking out into the street. He seemed to be a tall thin man—or was it by any chance a woman?—at least, it was someone who covered his or her head with some kind of drapery before going to bed, and, he thought, must be possessed of a red lampshade—and the lamp must be flickering very much. There was a distinct playing up and down of a dull red light on the opposite wall. He craned out a little to see if he could make any more of the figure, but beyond a fold of some light, perhaps white, material on the window-sill he could see nothing.

Now came a distant step in the street, and its approach seemed to recall Number 13 to a sense of his exposed position, for very swiftly and suddenly he swept aside from the window, and his red light went out. Anderson, who had been smoking a cigarette, laid the end of it on the window-sill and went to bed.

Next morning he was woke by the *stuepige* with hot water, etc. He roused himself, and after thinking out the correct Danish words, said as distinctly as he could:

'You must not move my portmanteau. Where is it?'

As is not uncommon, the maid laughed, and went away without making any distinct answer.

Anderson, rather irritated, sat up in bed, intending to call her back, but he remained sitting up, staring straight in front of him. There was his portmanteau on its trestle, exactly where he had seen the porter put it when he first arrived. This was a rude shock for a man who prided himself on his accuracy of observation. How it could possibly have escaped him the night before he did not pretend to understand; at any rate, there it was now.

The daylight showed more than the portmanteau; it let the true proportions of the room with its three windows appear, and satisfied its tenant that his choice after all had not been a bad one. When he was almost dressed he walked to the middle one of the three windows to look out at the weather. Another shock awaited him. Strangely unobservant he must have been last night. He could have sworn ten times over that he had been smoking at the right-hand window the last thing before he went to bed, and here was his cigarette-end on the sill of the middle window.

He started to go down to breakfast. Rather late, but Number 13 was later: here were his boots still outside his door—a gentleman's boots. So then Number 13 was a man, not a woman. Just then he caught sight of the number on the door. It was 14. He thought he must have passed Number 13 without noticing it. Three stupid mistakes in twelve hours were too much for a methodical, accurate-minded man, so he turned back to make sure. The next number to 14 was Number 12, his own room. There was no Number 13 at all.

After some minutes devoted to a careful consideration of everything he had had to eat and drink during the last twenty-four hours, Anderson decided to give the question up. If his eyes or his brain were giving way he would have plenty of opportunities for ascertaining that fact; if not, then he was evidently being treated to a very interesting experience. In either case the development of events would certainly be worth watching.

During the day he continued his examination of the episcopal correspondence which I have already summarized. To his disappointment, it was incomplete. Only one other letter could be found which referred to the affair of Mag Nicolas Francken. It was from the Bishop Jörgen Friis to Rasmus Nielsen. He said:

Although we are not in the least degree inclined to assent to your judgement concerning our court, and shall be prepared if need be to withstand you to the uttermost in that behalf, yet forasmuch as our trusty and well-beloved Mag Nicolas Francken, against whom you have dared to allege certain false and malicious charges, hath been suddenly removed from among us, it is apparent that the question for this time falls. But forasmuch as you further allege that the Apostle and Evangelist St John in his heavenly Apocalypse describes the Holy Roman Church under the guise and symbol of the Scarlet Woman, be it known to you, etc.

Search as he might, Anderson could find no sequel to this letter nor any clue to the cause or manner of the 'removal' of the *casus belli*. He could only suppose that Francken had died suddenly; and as there were only two days between the date of Nielsen's last letter—when Francken was evidently still in being—and that of the Bishop's letter, the death must have been completely unexpected.

In the afternoon he paid a short visit to Hald, and took his tea at Baekkelund; nor could he notice, though he was in a somewhat nervous frame of mind, that there was any indication of such a failure of eye or brain as his experiences of the morning had led him to fear.

At supper he found himself next to the landlord.

'What,' he asked him, after some indifferent conversation, 'is the reason why in most of the hotels one visits in this country the number thirteen is left out of the list of rooms? I see you have none here.'

The landlord seemed amused.

'To think that you should have noticed a thing like that! I've thought about it once or twice myself, to tell the truth. An educated man, I've said, has no business with these superstitious notions. I was brought up myself here in the high school of Viborg, and our old master was always a man to set his face against anything of that kind. He's been dead now this many years—a fine upstanding man he was, and ready with his hands as well as his head. I recollect us boys, one snowy day—'

Here he plunged into reminiscence.

'Then you don't think there is any particular objection to having a Number 13?' said Anderson.

'Ah! to be sure. Well, you understand, I was brought up to the business by my poor old father. He kept an hotel in Aarhuus first, and then, when we were born, he moved to Viborg here, which was his native place, and had the Phoenix here until he died. That was in 1876. Then I started business in Silkeborg, and only the year before last I moved into this house.'

Then followed more details as to the state of the house and business when first taken over.

'And when you came here, was there a Number 13?'

'No, no. I was going to tell you about that. You see, in a place like this, the commercial class—the travellers—are what we have to provide for in general. And put them in Number 13? Why, they'd as soon sleep in the street, or sooner. As far as I'm concerned myself, it wouldn't make a penny difference to me what the number of my room was, and so I've often said to them; but they stick to it that it brings them bad luck. Quantities of stories they have among them of men that have slept in a Number 13 and never been the same again, or lost their best customers, or—one thing and another,' said the landlord, after searching for a more graphic phrase.

'Then what do you use your Number 13 for?' said Anderson, conscious as he said the words of a curious anxiety quite disproportionate to the importance of the question.

'My Number 13? Why, don't I tell you that there isn't such a thing in the house? I thought you might have noticed that. If there was it would be next door to your own room.'

'Well, yes; only I happened to think—that is, I fancied last night that I had seen a door numbered thirteen in that passage; and, really, I am almost certain I must have been right, for I saw it the night before as well.'

Of course, Herr Kristensen laughed this notion to scorn, as Anderson had expected, and emphasized with much iteration the fact that no Number 13 existed or had existed before him in that hotel.

Anderson was in some ways relieved by his certainty, but still puzzled, and he began to think that the best way to make sure whether he had indeed been subject to an illusion or not was to invite the landlord to his room to smoke a cigar later on in the evening. Some photographs of English towns which he had with him formed a sufficiently good excuse.

Herr Kristensen was flattered by the invitation, and most willingly accepted it. At about ten o'clock he was to make his appearance, but before that Anderson had some letters to write, and retired for the purpose of writing them. He almost blushed to himself at confessing it, but he could not deny that it was the fact that he was becoming quite nervous about the question of the existence of Number 13; so much so that he approached his room by way of Number 11, in order that he might not be obliged to pass the door, or the place where the door ought to be. He looked quickly and suspiciously about the room when he entered it, but there was nothing, beyond that indefinable air of being smaller than usual, to warrant any misgivings. There was no question of the presence or absence of his portmanteau tonight. He had himself emptied it of its contents and lodged it under his bed. With a certain effort he dismissed the thought of Number 13 from his mind, and sat down to his writing.

His neighbours were quiet enough. Occasionally a door opened in the passage and a pair of boots was thrown out, or a bagman walked past humming to himself, and outside, from time to time a cart thundered over the atrocious cobblestones, or a quick step hurried along the flags.

Anderson finished his letters, ordered in whisky and soda, and then went to the window and studied the dead wall opposite and the shadows upon it.

As far as he could remember, Number 14 had been occupied by the lawyer, a staid man, who said little at meals, being generally engaged in studying a small bundle of papers beside his plate. Apparently, however, he was in the habit of giving vent to his animal spirits when alone. Why else should he be dancing? The shadow from the next room evidently showed that he was. Again and again his thin form crossed the window, his arms waved, and a gaunt leg was kicked up with surprising agility. He seemed to be barefooted, and the floor must be well laid, for no sound betrayed his movements. Sagförer Herr Anders Jensen, dancing at ten o'clock at night in a hotel bedroom, seemed a fitting subject for a historical painting in the grand style; and Anderson's thoughts, like those of Emily in the 'Mysteries of Udolpho', began to 'arrange themselves in the following lines':

When I return to my hotel,
     At ten o'clock p.m.,
The waiters think I am unwell;
     I do not care for them.
But when I've locked my chamber door,
     And put my boots outside,
I dance all night upon the floor.
And even if my neighbours swore,
I'd go on dancing all the more,
For I'm acquainted with the law,
And in despite of all their jaw,
     Their protests I deride.

Had not the landlord at this moment knocked at the door, it is probable that quite a long poem might have been laid before the reader. To judge from his look of surprise when he found himself in the room, Herr Kristensen was struck, as Anderson had been, by something unusual in its aspect. But he made no remark. Anderson's photographs interested him mightily, and formed the text of many autobiographical discourses. Nor is it quite clear how the conversation could have been diverted into the desired channel of Number 13, had not the lawyer at this moment begun to sing, and to sing in a manner which could leave no doubt in anyone's mind that he was either exceedingly drunk or raving mad. It was a high, thin voice that they heard, and it seemed dry, as if from long disuse. Of words or tune there was no question. It went sailing up to a surprising height, and was carried down with a despairing moan as of a winter wind in a hollow chimney, or an organ whose wind fails suddenly. It was a really horrible sound, and Anderson felt that if he had been alone he must have fled for refuge and society to some neighbour bagman's room.

The landlord sat open-mouthed.

'I don't understand it,' he said at last, wiping his forehead. 'It is dreadful. I have heard it once before, but I made sure it was a cat.'

'Is he mad?' said Anderson.

'He must be; and what a sad thing! Such a good customer, too, and so successful in his business, by what I hear, and a young family to bring up.'

Just then came an impatient knock at the door, and the knocker entered, without waiting to be asked. It was the lawyer, in *déshabille* and very rough-haired; and very angry he looked.

'I beg pardon, sir,' he said, 'but I should be much obliged if you would kindly desist—'

Here he stopped, for it was evident that neither of the persons before him was responsible for the disturbance; and after a moment's lull it swelled forth again more wildly than before.

'But what in the name of Heaven does it mean?' broke out the lawyer. 'Where is it? Who is it? Am I going out of my mind?'

'Surely, Herr Jensen, it comes from your room next door? Isn't there a cat or something stuck in the chimney?'

This was the best that occurred to Anderson to say and he realized its futility as he spoke; but anything was better than to stand and listen to that horrible voice, and look at the broad, white face of the landlord, all perspiring and quivering as he clutched the arms of his chair.

'Impossible,' said the lawyer, 'impossible. There is no chimney. I came here because I was convinced the noise was going on here. It was certainly in the next room to mine.'

'Was there no door between yours and mine?' said Anderson eagerly.

'No, sir,' said Herr Jensen, rather sharply. 'At least, not this morning.'

'Ah!' said Anderson. 'Nor tonight?'

'I am not sure,' said the lawyer with some hesitation.

Suddenly the crying or singing voice in the next room died away, and the singer was heard seemingly to laugh to himself in a crooning manner. The three men actually shivered at the sound. Then there was a silence.

'Come,' said the lawyer, 'what have you to say, Herr Kristensen? What does this mean?'

'Good Heaven!' said Kristensen. 'How should I tell! I know no more than you, gentlemen. I pray I may never hear such a noise again.'

'So do I,' said Herr Jensen, and he added something under his breath. Anderson thought it sounded like the last words of the Psalter, '*omnis spiritus laudet Dominum*,' but he could not be sure.

'But we must do something,' said Anderson—'the three of us. Shall we go and investigate in the next room?'

'But that is Herr Jensen's room,' wailed the landlord. 'It is no use; he has come from there himself.'

'I am not so sure,' said Jensen. 'I think this gentleman is right: we must go and see.'

The only weapons of defence that could be mustered on the spot were a stick and umbrella. The expedition went out into the passage, not without quakings. There was a deadly quiet outside, but a light shone from under the next door. Anderson and Jensen approached it. The latter turned the handle, and gave a sudden vigorous push. No use. The door stood fast.

'Herr Kristensen,' said Jensen, 'will you go and fetch the strongest servant you have in the place? We must see this through.'

The landlord nodded, and hurried off, glad to be away from the scene of action. Jensen and Anderson remained outside looking at the door.

'It *is* Number 13, you see,' said the latter.

'Yes; there is your door, and there is mine,' said Jensen.

'My room has three windows in the daytime,' said Anderson with difficulty, suppressing a nervous laugh.

'By George, so has mine!' said the lawyer, turning and looking at Anderson. His back was now to the door. In that moment the door opened, and an arm came out and clawed at his shoulder. It was clad in ragged, yellowish linen, and the bare skin, where it could be seen, had long grey hair upon it.

Anderson was just in time to pull Jensen out of its reach with a cry of disgust and fright, when the door shut again, and a low laugh was heard.

Jensen had seen nothing, but when Anderson hurriedly told him what a risk he had run, he fell into a great state of agitation, and suggested that they should retire from the enterprise and lock themselves up in one or other of their rooms.

However, while he was developing this plan, the landlord and two able-bodied men arrived on the scene, all looking rather serious and alarmed. Jensen met them with a torrent of description and explanation, which did not at all tend to encourage them for the fray.

The men dropped the crowbars they had brought, and said flatly that they were not going to risk their throats in that devil's den. The landlord was miserably nervous and undecided, conscious that if the danger were not faced his hotel was ruined, and very loth to face it himself. Luckily Anderson hit upon a way of rallying the demoralized force.

'Is this,' he said, 'the Danish courage I have heard so much of? It isn't a German in there, and if it was, we are five to one.'

The two servants and Jensen were stung into action by this, and made a dash at the door.

'Stop!' said Anderson. 'Don't lose your heads. You stay out here with the light, landlord, and one of you two men break in the door, and don't go in when it gives way.'

The men nodded, and the younger stepped forward, raised his crowbar, and dealt a tremendous blow on the upper panel. The result was not in the least what any of them anticipated. There was no cracking or rending of wood—only a dull sound, as if the solid wall had been struck. The man dropped his tool with a shout, and began rubbing his elbow. His cry drew their eyes upon him for a moment; then Anderson looked at the door again. It was gone; the plaster wall of the passage stared him in the face, with a considerable gash in it where the crowbar had struck it. Number 13 had passed out of existence.

For a brief space they stood perfectly still, gazing at the blank wall. An early cock in the yard beneath was heard to crow; and as Anderson glanced in the direction of the sound, he saw through the window at the end of the long passage that the eastern sky was paling to the dawn.

'Perhaps,' said the landlord, with hesitation, 'you gentlemen would like another room for tonight—a double-bedded one?'

Neither Jensen nor Anderson was averse to the suggestion. They felt inclined to hunt in couples after their late experience. It was found convenient, when each of them went to his room to collect the articles he wanted for the night, that the other should go with him and hold the candle. They noticed that both Number 12 and Number 14 had *three* windows.

Next morning the same party reassembled in Number 12. The landlord was naturally anxious to avoid engaging outside help, and yet it was imperative that the mystery attaching to that part of the house should be cleared up. Accordingly the two servants had been induced to take upon them the function of carpenters. The furniture was cleared away, and, at the cost of a good many irretrievably damaged planks, that portion of the floor was taken up which lay nearest to Number 14.

You will naturally suppose that a skeleton—say that of Mag Nicolas Francken—was discovered. That was not so. What they did find lying between the beams which supported the flooring was a small copper box. In it was a neatly folded vellum document, with about twenty lines of writing. Both Anderson and Jensen (who proved to be something of a palaeographer) were much excited by this discovery, which promised to afford the key to these extraordinary phenomena.

I possess a copy of an astrological work which I have never read. It has, by way of frontispiece, a woodcut by Hans Sebald Beham, representing a number of sages seated round a table. This detail may enable connoisseurs to identify the book. I cannot myself recollect its title, and it is not at this moment within reach; but the fly-leaves of it are covered with writing, and, during the ten years in which I have owned the volume, I have not been able to determine which way up this writing ought to be read, much less in what language it is. Not dissimilar was the position of Anderson and Jensen after the protracted examination to which they submitted the document in the copper box.

After two days' contemplation of it, Jensen, who was the bolder spirit of the two, hazarded the conjecture that the language was either Latin or Old Danish.

Anderson ventured upon no surmises, and was very willing to surrender the box and the parchment to the Historical Society of Viborg to be placed in their museum.

I had the whole story from him a few months later, as we sat in a wood near Upsala, after a visit to the library there, where we—or, rather, I—had laughed over the contract by which Daniel Salthenius (in later life Professor of Hebrew at Königsberg) sold himself to Satan. Anderson was not really amused.

'Young idiot!' he said, meaning Salthenius, who was only an under-graduate when he committed that indiscretion, 'how did he know what company he was courting?'

And when I suggested the usual considerations he only grunted. That same afternoon he told me what you have read; but he refused to draw any inferences from it, and to assent to any that I drew for him.

4

PERCEVAL LANDON

Railhead

This story was told me in Rangoon by a man whose name, I think, was Torrens, but I cannot remember very clearly, if indeed I ever knew. Really I hardly know anything about the man except that he was obviously convinced of its truth. He said that John Silbermeister told him the story himself, and I have no doubt that he did. So far as Torrens could recall the man, Silbermeister was an ordinary lanky man, of a singular directness of speech, and totally unable to see a joke. So, for that matter, was Torrens. He said that he had verified the story to this extent, that at the date that Silbermeister mentioned, the NP Railway would have reached Enderton; nor is it apparent what motive there could be for Silbermeister lying in the matter. Torrens hadn't the imagination of a 'rickshaw-wallah, so it isn't his lie either. At any rate, I give it for what it is worth.

Torrens was a little man who had taken up Christian Science somewhat earnestly a little beyond middle life. He was really a person of some importance on the railway, and I believe one of the Company's most efficient servants. To listen to him sometimes one would hardly believe that an accident could possibly occur on the railway, except as a mere delusion of the senses. I believe he died about two years after he told me the story, and for his own sake I hope that he was able to maintain his Christian Science doctrines to the end, for he had sore need of them. He died of cholera at Bhamo in 1904.

He had shown me round the curiosity-shops of Rangoon, and with his help I had disentangled one or two interesting pieces of work from the mass of modern substitutes—it is unfair to call them forgeries—which fill up the curio-shelves of Rangoon dealers. One of them was a

73

little bronze serpent, which sat on its rounded tail and blinked at me with ruby eyes as he told the story in the billiard-room of the 'Strand'; and I remember that the Calcutta boat was coming in from the Hastings shoal at the time, and from time to time wailed like a lost spirit up the river. The heat was intense. They have not in Rangoon the mosquito antidotes to which one is used in India. One buzzing electric fan supplied the entire room, but its sphere of influence was entirely monopolized by a pair of German diamond merchants and their jet-clad wives.

'Some years ago,' said Torrens, 'a man called Silbermeister came to me with excellent references, and asked if there was any chance of his being employed on the new construction towards the Yunnan frontier. That was before Curzon had put a stopper on the whole project. I dare say Curzon was right. The railway to the North-East, both on this side and on the other side of the frontier, would have been extremely expensive and possibly impracticable. There are deep ravines, "canyons", Silbermeister called them, across which our line had to be thrown. To zigzag down to the bottom by reversing stations and then up again seemed to be the only possible means of crossing them, and with such enormous initial expenditure it was doubtful whether the traffic would ever pay one per cent upon the capital. But we in Rangoon wanted to establish a definite connection with China for political reasons, and if the Indian Government had been willing to guarantee half the cost, the Burmah Railways would have gone on with the business.[1] Silbermeister, who had had a good deal of pioneer railway experience, would have been just the man for the job. While the matter was being decided in Calcutta he remained here, and I saw a good deal of him. One evening Silbermeister told me this story, and, so far as I can judge the man at all, I should say that he was telling me the truth.'

Some years ago, when the big New York Syndicate that employed Silbermeister, among thirty thousand others, was pushing forward the construction of the NP Railway in Nebraska, he was for about three months in charge of the railhead station at Enderton. This was merely

---

[1] Torrens was scarcely accurate in this matter.

a solidly built wooden hut by the side of the line. Trains ran up to it and nominally carried passengers, but as a matter of fact very few wanted to go further than Castleton, a raw pioneer clump of houses, which had already blossomed out into half a dozen stores, seven 'hotels', an electric generating shed, and thirty or forty pretentiously named wooden houses. Beyond Enderton the railway was at this time actually in course of construction. The navvies were chiefly Italian. It was a difficult piece of work, and about eight miles on matters had temporarily come to a standstill owing to a persistent subsidence along the edge of a small half-dry river. On one Thursday morning a piece of the embankment had given way, and an Italian workman had been killed. This was a matter of no great importance; all engineers know that their lives must be sacrificed to carry out any important work, and on the whole the loss of life on this section of the NP line had been less than might have been expected. There were the usual police guards in the navvies' camp, which contained between three to four hundred workmen.

On a Friday evening, between six and seven o'clock, Silbermeister was sitting in his station-house at Enderton running over the week's wages' account, when a light engine ran up from Castleton. Silbermeister was expecting the money with which to pay the navvies' weekly wages on the following day, and a sub-inspector got off the footplate carrying a canvas bag which contained the money that was needed. It was the usual weekend routine. At the same time, a couple of railwaymen took off the tender half a dozen large packing-cases containing materials that had been requisitioned for the work, and put them into the baggage-room, which composed one-half of the station-house. The inspector ran through Silbermeister's accounts, initialled them as correct, and then took a receipt for the money which he brought with him. Silbermeister proceeded to lock the money up in the safe in his own room, and then checked the packing-cases which had just been stored in the baggage-room. Among these cases was a somewhat gruesome object, a coffin sent up by the Company from Castleton in order that the victim of the late accident might be decently buried on Sunday morning.

Another receipt was signed for the cases, and then the inspector told the engine-driver he was ready to return. Before doing so, however, he turned to Silbermeister and said:

'Do you feel quite safe here with all that money? Shall I leave you a man to spend the night here with you?'

Silbermeister shrugged his shoulders, and with a smile declined the offer. He said that the police looked after the navvies' camp, that he and his negro servant had spent many nights together at the station, and that he had no fear of burglars. He had, he said, his revolver beside him, and the money would not remain with him more than that one night. The two men shook hands, and the inspector departed as he had come.

Silbermeister then rechecked the books, re-counted the money, saw that the doors were properly locked, sent away his negro servant for the night—the man had been getting the table ready for his supper while he was escorting the inspector back to the engine—and, after locking the door leading to the platform, occupied himself with some small duties now that his day's work was done. There was no further possibility of being rung up from Castleton, so he took this opportunity of cleaning and readjusting the telegraph instrument which stood on a table by the wall, and had not been working quite satisfactorily that morning. For this purpose he disconnected the instrument, and being a fairly skilled electrician—though of an old-fashioned school, Torrens said—he did nearly all that was needed in a few minutes. Leaving the instrument as it was, he lit a pipe and started to get ready his supper. By this time the night had begun to fall in earnest, and he lighted the kerosene lamp on the table. More from habit than from anything else, as he knew that he was not likely to need it, he also lighted the bull's-eye lantern which, on most evenings in the week, he took with him on his final rounds.

Silbermeister then opened the cupboard and took down a loaf of bread, a tin of canned meat, and a pot of marmalade. His preparations for supper were simple. It was a cold night, and he meant to have some hot grog before turning in, so he lighted the spirit lamp and filled his kettle from a pitcher of water. While the water was boiling he opened the tin of meat, cut himself a German slice of bread, and arranged the table. By this time the sun had entirely set, and only the last reflections from the dull western horizon still found their way through the windows. For a moment he looked out through the windows across the platform and the wide level waste beyond. There was not a living thing in sight—not a tree, hardly a bush. Then he shut up the house for the night, and fastened the shutters. He sat down at the table for his meal, propped up a book underneath the lamp, and made himself as comfortable as he could. The bully-beef was not a very appetizing dish, and it occurred to him that he had a bottle of sauce put away in a box at the side of the room. He got up, opened the box, and, in order to find the sauce, turned out upon the floor with some noise most of the contents of the trunk. While doing so, he did not notice that the telegraph instrument on the further table ticked out a short and sharp message: at least, it was only the last few strokes that attracted his attention. He turned from the box, before which he was kneeling, to listen, but the message had already stopped. Leaving the sauce undiscovered, he rose to his feet and muttered:

'I'm sure the thing was talking,' and went across to the table, to ask for a repetition from Castleton, only to discover, as he might have remembered, that he had himself disconnected the instrument while cleaning it. Dismissing the matter as an illusion, he returned to the box where the sauce was, and after a moment or two found what he wanted. He then resumed his seat at the table without thinking again of the telegraph instrument. He began his reading, and was in the middle of an engrossing sentence when the telegraph instrument spoke again. This time there could be no mistake. Silbermeister, who knew that when he had left the machine three minutes before it was entirely disconnected, laid down his knife and fork and listened like a man in a dream. There was no doubt about it.

'E—N—T.'

The signal for Enderton Station had been called up sharply, imperiously, unmistakably. He waited a moment, and then, in spite of the fact that he had not acknowledged the call, came the short message. He muttered the words as they were ticked out:

'*Watch the box.*'

For one full minute Silbermeister sat immovable. There was no question of the fact, yet the man's common sense refused to believe in what his ears had heard. The room was dead silent except for the hissing of the spirit lamp which had just begun to boil. Silbermeister felt that he was the victim of some nightmare. He would not believe his own senses, and decided to test the thing once more. He rose from the table, went across to the instrument, and brought it bodily away from its position. He put it on the table in front of him next the corned beef, and then, blowing out the spirit lamp in order that the silence might be more intense, he resumed his seat and waited, hanging over it with every sense on the alert. The lamp lighted up his angular jaw and deep-set eyes staring at the little contrivance of brass and wood. He had not to wait long. The instrument, with its connecting wires and plugs hanging over the side of his dinner-table, and still swinging to and fro beneath it, once again called out his station:

'E—N—T.'

The sweat leapt to Silbermeister's forehead, but he made no sign. It went on. It was the same message, short, clear, and beyond all doubt:

'*Watch the box.*'

Silbermeister passed a hand over his face and thought. Whatever the origin of this message was, the message itself was unmistakable. He reached for his bull's-eye lantern, saw it was burning well, turned out the lamp on the table, and rose silently. He moved across to the door that separated his living-room from the luggage-room, very quietly opened the door, and waited. One minute dragged its slow length along, then two, then three, and still Silbermeister stood in the darkness as motionless as the jamb of the door. There was no sound inside or outside the station-house. So still was the silence that, as Silbermeister said, a man could hear his blood circulating round the drum of his own ear—rather a good expression, Torrens thought.

At last the tension was relieved. There was a sound, more like the sound of a gnawing mouse than anything else, and Silbermeister sank silently to his knee to listen more intently. A touch which, infinitesimal though it was, could only have been made by iron upon iron, betrayed the whole circumstance to him. There was a man in the coffin, and the man had so contrived the lid that he could get out of the coffin without attracting the notice of Silbermeister till it was too late. There was at the same moment the sound of a cautiously planted footstep on the platform outside. Silbermeister acted at once. Some of the cases of railway material that had been sent up that evening contained steel tools, and were as much as two men could carry into the room. Silbermeister was a strong man, but he hardly knew how he managed unaided to drag down one of the packing-cases and set it on the top of the coffin with a crash that almost crushed it in.

The moment he had done so, all pretence was at an end, and the man within it shouted to his accomplice outside. The answer was a blow on the door like a battering-ram. The packing-case might hold down the man for some time yet, so Silbermeister leapt back into his living-room to meet the new danger, only to find the door on to the platform being battered through just above the bolt. He picked up his revolver, and in order to make sure there should be no attack from behind, aimed at the coffin and pulled the trigger. There was no response. It was clear that treachery had been at work. His black servant had seized the opportunity while Silbermeister escorted the inspector to the engine, of opening and emptying it—an easy task, as it was lying on the table. There was no time to turn back to the baggage-room. Seizing a small crowbar, Silbermeister had only just time to dash to the door, through the hole in which his negro servant's arm was now thrusting itself feeling for the bolt. He gripped the man's hand and pulled it into the room until the negro's arm-pit was forced up against the splintered hole in the door. He struck heavily with the crowbar, and the negro screamed in agony. He struck again, and again, and again. He hardly knows what happened during that awful minute. He went on striking blindly and mechanically at what had suddenly become a man's sleeve. In the baggage-room he had just left the tremendous exertions of the imprisoned man were making the room resound, and the packing-case on the top of the coffin rocked to and fro. Silbermeister paid no attention. He lost his head. Both lamps were now out, and all he could do in the darkness was to go on hitting at what he held.

Suddenly there was the whistle of an approaching engine. No train was due until the following morning, but Silbermeister admitted that at the moment he hardly regarded anything as unusual. A couple of armed men and the inspector leapt down on to the platform, collared the negro servant, who by that time was hanging half-unconscious from the hole in the door, and burst in just in time to intercept the man in the baggage-room who had at last overturned the packing-case above him and was crashing his way out through the lid of the coffin. It was an extraordinary scene.

The inspector pulled the negro servant, with his arm one pulp of splintered bone and blood, into the room and thrust him roughly aside. He fell without a moan into the corner. The two men then brought the burglar into the living-room between them. Silbermeister went back to the table, sat down, and put his head between his hands. The inspector looked at him for a moment in amazement as he raised his head and said: 'Thank God!' After a pause he added: 'Why did you come?'

The inspector answered:

'Your telegram caught us just before we left Castleton again. It was lucky, wasn't it?' he added grimly.

Silbermeister again raised his head from his hands, and as if he had heard nothing, said:

'But why did you come?'

The inspector, a trifle gravely, said:

'I told you, your telegram just reached us in time.'

There was another pause of ten seconds, and then Silbermeister pointed to the disconnected instrument, and said once more:

'Why did you come?' His eyes turned in his head: 'I sent no message'; and then he fell on the floor in a dead faint.

That is all I know about it. That is the story that Torrens told me, and the story that undoubtedly Torrens believed.

5

W. W. JACOBS

The Toll-House

'It's all nonsense,' said Jack Barnes. 'Of course people have died in the house; people die in every house. As for the noises—wind in the chimney and rats in the wainscot are very convincing to a nervous man. Give me another cup of tea, Meagle.'

'Lester and White are first,' said Meagle, who was presiding at the tea-table of the Three Feathers Inn. 'You've had two.'

Lester and White finished their cups with irritating slowness, pausing between sips to sniff the aroma, and to discover the sex and dates of arrival of the 'strangers' which floated in some numbers in the beverage. Mr Meagle served them to the brim, and then, turning to the grimly expectant Mr Barnes, blandly requested him to ring for hot water.

'We'll try and keep your nerves in their present healthy condition,' he remarked. 'For my part I have a sort of half-and-half belief in the supernatural.'

'All sensible people have,' said Lester. 'An aunt of mine saw a ghost once.'

White nodded.

'I had an uncle that saw one,' he said.

'It always is somebody else that sees them,' said Barnes.

'Well, there is the house,' said Meagle, 'a large house at an absurdly low rent, and nobody will take it. It has taken toll of at least one life of every family that has lived there—however short the time—and since it has stood empty caretaker after caretaker has died there. The last caretaker died fifteen years ago.'

'Exactly,' said Barnes. 'Long enough ago for legends to accumulate.'

81

'I'll bet you a sovereign you won't spend the night there alone, for all your talk,' said White suddenly.

'And I,' said Lester.

'No,' said Barnes slowly. 'I don't believe in ghosts nor in any supernatural things whatever; all the same, I admit that I should not care to pass a night there alone.'

'But why not?' enquired White.

'Wind in the chimney,' said Meagle, with a grin.

'Rats in the wainscot,' chimed in Lester.

'As you like,' said Barnes, colouring.

'Suppose we all go?' said Meagle. 'Start after supper, and get there about eleven? We have been walking for ten days now without an adventure—except Barnes's discovery that ditchwater smells longest. It will be a novelty, at any rate, and, if we break the spell by all surviving, the grateful owner ought to come down handsome.'

'Let's see what the landlord has to say about it first,' said Lester. 'There is no fun in passing a night in an ordinary empty house. Let us make sure that it is haunted.'

He rang the bell, and, sending for the landlord, appealed to him in the name of our common humanity not to let them waste a night watching in a house in which spectres and hobgoblins had no part. The reply was more than reassuring, and the landlord, after describing with considerable art the exact appearance of a head which had been seen hanging out of a window in the moonlight, wound up with a polite but urgent request that they would settle his bill before they went.

'It's all very well for you young gentlemen to have your fun,' he said indulgently; 'but, supposing as how you are all found dead in the morning, what about me? It ain't called the Toll-House for nothing, you know.'

'Who died there last?' enquired Barnes, with an air of polite derision.

'A tramp,' was the reply. 'He went there for the sake of half-a-crown, and they found him next morning hanging from the balusters, dead.'

'Suicide,' said Barnes. 'Unsound mind.'

The landlord nodded. 'That's what the jury brought it in,' he said slowly; 'but his mind was sound enough when he went in there.

I'd known him, off and on, for years. I'm a poor man, but I wouldn't spend the night in that house for a hundred pounds.'

He repeated this remark as they started on their expedition a few hours later. They left as the inn was closing for the night; bolts shot noisily behind them, and, as the regular customers trudged slowly homewards, they set off at a brisk pace in the direction of the house. Most of the cottages were already in darkness, and lights in others went out as they passed.

'It seems rather hard that we have got to lose a night's rest in order to convince Barnes of the existence of ghosts,' said White.

'It's in a good cause,' said Meagle. 'A most worthy object; and something seems to tell me that we shall succeed. You didn't forget the candles, Lester?'

'I have brought two,' was the reply; 'all the old man could spare.'

There was but little moon, and the night was cloudy. The road between high hedges was dark, and in one place, where it ran through a wood, so black that they twice stumbled in the uneven ground at the side of it.

'Fancy leaving our comfortable beds for this!' said White again. 'Let me see; this desirable residential sepulchre lies to the right, doesn't it?'

'Further on,' said Meagle.

They walked on for some time in silence, broken only by White's tribute to the softness, the cleanliness, and the comfort of the bed which was receding further and further into the distance. Under Meagle's guidance they turned off at last to the right, and, after a walk of a quarter of a mile, saw the gates of the house before them.

The lodge was almost hidden by overgrown shrubs and the drive was choked with rank growths. Meagle leading, they pushed through it until the dark pile of the house loomed above them.

'There is a window at the back where we can get in, so the landlord says,' said Lester, as they stood before the hall door.

'Window?' said Meagle. 'Nonsense. Let's do the thing properly. Where's the knocker?'

He felt for it in the darkness and gave a thundering rat-tat-tat at the door.

'Don't play the fool,' said Barnes crossly.

'Ghostly servants are all asleep,' said Meagle gravely, 'but *I'll* wake them up before I've done with them. It's scandalous keeping us out here in the dark.'

He plied the knocker again, and the noise volleyed in the emptiness beyond. Then with a sudden exclamation he put out his hands and stumbled forward.

'Why, it was open all the time,' he said, with an odd catch in his voice. 'Come on.'

'I don't believe it was open,' said Lester, hanging back. 'Somebody is playing us a trick.'

'Nonsense,' said Meagle sharply. 'Give me a candle. Thanks. Who's got a match?'

Barnes produced a box and struck one, and Meagle, shielding the candle with his hand, led the way forward to the foot of the stairs. 'Shut the door, somebody,' he said; 'there's too much draught.'

'It is shut,' said White, glancing behind him.

Meagle fingered his chin. 'Who shut it?' he enquired, looking from one to the other. 'Who came in last?'

'I did,' said Lester, 'but I don't remember shutting it—perhaps I did, though.'

Meagle, about to speak, thought better of it, and, still carefully guarding the flame, began to explore the house, with the others close behind. Shadows danced on the walls and lurked in the corners as they proceeded. At the end of the passage they found a second staircase, and ascending it slowly gained the first floor.

'Careful!' said Meagle, as they gained the landing.

He held the candle forward and showed where the balusters had broken away. Then he peered curiously into the void beneath.

'This is where the tramp hanged himself, I suppose,' he said thoughtfully.

'You've got an unwholesome mind,' said White, as they walked on. 'This place is quite creepy enough without you remembering that. Now let's find a comfortable room and have a little nip of whisky apiece and a pipe. How will this do?'

He opened a door at the end of the passage and revealed a small square room. Meagle led the way with the candle, and, first melting a drop or two of tallow, stuck it on the mantelpiece. The others seated themselves on the floor and watched pleasantly as White drew from his pocket a small bottle of whisky and a tin cup.

'H'm! I've forgotten the water,' he exclaimed.

'I'll soon get some,' said Meagle.

He tugged violently at the bell-handle, and the rusty jangling of a bell sounded from a distant kitchen. He rang again.

'Don't play the fool,' said Barnes roughly.

Meagle laughed. 'I only wanted to convince you,' he said kindly. 'There ought to be, at any rate, one ghost in the servants' hall.'

Barnes held up his hand for silence.

'Yes?' said Meagle, with a grin at the other two. 'Is anybody coming?'

'Suppose we drop this game and go back,' said Barnes suddenly. 'I don't believe in spirits, but nerves are outside anybody's command. You may laugh as you like, but it really seemed to me that I heard a door open below and steps on the stairs.'

His voice was drowned in a roar of laughter.

'He is coming round,' said Meagle, with a smirk. 'By the time I have done with him he will be a confirmed believer. Well, who will go and get some water? Will, you, Barnes?'

'No,' was the reply.

'If there is any it might not be safe to drink after all these years,' said Lester. 'We must do without it.'

Meagle nodded, and taking a seat on the floor held out his hand for the cup. Pipes were lit, and the clean, wholesome smell of tobacco filled the room. White produced a pack of cards; talk and laughter rang through the room and died away reluctantly in distant corridors.

'Empty rooms always delude me into the belief that I possess a deep voice,' said Meagle. 'Tomorrow I——'

He started up with a smothered exclamation as the light went out suddenly and something struck him on the head. The others sprang to their feet. Then Meagle laughed.

'It's the candle,' he exclaimed. 'I didn't stick it enough.'

Barnes struck a match, and relighting the candle, stuck it on the mantelpiece, and sitting down took up his cards again.

'What was I going to say?' said Meagle. 'Oh, I know; tomorrow I——'

'Listen!' said White, laying his hand on the other's sleeve. 'Upon my word I really thought I heard a laugh.'

'Look here!' said Barnes. 'What do you say to going back? I've had enough of this. I keep fancying that I hear things too; sounds of something moving about in the passage outside. I know it's only fancy, but it's uncomfortable.'

'You go if you want to,' said Meagle, 'and we will play dummy. Or you might ask the tramp to take your hand for you, as you go downstairs.'

Barnes shivered and exclaimed angrily. He got up, and, walking to the half-closed door, listened.

'Go outside,' said Meagle, winking at the other two. 'I'll dare you to go down to the hall door and back by yourself.'

Barnes came back, and, bending forward, lit his pipe at the candle.

'I am nervous, but rational,' he said, blowing out a thin cloud of smoke. 'My nerves tell me that there is something prowling up and down the long passage outside; my reason tells me that that is all nonsense. Where are my cards?'

He sat down again, and, taking up his hand, looked through it carefully and led.

'Your play, White,' he said, after a pause.

White made no sign.

'Why, he is asleep,' said Meagle. 'Wake up, old man. Wake up and play.'

Lester, who was sitting next to him, took the sleeping man by the arm and shook him, gently at first and then with some roughness; but White, with his back against the wall and his head bowed, made no sign. Meagle bawled in his ear, and then turned a puzzled face to the others.

'He sleeps like the dead,' he said, grimacing. 'Well, there are still three of us to keep each other company.'

'Yes,' said Lester, nodding. 'Unless—Good Lord! suppose——'

He broke off, and eyed them, trembling.

'Suppose what?' enquired Meagle.

'Nothing,' stammered Lester. 'Let's wake him. Try him again. *White!* WHITE!'

'It's no good,' said Meagle seriously; 'there's something wrong about that sleep.'

'That's what I meant,' said Lester; 'and if *he* goes to sleep like that, why shouldn't——'

Meagle sprang to his feet. 'Nonsense,' he said roughly. 'He's tired out; that's all. Still, let's take him up and clear out. You take his legs and Barnes will lead the way with the candle. *Yes? Who's that?*'

He looked up quickly towards the door. 'Thought I heard somebody tap,' he said, with a shamefaced laugh. 'Now, Lester, up with him. One, two—*Lester! Lester!*'

He sprang forward too late; Lester, with his face buried in his arms, had rolled over on the floor fast asleep, and his utmost efforts failed to awake him.

'He—is—asleep,' he stammered, 'Asleep!'

Barnes, who had taken the candle from the mantelpiece, stood peering at the sleepers in silence and dropping tallow over the floor.

'We must get out of this,' said Meagle. 'Quick!'

Barnes hesitated. 'We can't leave them here—' he began.

'We must,' said Meagle, in strident tones. 'If you go to sleep I shall go—Quick! Come!'

He seized the other by the arm and strove to drag him to the door. Barnes shook him off, and, putting the candle back on the mantelpiece, tried again to arouse the sleepers.

'It's no good,' he said at last, and, turning from them, watched Meagle. 'Don't you go to sleep,' he said anxiously.

Meagle shook his head, and they stood for some time in uneasy silence. 'May as well shut the door,' said Barnes at last.

He crossed over and closed it gently. Then at a scuffling noise behind him he turned and saw Meagle in a heap on the hearthstone.

With a sharp catch in his breath he stood motionless. Inside the room the candle, fluttering in the draught, showed dimly the grotesque attitudes of the sleepers. Beyond the door there seemed to his overwrought imagination a strange and stealthy unrest. He tried to whistle, but his lips were parched, and in a mechanical fashion he stooped, and began to pick up the cards which littered the floor.

He stopped once or twice and stood with bent head listening. The unrest outside seemed to increase; a loud creaking sounded from the stairs.

'Who is there?' he cried loudly.

The creaking ceased. He crossed to the door, and, flinging it open, strode out into the corridor. As he walked his fears left him suddenly.

'Come on!' he cried, with a low laugh.

'All of you! All of you! Show your faces—your infernal ugly faces! Don't skulk!'

He laughed again and walked on; and the heap in the fireplace put out its head tortoise fashion and listened in horror to the retreating footsteps. Not until they had become inaudible in the distance did the listener's features relax.

'Good Lord, Lester, we've driven him mad,' he said, in a frightened whisper. 'We must go after him.'

There was no reply. Meagle sprang to his feet.

'Do you hear?' he cried. 'Stop your fooling now; this is serious. White! Lester! Do you hear?'

He bent and surveyed them in angry bewilderment. 'All right,' he said, in a trembling voice. 'You won't frighten me, you know.'

He turned away and walked with exaggerated carelessness in the direction of the door. He even went outside and peeped through the crack, but the sleepers did not stir. He glanced into the blackness behind, and then came hastily into the room again.

He stood for a few seconds regarding them. The stillness in the house was horrible; he could not even hear them breathe. With a sudden resolution he snatched the candle from the mantelpiece and held the flame to White's finger. Then as he reeled back stupefied, the footsteps again became audible.

He stood with the candle in his shaking hand, listening. He heard them ascending the further staircase, but they stopped suddenly as he went to the door. He walked a little way along the passage, and they went scurrying down the stairs and then at a jog-trot along the corridor below. He went back to the main staircase, and they ceased again.

For a time he hung over the balusters, listening and trying to pierce the blackness below; then slowly, step by step, he made his way downstairs, and, holding the candle above his head, peered about him.

'Barnes!' he called. 'Where are you?'

Shaking with fright, he made his way along the passage, and summoning up all his courage, pushed open doors and gazed fearfully into empty rooms. Then, quite suddenly, he heard the footsteps in front of him.

He followed slowly for fear of extinguishing the candle, until they led him at last into a vast bare kitchen, with damp walls and a broken floor. In front of him a door leading into an inside room had just closed. He ran towards it and flung it open, and a cold air blew out the candle. He stood aghast.

'Barnes!' he cried again. 'Don't be afraid! It is I—Meagle!'

There was no answer. He stood gazing into the darkness, and all the time the idea of something close at hand watching was upon him. Then suddenly the steps broke out overhead again.

He drew back hastily, and passing through the kitchen groped his way along the narrow passages. He could now see better in the darkness, and finding himself at last at the foot of the staircase, began to ascend it noiselessly. He reached the landing just in time to see a figure disappear round the angle of a wall. Still careful to make no noise, he followed the sound of the steps until they led him to the top floor, and he cornered the chase at the end of a short passage.

'Barnes!' he whispered. 'Barnes!'

Something stirred in the darkness. A small circular window at the end of the passage just softened the blackness and revealed the dim outlines of a motionless figure. Meagle, in place of advancing, stood almost as still as a sudden horrible doubt took possession of him. With his eyes fixed on the shape in front he fell back slowly, and, as it advanced upon him, burst into a terrible cry.

'Barnes! For God's sake! Is it *you?*'

The echoes of his voice left the air quivering, but the figure before him paid no heed. For a moment he tried to brace his courage up to endure its approach, then with a smothered cry he turned and fled.

The passages wound like a maze, and he threaded them blindly in a vain search for the stairs. If he could get down and open the hall door——

He caught his breath in a sob; the steps had begun again. At a lumbering trot they clattered up and down the bare passages, in and out, up and down, as though in search of him. He stood appalled, and then as they drew near entered a small room and stood behind the door as they rushed by. He came out and ran swiftly and noiselessly in the other direction, and in a moment the steps were after him. He found the long corridor and raced along it at top speed. The stairs he knew were at the end, and with the steps close behind he descended them in blind haste. The steps gained on him, and he shrank to the side to let them pass, still continuing his headlong flight. Then suddenly he seemed to slip off the earth into space.

Lester awoke in the morning to find the sunshine streaming into the room, and White sitting up and regarding with some perplexity a badly blistered finger.

'Where are the others?' enquired Lester.

'Gone, I suppose,' said White. 'We must have been asleep.'

Lester arose, and, stretching his stiffened limbs, dusted his clothes with his hands and went out into the corridor. White followed. At the noise of their approach a figure which had been lying asleep at the other end sat up and revealed the face of Barnes. 'Why, I've been asleep,' he said, in surprise. 'I don't remember coming here. How did I get here?'

'Nice place to come for a nap,' said Lester severely, as he pointed to the gap in the balusters. 'Look there! Another yard and where would you have been?'

He walked carelessly to the edge and looked over. In response to his startled cry the others drew near, and all three stood staring at the dead man below.

6

E. F. BENSON

The Face

Hester Ward, sitting by the open window on this hot afternoon in June, began seriously to argue with herself about the cloud of foreboding and depression which had encompassed her all day, and, very sensibly, she enumerated to herself the manifold causes for happiness in the fortunate circumstances of her life. She was young, she was extremely good-looking, she was well-off, she enjoyed excellent health, and above all, she had an adorable husband and two small, adorable children. There was no break, indeed, anywhere in the circle of prosperity which surrounded her, and had the wishing-cap been handed to her that moment by some beneficent fairy, she would have hesitated to put it on her head, for there was positively nothing that she could think of which would have been worthy of such solemnity. Moreover, she could not accuse herself of a want of appreciation of her blessings; she appreciated enormously, she enjoyed enormously, and she thoroughly wanted all those who so munificently contributed to her happiness to share in it.

She made a very deliberate review of these things, for she was really anxious, more anxious, indeed, than she admitted to herself, to find anything tangible which could possibly warrant this ominous feeling of approaching disaster. Then there was the weather to consider; for the last week London had been stiflingly hot, but if that was the cause, why had she not felt it before? Perhaps the effect of these broiling, airless days had been cumulative. That was an idea, but, frankly, it did not seem a very good one, for, as a matter of fact, she loved the heat; Dick, who hated it, said that it was odd he should have fallen in love with a salamander.

She shifted her position, sitting up straight in this low window-seat, for she was intending to make a call on her courage. She had known from the moment she awoke this morning what it was that lay so heavy on her, and now, having done her best to shift the reason of her depression on to anything else, and having completely failed, she meant to look the thing in the face. She was ashamed of doing so, for the cause of this leaden mood of fear which held her in its grip, was so trivial, so fantastic, so excessively silly.

'Yes, there never was anything so silly,' she said to herself. 'I must look at it straight, and convince myself how silly it is.' She paused a moment, clenching her hands.

'Now for it,' she said.

She had had a dream the previous night, which, years ago, used to be familiar to her, for again and again when she was a child she had dreamed it. In itself the dream was nothing, but in those childish days, whenever she had this dream which had visited her last night, it was followed on the next night by another, which contained the source and the core of the horror, and she would awake screaming and struggling in the grip of overwhelming nightmare. For some ten years now she had not experienced it, and would have said that, though she remembered it, it had become dim and distant to her. But last night she had had that warning dream, which used to herald the visitation of the nightmare, and now that whole storehouse of memory crammed as it was with bright things and beautiful contained nothing so vivid.

The warning dream, the curtain that was drawn up on the succeeding night, and disclosed the vision she dreaded, was simple and harmless enough in itself. She seemed to be walking on a high sandy cliff covered with short down-grass; twenty yards to the left came the edge of this cliff, which sloped steeply down to the sea that lay at its foot. The path she followed led through fields bounded by low hedges, and mounted gradually upwards. She went through some half-dozen of these, climbing over the wooden stiles that gave communication; sheep grazed there, but she never saw another human being, and always it was dusk, as if evening was falling, and she had to hurry on, because someone (she knew not whom) was waiting for her, and had been waiting not a few minutes only, but for many years.

Presently, as she mounted this slope, she saw in front of her a copse of stunted trees, growing crookedly under the continual pressure of the wind that blew from the sea, and when she saw those she knew her journey was nearly done, and that the nameless one, who had been waiting for her so long was somewhere close at hand. The path she followed was cut through this wood, and the slanting boughs of the trees on the seaward side almost roofed it in; it was like walking through a tunnel. Soon the trees in front began to grow thin, and she saw through them the grey tower of a lonely church. It stood in a graveyard, apparently long disused, and the body of the church, which lay between the tower and the edge of the cliff, was in ruins, roofless, and with gaping windows, round which ivy grew thickly.

At that point this prefatory dream always stopped. It was a troubled, uneasy dream, for there was over it the sense of dusk and of the man who had been waiting for her so long, but it was not of the order of nightmare. Many times in childhood had she experienced it, and perhaps it was the subconscious knowledge of the night that so surely followed it, which gave it its disquiet. And now last night it had come again, identical in every particular but one. For last night it seemed to her that in the course of these ten years which had intervened since last it had visited her, the glimpse of the church and churchyard was changed. The edge of the cliff had come nearer to the tower, so that it now was within a yard or two of it, and the ruined body of the church, but for one broken arch that remained, had vanished. The sea had encroached, and for ten years had been busily eating at the cliff.

Hester knew well that it was this dream and this alone which had darkened the day for her, by reason of the nightmares that used to follow it, and, like a sensible woman, having looked it once in the face, she refused to admit into her mind any conscious calling-up of the sequel. If she let herself contemplate that, as likely or not the very thinking about it would be sufficient to ensure its return, and of one thing she was very certain, namely, that she didn't at all want it to do so. It was not like the confused jumble and jangle of ordinary nightmare, it was very simple, and she felt it concerned the nameless one who waited for her. . . . But she must not think of it; her whole will and intention was set on not thinking of it, and to aid her resolution, there was the rattle of Dick's latch-key in the front-door, and his voice calling her.

She went out into the little square front hall; there he was, strong and large, and wonderfully undreamlike.

'This heat's a scandal, it's an outrage, it's an abomination of desolation,' he cried, vigorously mopping. 'What have we done that Providence should place us in this frying-pan? Let us thwart him, Hester! Let us drive out of this inferno and have our dinner at—I'll whisper it so that he shan't overhear—at Hampton Court!'

She laughed: this plan suited her excellently. They would return late, after the distraction of a fresh scene; and dining out at night was both delicious and stupefying.

'The very thing,' she said, 'and I'm sure Providence didn't hear. Let's start now!'

'Rather. Any letters for me?'

He walked to the table where there were a few rather uninteresting-looking envelopes with half penny stamps.

'Ah, receipted bill,' he said. 'Just a reminder of one's folly in paying it. Circular . . . unasked advice to invest in German marks. . . . Circular begging letter, beginning "Dear Sir or Madam." Such impertinence to ask one to subscribe to something without ascertaining one's sex. . . . Private view, portraits at the Walton Gallery. . . . Can't go: business meetings all day. You might like to have a look in, Hester. Some one told me there were some fine Vandycks. That's all: let's be off.'

Hester spent a thoroughly reassuring evening, and though she thought of telling Dick about the dream that had so deeply imprinted itself on her consciousness all day, in order to hear the great laugh he would have given her for being such a goose, she refrained from doing so, since nothing that he could say would be so tonic to these fantastic fears as his general robustness. Besides, she would have to account for its disturbing effect, tell him that it was once familiar to her, and recount the sequel of the nightmares that followed. She would neither think of them, nor mention them: it was wiser by far just to soak herself in his extraordinary sanity, and wrap herself in his affection. . . . They dined out-of-doors at a riverside restaurant and strolled about afterwards, and it was very nearly midnight when, soothed with coolness and fresh air, and the vigour of his strong companionship, she let herself into the house, while he took the car back to the garage. And now she marvelled at the mood which had beset her all day, so distant and unreal had it become. She felt as if she had dreamed of shipwreck, and had awoke to find herself in some secure and sheltered garden where no tempest raged nor waves beat. But was there, ever so remotely, ever so dimly, the noise of far-off breakers somewhere?

He slept in the dressing-room which communicated with her bedroom, the door of which was left open for the sake of air and coolness, and she fell asleep almost as soon as her light was out, and while his was still burning. And immediately she began to dream.

She was standing on the seashore; the tide was out, for level sands strewn with stranded jetsam glimmered in a dusk that was deepening into night. Though she had never seen the place it was awfully familiar to her. At the head of the beach there was a steep cliff of sand, and perched on the edge of it was a grey church tower. The sea must have encroached and undermined the body of the church, for tumbled blocks of masonry lay close to her at the bottom of the cliff, and there were gravestones there, while others still in place were silhouetted whitely against the sky. To the right of the church tower there was a wood of stunted trees, combed sideways by the prevalent sea-wind, and she knew that along the top of the cliff a few yards inland there lay a path through fields, with wooden stiles to climb, which led through a tunnel of trees and so out into the churchyard. All this she saw in a glance, and waited, looking at the sand-cliff crowned by the church tower, for the terror that was going to reveal itself. Already she knew what it was, and, as so many times before, she tried to run away. But the catalepsy of nightmare was already on her; frantically she strove to move, but her utmost endeavour could not raise a foot from the sand. Frantically she tried to look away from the sand-cliffs close in front of her, where in a moment now the horror would be manifested. . . .

It came. There formed a pale oval light, the size of a man's face, dimly luminous in front of her and a few inches above the level of her eyes. It outlined itself, short reddish hair grew low on the forehead, below were two grey eyes, set very close together, which steadily and fixedly regarded her. On each side the ears stood noticeably away from the head, and the lines of the jaw met in a short pointed chin. The nose was straight and rather long, below it came a hairless lip, and last of all the mouth took shape and colour, and there lay the crowning terror. One side of it, soft-curved and beautiful, trembled into a smile, the other side, thick and gathered together as by some physical deformity, sneered and lusted.

The whole face, dim at first, gradually focused itself into clear outline: it was pale and rather lean, the face of a young man. And then the lower lip dropped a little, showing the glint of teeth, and there was the sound of speech. 'I shall soon come for you now,' it said, and on the words it drew a little nearer to her, and the smile broadened. At that the full hot blast of nightmare poured in upon her. Again she tried to run, again she tried to scream, and now she could feel the breath of that terrible mouth upon her. Then with a crash and a rending like the tearing asunder of soul and body she broke the spell, and heard her own voice yelling, and felt with her fingers for the switch of her light. And then she saw that the room was not dark, for Dick's door was open, and the next moment, not yet undressed, he was with her.

'My darling, what is it?' he said. 'What's the matter?'

She clung desperately to him, still distraught with terror.

'Ah, he has been here again,' she cried. 'He says he will soon come to me. Keep him away, Dick.'

For one moment her fear infected him, and he found himself glancing round the room.

'But what do you mean?' he said. 'No one has been here.'

She raised her head from his shoulder.

'No, it was just a dream,' she said. 'But it was the old dream, and I was terrified. Why, you've not undressed yet. What time is it?'

'You haven't been in bed ten minutes, dear,' he said. 'You had hardly put out your light when I heard you screaming.'

She shuddered.

'Ah, it's awful,' she said. 'And he will come again. . . .'

He sat down by her.

'Now tell me all about it,' he said.

She shook her head.

'No, it will never do to talk about it,' she said, 'it will only make it more real. I suppose the children are all right, are they?'

'Of course they are. I looked in on my way upstairs.'

'That's good. But I'm better now, Dick. A dream hasn't anything real about it, has it? It doesn't mean. anything?'

He was quite reassuring on this point, and soon she quieted down. Before he went to bed he looked in again on her, and she was asleep.

Hester had a stern interview with herself when Dick had gone down to his office next morning. She told herself that what she was afraid of was nothing more than her own fear. How many times had that ill-omened face come to her in dreams, and what significance had it ever proved to possess? Absolutely none at all, except to make her afraid. She was afraid where no fear was: she was guarded, sheltered, prosperous, and what if a nightmare of childhood returned? It had no more meaning now than it had then, and all those visitations of her childhood had passed away without trace. . . . And then, despite herself, she began thinking over that vision again. It was grimly identical with all its previous occurrences, except . . . And then, with a sudden shrinking of the heart, she remembered that in earlier years those terrible lips had said: 'I shall come for you when you are older,' and last night they had said: 'I shall soon come for you now.' She remembered, too, that in the warning dream the sea had encroached, and it had now demolished the body of the church. There was an awful consistency about these two changes in the otherwise identical visions. The years had brought their change to them, for in the one the encroaching sea had brought down the body of the church, in the other the time was now near. . . .

It was no use to scold or reprimand herself, for to bring her mind to the contemplation of the vision meant merely that the grip of terror closed on her again; it was far wiser to occupy herself, and starve her fear out by refusing to bring it the sustenance of thought. So she went about her household duties, she took the children out for their airing in the park, and then, determined to leave no moment unoccupied, set off with the card of invitation to see the pictures in the private view at the Walton Gallery. After that her day was full enough, she was lunching out, and going on to a matinée, and by the time she got home Dick would have returned, and they would drive down to his little house at Rye for the weekend. All Saturday and Sunday she would be playing golf, and she felt that fresh air and physical fatigue would exorcize the dread of these dreaming fantasies.

The gallery was crowded when she got there; there were friends among the sightseers, and the inspection of the pictures was diversified by cheerful conversation. There were two or three fine Raeburns, a couple of Sir Joshuas, but the gems, so she gathered, were three Vandycks that hung in a small room by themselves. Presently she strolled in there, looking at her catalogue. The first of them, she saw, was a portrait of Sir Roger Wyburn. Still chatting to her friend she raised her eye and saw it. . . .

Her heart hammered in her throat, and then seemed to stand still altogether. A qualm, as of some mental sickness of the soul overcame her, for there in front of her was he who would soon come for her. There was the reddish hair, the projecting ears, the greedy eyes set close together, and the mouth smiling on one side, and on the other gathered up into the sneering menace that she knew so well. It might have been her own nightmare rather than a living model which had sat to the painter for that face.

'Ah, what a portrait, and what a brute!' said her companion. 'Look, Hester, isn't that marvellous?'

She recovered herself with an effort. To give way to this ever-mastering dread, would have been to allow nightmare to invade her waking life, and there, for sure, madness lay. She forced herself to look at it again, but there were the steady and eager eyes regarding her; she could almost fancy the mouth began to move. All round her the crowd bustled and chattered, but to her own sense she was alone there with Roger Wyburn.

And yet, so she reasoned with herself, this picture of him—for it was he and no other—should have reassured her. Roger Wyburn, to have been painted by Vandyck, must have been dead near on two hundred years; how could he be a menace to her? Had she seen that portrait by some chance as a child; had it made some dreadful impression on her, since overscored by other memories, but still alive in the mysterious subconsciousness, which flows eternally, like some dark underground river, beneath the surface of human life? Psychologists taught that these early impressions fester or poison the mind like some hidden abscess. That might account for this dread of one, nameless no longer, who waited for her.

That night down at Rye there came again to her the prefatory dream, followed by the nightmare, and clinging to her husband as the terror began to subside, she told him what she had resolved to keep to herself. Just to tell it brought a measure of comfort, for it was so outrageously fantastic, and his robust common sense upheld her. But when on their return to London there was a recurrence of these visions, he made short work of her demur and took her straight to her doctor.

'Tell him all, darling,' he said. 'Unless you promise to do that, I will. I can't have you worried like this. It's all nonsense, you know, and doctors are wonderful people for curing nonsense.'

She turned to him.

'Dick, you're frightened,' she said quietly.

He laughed.

'I'm nothing of the kind,' he said, 'but I don't like being awakened by your screaming. Not my idea of a peaceful night. Here we are.'

The medical report was decisive and peremptory. There was nothing whatever to be alarmed about; in brain and body she was perfectly healthy, but she was run down. These disturbing dreams were, as likely as not, an effect, a symptom of her condition, rather than the cause of it, and Dr Baring unhesitatingly recommended a complete change to some bracing place. The wise thing would be to send her out of this stuffy furnace to some quiet place to where she had never been. Complete change; quite so. For the same reason her husband had better not go with her; he must pack her off to, let us say, the East coast. Sea-air and coolness and complete idleness. No long walks; no long bathings; a dip, and a deckchair on the sands. A lazy, soporific life. How about Rushton? He had no doubt that Rushton would set her up again. After a week or so, perhaps, her husband might go down and see her. Plenty of sleep—never mind the nightmares—plenty of fresh air.

Hester, rather to her husband's surprise, fell in with this suggestion at once, and the following evening saw her installed in solitude and tranquillity. The little hotel was still almost empty, for the rush of summer tourists had not yet begun, and all day she sat out on the beach with the sense of a struggle over. She need not fight the terror any more; dimly it seemed to her that its malignancy had been relaxed. Had she in some way yielded to it and done its secret bidding? At any rate no return of its nightly visitations had occurred, and she slept long and dreamlessly, and woke to another day of quiet. Every morning there was a line for her from Dick, with good news of himself and the children, but he and they alike seemed somehow remote, like memories of a very distant time. Something had driven in between her and them, and she saw them as if through glass. But equally did the memory of the face of Roger Wyburn, as seen on the master's canvas or hanging close in front of her against the crumbling sand-cliff, become blurred and indistinct, and no return of her nightly terrors visited her. This truce from all emotion reacted not on her mind alone, lulling her with a sense of soothed security, but on her body also, and she began to weary of this day-long inactivity.

The village lay on the lip of a stretch of land reclaimed from the sea. To the north the level marsh, now beginning to glow with the pale bloom of the sea-lavender, stretched away featureless till it lost itself in distance, but to the south a spur of hill came down to the shore ending in a wooded promontory. Gradually, as her physical health increased, she began to wonder what lay beyond this ridge which cut short the view, and one afternoon she walked across the intervening level and strolled up its wooded slopes. The day was close and windless, the invigorating sea-breeze which till now had spiced the heat with freshness had died, and she looked forward to finding a current of air stirring when she had topped the hill. To the south a mass of dark cloud lay along the horizon, but there was no imminent threat of storm. The slope was easily surmounted, and presently she stood at the top and found herself on the edge of a tableland of wooded pasture, and following the path, which ran not far from the edge of the cliff, she came out into more open country. Empty fields, where a few sheep were grazing, mounted gradually upwards. Wooden stiles made a communication in the hedges that bounded them. And there, not a mile in front of her, she saw a wood, with trees growing slantingly away from the push of the prevalent sea winds, crowning the upward slope, and over the top of it peered a grey church tower.

For the moment, as the awful and familiar scene identified itself, Hester's heart stood still: the next a wave of courage and resolution poured in upon her. Here, at last was the scene of that prefatory dream, and here was she presented with the opportunity of fathoming and dispelling it. Instantly her mind was made up, and under the strange twilight of the shrouded sky, she walked swiftly on through the fields she had so often traversed in sleep, and up to the wood, beyond which he was waiting for her. She closed her ears against the clanging bell of terror, which now she could silence for ever, and unfalteringly entered that dark tunnel of wood. Soon in front of her the trees began to thin, and through them, now close at hand, she saw the church tower. In a few yards further she came out of the belt of trees, and round her were the monuments of a graveyard long disused. The cliff was broken off close to the church tower: between it and the edge there was no more of the body of the church than a broken arch, thick hung with ivy. Round this she passed and saw below the ruin of fallen masonry, and the level sands strewn with headstones and disjected rubble, and at the edge of the cliff were graves already cracked and toppling. But there was no one here, none waited for her, and the churchyard where she had so often pictured him was as empty as the fields she had just traversed.

A huge elation filled her; her courage had been rewarded, and all the terrors of the past became to her meaningless phantoms. But there was no time to linger, for now the storm threatened, and on the horizon a blink of lightning was followed by a crackling peal. Just as she turned to go her eye fell on a tombstone that was balanced on the very edge of the cliff, and she read on it that here lay the body of Roger Wyburn.

Fear, the catalepsy of nightmare, rooted her for the moment to the spot; she stared in stricken amazement at the moss-grown letters; almost she expected to see that fell terror of a face rise and hover over his resting-place. Then the fear which had frozen her lent her wings, and with hurrying feet she sped through the arched pathway in the wood and out into the fields. Not one backward glance did she give till she had come to the edge of the ridge above the village, and, turning saw the pastures she had traversed empty of any living presence. None had followed; but the sheep, apprehensive of the coming storm, had ceased to feed, and were huddling under shelter of the stunted hedges.

Her first idea, in the panic of her mind, was to leave the place at once, but the last train for London had left an hour before, and besides, where was the use of flight if it was the spirit of a man long dead from which she fled? The distance from the place where his bones lay did not afford her safety; that must be sought for within. But she longed for Dick's sheltering and confident presence; he was arriving in any case tomorrow, but there were long dark hours before tomorrow, and who could say what the perils and dangers of the coming night might be? If he started this evening instead of tomorrow morning, he could motor down here in four hours, and would be with her by ten o'clock or eleven. She wrote an urgent telegram: 'Come at once,' she said. 'Don't delay.'

The storm which had flickered on the south now came quickly up, and soon after it burst in appalling violence. For preface there were but a few large drops that splashed and dried on the roadway as she came back from the post-office, and just as she reached the hotel again the roar of the approaching rain sounded, and the sluices of heaven were opened. Through the deluge flared the fire of the lightning, the thunder crashed and echoed overhead, and presently the street of the village was a torrent of sandy turbulent water, and sitting there in the dark one picture leapt floating before her eyes, that of the tombstone of Roger Wyburn, already tottering to its fall at the edge of the cliff of the church tower. In such rains as these, acres of the cliffs were loosened; she seemed to hear the whisper of the sliding sand that would precipitate those perished sepulchres and what lay within to the beach below.

By eight o'clock the storm was subsiding, and as she dined she was handed a telegram from Dick, saying that he had already started and sent this off en route. By half-past ten, therefore, if all was well, he would be here and somehow he would stand between her and her fear. Strange how a few days ago both it and the thought of him had become distant and dim to her; now the one was as vivid as the other, and she counted the minutes to his arrival. Soon the rain ceased altogether, and looking out of the curtained window of her sitting-room where she sat watching the slow circle of the hands of the clock, she saw a tawny moon rising over the sea. Before it had climbed to the zenith, before her clock had twice told the hour again, Dick would be with her.

It had just struck ten when there came a knock at her door, and the page-boy entered with the message that a gentleman had come for her. Her heart leaped at the news; she had not expected Dick for half an hour yet, and now the lonely vigil was over. She ran downstairs, and there was the figure standing on the step outside. His face was turned away from her; no doubt he was giving some order to his chauffeur. He was outlined against the white moonlight, and in contrast with that, the gas-jet in the entrance just above his head gave his hair a warm, reddish tinge.

She ran across the hall to him.

'Ah, my darling, you've come,' she said. 'It was good of you. How quick you've been!' Just as she laid her hand on his shoulder he turned. His arm was thrown out round her, and she looked into a face with eyes close set, and a mouth smiling on one side, the other, thick and gathered together as by some physical deformity, sneered and lusted.

The nightmare was on her; she could neither run nor scream, and supporting her dragging steps, he went forth with her into the night.

Half an hour later Dick arrived. To his amazement he heard that a man had called for his wife not long before, and that she had gone out with him. He seemed to be a stranger here, for the boy who had taken his message to her had never seen him before, and presently surprise began to deepen into alarm; enquiries were made outside the hotel, and it appeared that a witness or two had seen the lady whom they knew to be staying there walking, hatless, along the top of the beach with a man whose arm was linked in hers. Neither of them knew him, but one had seen his face and could describe it.

The direction of the search thus became narrowed down, and though with a lantern to supplement the moonlight they came upon footprints which might have been hers, there were no marks of any who walked beside her. But they followed these until they came to an end, a mile away, in a great landslide of sand, which had fallen from the old churchyard on the cliff, and had brought down with it half the tower and a gravestone, with the body that had lain below.

The gravestone was that of Roger Wyburn, and his body lay by it, untouched by corruption or decay, though two hundred years had elapsed since it was interred there. For a week afterwards the work of searching the landslide went on, assisted by the high tides that gradually washed it away. But no further discovery was made.

7

W. F. HARVEY

The Tool

I like the long south corridor, with its light-coloured walls and low windows looking on to the garden. I do my writing there, for it is very quiet, especially when Jellerby is off colour and is obliged to keep to his room. He calls himself a Social Democrat, and is eloquent on the rights of man—a wonderfully fluent speaker, with facts and figures at his fingertips to drive home every argument. But one tires of that sort of thing very easily. Of the two I would rather listen to Charlie Lovel recite his endless pedigree, as he sits dribbling over his knitting.

I cannot help smiling to myself when I think of yesterday's sermon. Canon Eldred was the preacher, and was obviously ill at ease, as indeed I should have been in similar circumstances. He has a red cheerful face, with comfortable folds of flesh about the chin; a typical healthy-minded Philistine, whom it did one good to see. However, he was there to speak to us. He took as his theme the Duty of Cheerfulness. The subject was excellent, and what he said was to the point; but I could not help wondering whether he had the slightest idea of the condition of those whom he addressed. Evidently he realized our need, but there was a tendency to regard us less as men than as children. He spoke incautiously of the man in the street, and, in so doing, showed the falsity of his position. We have no use for arguments calculated to satisfy the ordinary man, since we are extraordinary men in an extraordinary position.

No, 'the man in the street' was, to say the least of it, a most unhappy phrase!

I should like to tell Canon Eldred my own story. He told us that next week he was going away to enjoy a well-earned holiday. Two years ago I was taking my summer holiday too. Autumn holiday it was, in fact, for our vicar—I was senior curate at the time in a big working-class parish in the North of England—had gone off to the sea with his children in July, and Legge, my junior, had claimed August for the Tyrol.

I had made no definite plans for myself that year. Something, I felt sure, would turn up, and if all my friends were booked elsewhere, I knew that I could depend on ten days at my uncle's place in Devonshire, or a fortnight of fresh air and plain living on Bob's disreputable old ketch. But somehow everything fell through. My uncle, who was beginning to be troubled about death duties, had let the shooting for the first time in fifty years; Bob was busy running his craft aground on Danish shoals, and I was left to my own resources. I set off finally at twelve hours' notice on a ten days' walking-tour, determined to hunt out some weatherproof barn within easy distance of a river or the sea, where Legge and I could take our boys to camp at Easter.

I left on a Monday (and I would have Canon Eldred, if he ever reads this, to note the date, because the dates are an important part of my narrative) and Legge came with me to the station, for I had several matters to arrange with him connected with the parish work. I took a ten days' ticket. It was stamped 22nd September, and, as I said, the 22nd was a Monday.

That night I slept at Dunsley. It was the end of the season. Nearly all the visitors had left the place, but the harbour was jammed with the herring fleet, storm-bound for over three days, and all the alleyways in the old town were crowded with fishermen. On the Tuesday I started off with my rucksack, intending to follow the line of the cliff, but the easterly gale was too much for me, and I struck inland on to the moors. I walked the whole of the day, a good thirty-five miles, and towards dusk got a lift in a farmer's cart. He was going to Chedsholme, and there I spent the night at the Ship Inn, a stone's-throw from the abbey-church. I felt disinclined for a long tramp on Wednesday, so I walked on into Rapmoor in the morning, left my things with old Mr Robinson at the 'Crown', borrowed a rod and tackle from him, and spent the afternoon fishing the Lansdale Beck. I found a splendid camping-ground, but no barn or building, and saw the farmer, a churchwarden, who readily gave permission for the setting-up of our tents, if ever we brought the boys that way. Wednesday night I spent at Rapmoor, Thursday at Frankstone Edge, where I dined with the vicar, a college friend of Legge's, and Friday at Gorton. The landlady of the inn at Gorton kept a green parrot in a cage in the parlour. It was remarkably tame, and though I am not usually fond of such birds, I remember spending quite a long time talking to it in the evening.

I set out on the morning of Saturday prepared for a long walk and a probable soaking. Not that the rain was falling, but there was a mist sweeping inland over the moors from the sea, which I was obliged to face, since my track lay eastwards. I followed up the road to the end of the dale, and then took a rough path that skirted a plantation of firs past a disused quarry on to the moor. By noon I was right on the top of the tableland. I ate my sandwiches in the shelter of a peat shooting-butt, while I tried to find my exact position on the map. It was not altogether easy, but I made a rough approximation, and then looked to see which was the nearest village where I could find lodging for the night. Chedsholme, where I had slept on Tuesday, seemed to be the easiest of access, and though they had charged me just double of what was reasonable for supper, bed and breakfast, the fare was good and the house quiet, no small consideration on a Saturday night.

It was after two when I left the shelter of the butt. I had at first some difficulty in finding my way. There were no landmarks on the moor to guide me; the flat expanse was only broken by mound after mound of unclothed shale, running in parallel lines from north to south, which marked the places where men had searched for ironstone many years before. Gradually the mounds grew less and less frequent, and I was beginning to think that I had left them all behind, when one larger than the rest loomed up out of the mist.

Every man has experienced at some period of his life that strange intuition of danger which compels us, if only it be strong enough, to alter some course of action, substituting for a reasonable motive the blind force of fear. I was walking straight towards the mound, when I came to a standstill. Something seemed to repel me from the spot, while at the same time I became conscious of my intense isolation, alone on the moor miles away from any fellow-creature. I stopped for half a minute, half in doubt as to whether to proceed. Then I told myself that fear is always strongest when in pursuit and, smiling at my folly, I went on.

At the further side of the mound was the body of a dead man. He was a foreigner, with dark skin and long, oily locks of hair. A scarlet handkerchief was tied loosely round his throat. There were ear-rings in his ears. He lay on his back, with his eyes wide open and glazed.

My first feeling was one, not of surprise or pity, but of intense, over-powering nausea. Then with an effort I pulled myself together and examined the body more closely. I could see at once that he had been dead several days. The hands were white and cold, and the limbs strangely limp. His clothes were little more than rags. The shirt was torn open and tattooed on the chest—even in my horror I could not help but marvel at the skill with which the thing was done—was a great green parrot with wings outstretched.

At first I could see no sign of how the man had met his death. It was not until I turned the body over that I noticed an ugly wound at the back of the skull, that might have been made by some blunt instrument or a stone. There was nothing for me to do except report the matter to the police as quickly as possible. The nearest constable would be stationed at Chedsholme, ten miles away; and I decided that the best way of getting there in the mist would be to walk eastwards until I struck the mineral line that runs from the Bleadale ironstone quarries. This I did; and I shall not easily forget the joyful feeling of companionship in a living world that I experienced on hearing the distant whistle of an engine, and saw five minutes later through a break in the clouds the long train of trucks crawling along the skyline.

Once on the permanent way my progress became less slow. Freed from the necessity of maintaining a sense of direction, I began to think more of my horrible discovery. Who could the man be, and why had he been killed? He seemed to have nothing in common with this wild, cold country—a mariner, whom one might have seen without surprise in the days of the Spanish Main, marooned with empty treasure-chests on some spit of dazzling, shadeless sand. And then, the man being killed, why had the murderer done nothing to hide the traces of his crime? What could have been easier than to have covered the body with the loose shale from the mound? 'I could have done the thing in five minutes,' I said to myself, 'if only I had a trowel.' But it was useless for me to wonder what might be the meaning of this illustration to a story I could never hope to read. I left the line at the point where it crossed the road, and then followed the latter down the ridge to Chedsholme. I must have been a mile or more from the village, when the silence of the late afternoon was suddenly broken by the tolling of a bell.

I remember once on Bob's ketch being overtaken by a sea fog. The current was running strong, and Bob was a stranger to the coast. 'It's all right; we shall worry through!' he said, and had hardly finished speaking when we heard the wild, mad clanging of the bell-buoy. I did not soon forget the look of utter surprise on Bob's face. 'There's some mistake,' he said, with all his old lack of logic; 'it's no earthly business to be there.'

That was how I felt on that September evening two years ago. What right had the church-bell to be ringing? There would be no evening service on Saturday in a place the size of Chedsholme. It was too late in the day for a funeral. And yet what else could it be? For, as I passed down the village street, I noticed that the windows of the shops were shuttered. There were men, too, hanging about the green, dressed in their Sunday black.

I found the police-station without difficulty, or rather the cottage where the constable lived. He was away, so his wife told me, but would be back in the morning, and as there seemed to be no way of communicating with the authorities I was obliged, for the time being, to keep my secret to myself.

The door of the Ship Inn was shut, and I had to knock twice before the landlady appeared. She recognized me at once. 'Yes,' she said, 'we can put you up, to be sure. You can have the same room as before. Number Three, to the right at the top of the stair. The girl's out, so I'm afraid I can only give you a cold supper.'

Ten minutes later I was standing before a cheerful fire in the parlour, while Mrs Shaftoe spread the cloth, dealing out to me in the meantime the gossip of the week. There were few visitors now; the season was too late, but she expected to have a houseful in a fortnight's time, when Mr Somerset from Steelborough was coming back with a party for another week's shooting. 'It's a pity we only get people in the spring and summer,' she said. 'A village like this is terrible poor, and every visitor makes a difference. I suppose they find it too lonely; but, bless my life, there's nothing to be afraid of on these moors. You could walk all day without meeting anybody. There's no-one to harm you. Well, sir, there's your supper ready. If you want anything, you've only got to touch the bell.'

'How is it,' I asked, as I sat down, 'that the place is so quiet tonight? I always thought that Saturday evenings were your busiest times.'

'So they are,' said Mrs Shaftoe; 'we do very little business on a Sunday. It's only a six days' licence, you see. If you'll excuse me, sir, I think that's one of the children calling; I'm only single-handed just at present, for the girl's away at church.'

She left the room, seeing nothing of the effect that her words had on me. 'Sunday!' I thought. 'What can she mean? Surely she must be mistaken!' Yet there in front of me was the calendar; Sunday, the 28th. Less than an hour before I had heard the church-bell calling to evening prayer. The men whom I had seen lounging about the street were only the ordinary Sunday idlers. Somewhere in the last week I must have missed a day.

But where? I pulled out my pocket-diary. The space allotted to each day was filled with brief notes. 'First,' I said to myself, 'let me make certain of a date from which to reckon.' I was positive that I had started on my holiday on Monday, the 22nd. For further information there was the return half of my ticket stamped with the date. On Monday I slept at Dunsley; Tuesday at this same inn at Chedsholme, Wednesday at Rapmoor, Thursday at Frankstone Edge, and Friday at Gorton. Each day, as I looked back, seemed well filled; my recollection of each was clearly defined. And yet somewhere there was a gap of twenty-four hours about which I knew nothing.

I have always been absent-minded—ludicrously so, my friends might say—it is, in fact, a trait in my character that has on more than one occasion put me into an embarrassing situation; but here was something of a nature completely different. In vain I groped about in my memory, in search for even the shadow of an explanation. The week came back to me as no sequence of indistinguishable grey days, but the clearest of well-ordered processions. But was it really Sunday? Could the whole thing be a hoax, explicable as the result of some absurd wager? In default of a better the hypothesis was worth testing.

I made a pretence of finishing the meal, and, taking my hat from the stand, hurried out of the house. I walked in the direction of the church, but as I approached the building my heart sank within me. I passed half a dozen young fellows hanging about the churchyard gate, waiting to walk back home with their girls. 'It's been a dreary Sunday,' I said, and one stopped in the act of lighting a cigarette to agree. I stood in the porch to listen. They were singing Bishop Ken's evening hymn. Then came the thin piping voice of the priest, asking for defence against the perils and dangers of the night.

Under a feeling of almost unbearable depression, I made my way back to the inn and its empty parlour.

'After all,' I said to myself, 'there's nothing that I can do. Other men before now have lost their memory. I should be thankful for regaining it so quickly, and that no harm has been done. No good, at any rate, can result from my pondering over the thing.' But in spite of my resolution I found it impossible to control my thoughts. Again and again I found myself returning to the subject, fascinated by this sudden break in the past and the possibilities that sprang from it. Where had I been? What had I done?

I believe that it was the sight of an ordinary cottage hospital collecting-box on the mantelpiece that suggested to me a new way of approaching the problem. I have always kept accurate accounts, jotting down the expenses of each day, not in my diary, but in a separate pocket cash-book. This, I thought, might throw new light on the matter. I took it out and hastily turned over the pages. At first sight it told me nothing. There was the same list of villages and their inns; no new names appeared. Then I read it through again. This time I made a discovery. The amounts I had paid in bills for a night's lodging, for supper, bed and breakfast, were much the same at all the inns, with the exception of the 'Ship' at Chedsholme. The bill there seemed to be just twice as much as what it should have been. I only remembered to have spent one night there, Tuesday. It might be that I had spent Wednesday night as well.

I rang the bell and ordered what I wanted for breakfast; then, as Mrs Shaftoe was leaving the room, I asked when it was that I had slept at the inn.

'Tuesday and Wednesday,' she said. 'You left us on Thursday

morning for Rapmoor. Goodnight, sir! I'll see that you are called at half-past seven.'

So my supposition was right. The day had been lost at Chedsholme. I wished, as soon as she had gone, that I had asked the woman more. She might have told me something of what I had done. And yet how could I have asked such questions except in the most general terms, without arousing the suspicion that I was mad! From her behaviour it was evident that I had conducted myself in a normal fashion. Very likely I had been out all day walking, only to return to the inn at night dead tired. Why should I worry about this thing, so small compared to the tragedy that centred in my discovery of the afternoon?

It was clear, however, that I should not find peace sitting by the fire in the parlour. The clock had struck half-past nine; I took my candle from the sideboard and went upstairs to bed.

My room was much the same as other rooms in country inns, but there was a hanging bookshelf in the corner, holding half a dozen books: Dr Meiklejohn's *Sermons in Advent*, *Gulliver's Travels*, *Yorkshire Anecdotes*, *The House by the Sea*, and two bound volumes, one of the *Boy's Own Paper*, and the other of some American magazine. The latter I took down and, turning over the pages, saw that the type was good and that the stories were illustrated by some fine half-tone engravings. I got into bed and, placing the candle on the chair by my side, began to read. The story dealt with a young Methodist minister in a New England town. The girl he loved had promised herself in marriage to a sailor, who had been washed ashore from a stranded brig, bound for Baltimore from Smyrna. Maddened by the girl's love for the foreigner, he forged a letter arranging for a rendezvous on the sand dunes, met his rival there, and shot him through the heart. There was nothing remarkable about the story. I read it to the end unmoved. But on turning the last page over I came across a full-page illustration that held me fascinated.

It showed the scene on the dunes; the minister in his suit of black gazing down on the dead body of the Syrian sailor, just as I had stood that afternoon, and underneath were the words, taken from the letterpress of the story:

'What would he not have given to blot out the sight from his memory?'

I suppose that up to the time of which I am writing, my life had been a very ordinary one, filled with ordinary weekday pleasures and cares, regulated by ordinary routine. Within the space of a few hours I had experienced two great emotional shocks, the sudden discovery of the body on the moor, and this inexplicable loss of memory. Each by itself had proved sufficiently disturbing, but I had at least looked upon them as unconnected. A mere chance had shown me that I might be mistaken. I had stood, as it were, on the watershed at the source of two rivers. I had assumed that they flowed into two oceans. The clouds lifted, and I saw that they joined each other to form a torrent of irresistible force that would inevitably overwhelm me.

The whole thing seemed impossible; but I had a sickening feeling that the impossible was true, that I was the instrument, the unwilling tool, in this ghastly tragedy.

It was useless to lie in bed. I got up and paced the room. Again and again I tried to shut in the horrible thought behind a high wall of argument, built so carefully that there seemed to be no loophole for its escape. My best efforts were of no avail. I was seized with an over-mastering fear of myself and the deed I might have done. I could think of only one thing to do, to report the whole matter to the police, to inform them of my inability to account for my doings on the Wednesday, and to welcome every investigation. 'Anything', I told myself, 'is better than this intolerable uncertainty.'

And yet it seemed a momentous step to take. Supposing that I had nothing to do with this man's death, but at the same time had been the last person seen with him, I might run the risk of being punished for another's crime. I owed something to the position I held, to my future career; and so at last, dazed and weary, I lay down to wait for sleep. I did so with the firm determination that on the morrow I would retrace the path I had followed that afternoon. I might discover some fresh clue to the tragedy. I might find that the whole thing was but the fancy of an overwrought brain.

Slowly I became aware of a narrowing of the field of consciousness. A warm soft mist surrounded me and enfolded me. I heard the church clock strike the hour, but was too weary to count the strokes. The bell seemed to be tolling, tolling; every note grew fainter and I fell asleep.

When I awoke it was nine o'clock. The sun was shining in through the window and, pulling up the blind, I saw a sky of cloudless blue. Sleep had brought hope. I dressed quickly, laughing at the night's fears. In certain moods nothing is so strong as the force of unexpected coincidence. I told myself that I had been in a morbidly sensitive mood on the preceding evening; and in the clear light of day I took up the bound volume which had been the source of so much uneasiness. Really there was nothing in the story of the Methodist minister and the sailor, and as to the illustration, I turned the last page over and found that the illustration did not exist. Evidently I had imagined the whole thing.

'Another lovely day!' said Mrs Shaftoe, as she brought in the breakfast. 'Will you be out walking again, sir? If you like, I could put up some sandwiches for you.' I thought the idea a good one, and telling her I should not be back until four or five, set out soon after eleven.

For the first few miles I had no difficulty in retracing my steps, but after I crossed the mineral line there were no landmarks to guide me. More than once I asked myself why I went on. I could give no satisfactory reply. I think now it must have been the desire to be brought face to face with facts that impelled me. I had had enough of the unbridled fancies of the preceding evening, and longed to discover some clue to the mystery, however faint.

At last I found myself among the old ironstone workings. There was the long line of mounds, thrown up like ramparts, and there was the one standing alone in advance of the rest, beside which the body lay. Slowly I walked towards it. It seemed smaller in the light of a cloudless noon than in Sunday's mists. What was I to find? With beating heart I scrambled up the slope of shale. I stood on the top and looked around. There was nothing, only the wide expanse of moor and sky.

My first thought was that I had mistaken the place. Eagerly I scanned the ground for footprints. I found them almost immediately. They corresponded exactly to my nailed walking-boots. Evidently the place was the same.

Then what had happened? There was but one explanation possible—that I had imagined the whole thing.

And strange as it may seem, I accepted the explanation gladly, for it was the cold reality that I dreaded, linked as it had been with the awful idea that I had done the deed myself in a fit of unconscious frenzy; and in my thankfulness I knelt down on the heather and praised the God of the blue sky and sunlight for having saved me from the terrors of the night.

With a mind at peace with itself I walked back across the moor. I determined to end my holiday on the morrow, to consult some nerve specialist and, if need be, to go abroad for a month or two. I dined that night at the Ship Inn with a talkative old gentleman, who succeeded in keeping me from thinking of my own affairs, and, feeling sure of sleep, went early to bed.

My story does not end there. I wish that it did; but, as Canon Eldred said in yesterday's sermon, it is often our duty to accept things as they are, not to waste the limited amount of energy that is given for the day's work in vain regret or morbid anticipation.

For, as I was sitting at breakfast on the morrow, I heard a man in the bar ask Mrs Shaftoe for the morning's paper. She told him that the gentleman in the parlour was reading it, but that Tuesday's was in the kitchen.

'Tuesday's?' I said to myself. 'Monday's, she means. Today is Tuesday'; and I looked at the calendar on the mantelpiece. The calendar said Wednesday. I looked at the newspaper and saw on every page, 'Wednesday, 1st October'. I got up half-dazed and walked into the bar. I suppose Mrs Shaftoe must have seen that there was something wrong, for, before I spoke, she offered me a glass of brandy.

'I'm losing my memory,' I said. 'I think I can't be quite well. I can't remember anything I did yesterday.'

'Why, bless you, sir!' she said, 'you were out on the moors all day. I made you some sandwiches, and in the evening you were talking to the old gentleman who left this morning on Free Trade and Protection.'

'Then what did I do on Monday? I thought that was Monday.'

'Oh! Monday!' said Mrs Shaftoe. 'You were out on the moors all that day too. Don't you recollect borrowing my trowel? There was something you wanted to bury, a green parrot, I think you said it was. I remember, because it seemed so strange. You came in quite late in the evening, and looked regular knocked up, just the same as last week. It's my belief, sir, that you've been walking too far.'

I asked for my account and, while she was making it out, I went upstairs to my bedroom. I took down the bound volume from the shelf and turned to the story of the Methodist minister. The illustration at the end was certainly not there, but on close inspection I found that a page was missing. For some reason it had been carefully removed. I turned to the index of illustrations, and saw that the picture with the words beneath that had so strangely affected me, should have been found on the missing page.

I walked to the nearest station and took the train to Steelborough, where I told my story to an inspector of police, who evidently disbelieved it. But in the course of a day or two they made discoveries. The body of an unknown sailor, a foreigner, with curiously distinctive tattooings on the breast, was found in the place I described. For some time there was nothing to connect me with the crime. Then a gamekeeper came forward, who said that on Wednesday, the 24th, he had seen two men, one of whom seemed to be a clergyman, the other a tramp, walking across the moor. He had called to them, but they had not stopped. I stood my trial. I was examined, of course, by alienists, and here I am. No, Canon Eldred, the world is a little more complicated than you think. I agree with you as to the necessity for cheerfulness, but I want better reasons than yours. These are mine—they may be only a poor lunatic's, but they are none the worse for that.

The world, I consider, is governed by God through a hierarchy of spirits. Little Charlie Lovel, by the way, says that he saw the Archangel Gabriel yesterday evening, as he was coming from the bathroom, and for all I know he may be right. It is governed by a hierarchy of spirits, some greater and more wise than others, and to each is given its appointed task. I suppose that for some reason, which I may never know, it was necessary for that sailorman to die. It may have been necessary for his salvation that he should die in a certain way, that his soul at the last might be purged by sudden terror. I cannot say, for I was only the tool. The great and powerful (but not all-powerful) spirit did his work as far as concerned the sailor, and then, with a workman's love for his tool, he thought of me. It was not needful that I should remember what I had done—I had been lent by God, as Gog was lent to Satan,—but, my work finished, this spirit in his pity took from me all memory of my deed. But, as I said before, he was not omnipotent, and I suppose the longing of the brute in me to see again his handi-work guided me unconsciously to the bank of shale on the moor, though even at the last minute I had felt something urging me not to go on. That and the chance reading of an idle magazine story had been my undoing; and, when for the second time I lost my memory, and some power outside myself took control in order to cover up the traces before I revisited the scene, the issue of events had passed into other hands.

Sometimes I find myself wondering who that sailor was and what his life had been.

Nobody knows.

8

H. RUSSELL WAKEFIELD

'Look Up There'

Why *did* he always stare up? And why did he so worry Mr Packard by doing it? The latter had come to Brioni to read and to rest, and to take the bare minimum of notice of his fellow men. Doctor's orders! And here he was preoccupied, almost obsessed, by the garish idiosyncrasy of this tiny, hen-eyed fellow. He was not a taking specimen of humanity, for his forehead was high and receding, his nose beaked fantastically and the skin stretched so tightly across it that it seemed as if it might be ripped apart at any moment. Then, he had a long, thin-lipped mouth always slightly open, and a pointed beard which, like his hair, was fussy and unkempt. He was for ever in the company of a stalwart yokel—a south-country enlisted Guardsman to the life; a slow-moving, massive, red-faced plebeian who seemed a master of the desirable art of aphasia, for no word ever seemed to pass his lips. But, good heavens! how he ploughed and furrowed the menu!

Mr Packard was a very important Civil servant, and, contrary to the opinion of the vulgar, Civil servants sometimes overwork. The notion that they arrive at their offices just in time for lunch, and return again to them just in time to sign a few letters and catch a train home, is a fantasy derived from newspapers, and therefore from newspaper proprietors—idle fellows as a rule, for all they have to do is to propagate ideas and employ other people to carry them out. Anyone can have ideas; it is the carrying them out which means work. Mr Packard had ideas, usually very judicious and admirable ideas, and he also had to carry them out, which meant work—eventually overwork, a threatened nervous breakdown, peremptory advice from a specialist, and three months' leave. He had been recommended Brioni in June because it was between seasons for that green and placid isle, and there was plenty of sun; gentle breezes blown over a purple sea, very purple, very warm, very salt; a golf course, with seven short holes, and a reasonable tariff. Perched primly in the Adriatic, it offered every possible advantage, every chance of speedy convalescence to an over-worked bachelor fifty-two years of age, with nothing whatsoever organically wrong with him. So Mr Packard had found it till his eye had been caught by this curious couple: one who never spoke, but stolidly filled his belly, the other who was no more communicative, and for ever stared upwards at an angle of thirty-five degrees, for such Mr Packard, after an exasperating calculation, estimated it to be. On the first occasion he had noticed him, Mr Packard had instinctively stared up also, wondering what object of interest was to be found on the bare, brimstone-tinted wall of the dining room at an angle of thirty-five degrees about. But there was nothing. Yet this midget had continued to gaze up, even while eating his fish and emptying his glass. And his companion, that burly proletarian, appeared entirely uncon-cerned. Again Mr Packard's eyes tilted in sympathy, only to encounter a bare brimstone wall. It then occurred to him that this angular obses-sion must be of long standing, for its victim most expertly neutralized what must have been a heavy handicap to accur-ate feeding by an impressive dexterity in the manipulation of knives and forks and spoons, though his appetite seemed as slender as his physical frame.

So stern and uncompromising had been the specialist's fiat, that Mr Packard had been genuinely alarmed about his nerves; so much so that he almost entertained the possibility that this upward-peering absurdity was a figment of his disordered imagination—a very unlovely thought—but he had dismissed it with a very comforting reassurance when he saw that others among the sparse company then visiting Brioni were also puzzled by this singular prepossession of the hen-eyed fellow.

What an incongruous couple they were! And why didn't the lusty rustic turn his eyes up too—or do something about it? Well, let him take a leaf out of his book, and pay no regard to what was none of his business, and certainly no part of his cure.

If the fellow wanted to stare up, let him. So, by making a consider-able effort, Mr Packard looked away. All the same, he was charged with a tantalizing and hard-to-exorcize curiosity about this couple, their circumstances, the connection between them—all this—but, above all, why the devil the tiny one stared up. Knowing such wonderings could only delay the healing of the lesion in his nervous system, he made quite elaborate plans for avoiding the pair. He changed the times of his meals, and if he saw them in a room he went to another, and if he observed them coming towards him he turned on his heel. By these means he freed his mind of them to some extent, but a sneaking, insidious inquisitiveness endured. However, the sun and air and peace of Brioni rapidly restored him, and once again he slept an unbroken eight hours; he found himself with such an appetite as he had not known for twenty years, and the idea that there was someone standing just behind him all the time—a very irritating symptom, this—most absolutely and blessedly ceased. So, reassuringly soon, his inner eye began to turn longingly to a snug though austere office in Whitehall, with neatly raised pyramids of 'jackets' and official documents of undeniable secrecy and import. And to that leisurely stroll up to the club at one o'clock so punctually, and that carefully chosen little lunch, and perhaps a game of chess with Lenton, some gossip, and a leisurely stroll back to the Home Office, where there would be decisions to make, questions in the House to consider, a feeling of slight but pleasing importance, and all that regulated system and ordered regime which suited him temperamentally so perfectly.

A holiday in August seemed a justifiable weakness to him, but to idle about in dreamy, flushing, dark-green islands in June was abnormal—a process which should not be prolonged for an unnecessary second. He would stick it out for a week or two longer, and count the days till the hour of his release should strike—release from indolence, strolling about, and from an inclination to uneasy, vague surmisings concerning an ill-assorted couple, one of whom for ever raised his eyes in a sort of viewless intensity, and the other who never spoke but was for ever at his side.

On the evening before his departure, about six o'clock, Mr Packard strolled along the path through the holm oaks towards the bathing place and sat down on a seat overlooking the shadowed and darkening straits of the Istrian shore. Shadowed and darkening because a slowly marshalling army of clouds was rising above the Dolomites and frowning down over Trieste. The sun, resisting and not yet over-powered, hurled red and gold shafts up through the advancing host. The spectacle had a certain sombre sublimity, and its leisurely shifting pattern pleasantly absorbed Mr Packard's attention, so much so that when a rather high-pitched and deliberate voice remarked, 'Some persons have found in such spectacles evidence of the existence of a God', he started abruptly and half rose from his seat. He must have been half-asleep, for he found sitting on the same seat beside him that enigmatic pair, the little one next to him and the yokel—on his other side—smoking a pipe and staring out to sea. Mr Packard was irritated and taken by surprise, but his natural good manners and subcon-scious curiosity prevented him from uttering the tart and 'snubby' retort which half rose to his lips. Instead, he said dryly, 'The particular deity concerned is most certainly Jupiter Pluvius. I imagine that Trieste will get the full benefit of that storm soon and it will be our turn in an hour or so.'

'From your tone,' suggested the little man, 'I judge you are of a sceptical turn of mind.'

('And what the devil has it got to do with you if I am?') thought Mr Packard. 'If you mean,' he said, 'that I do not see why all that is beautiful should be put to the credit of what you call "God", that is so. For in whom do you lodge the responsibility for the somewhat less palatable spectacles provided by bullfights and battlefields? Unless you are a dualist.'

'Very possibly I am,' said the little man, staring up at the fading sun, now drowning in a majestically pacing cloud ocean.

'Well,' said Mr Packard, 'it will be the devil's turn soon enough. Storms in this region are no joke.'

'I think I have reason to believe in the devil,' continued the little man, taking off his rusty panama and placing it on the ground beside him. As he said this the yokel looked at him sharply, then knocked out his pipe on his boot and began filling it again from an aluminium box.

'Oh, indeed,' replied Mr Packard, his curiosity rising. 'I have myself deduced him logically, but I take it you have had a closer view of him.'

'Yes,' answered the little man, his eyes on the rim of the advancing storm, 'I think I can say that. Would you like to hear about it?'

'Certainly,' said Mr Packard.

'I'm glad of that, because it is a relief to me to tell it now and again. Does Gauntry Hall convey anything to you?'

'Gauntry Hall,' repeated Mr Packard uncertainly. 'The name seems vaguely familiar.'

'It was a famous show place burnt down in 1904. I was there that night.'

'Oh, I remember now,' said Mr Packard. 'Middle Tudor, near Leicester, famous chiefly for its Long Gallery; and wasn't there some legend about it?'

'Yes,' replied the little man; 'and the fact that you can recall so much is a great tribute to your memory.'

'Oh, I was rather keen on that period once upon a time when I was less busy.'

'I went up to Oxford the same term as Jack Gauntry, and to the same college—Oriel,' continued the little man, his eyes narrowed and shifting and busy with the sky. 'In those days I was keenly interested in the occult: I believe it to have been somewhat of a pose—a dangerous pose. I knew there was some queer story about Gauntry Hall, and made up my mind I would get Jack to tell me about it; not a very creditable ambition, but I was young and foolish, and I have been punished enough. We became great friends, and one evening I had my chance. He came up to my rooms rather late one night, late in November 1896, after dining out. He was a little drunk, and still thirsty. I filled him up, and finally brought the subject round to Gauntry Hall.

' "Funny you should mention it," he said; "my people did the annual trek to London today."

' "How do you mean—'annual trek'?" I asked.

'He did not answer for a moment, and I could see he was torn between two impulses—one to cleanse his bosom of this family obsession, the other to keep his mouth dutifully shut. So I gave him another whisky-and-soda. He drank it in a gulp and then became muzzy and garrulous. I could see he would find relief in being unrestrainedly indiscreet. I'm not boring you?'

'Not in the least,' Mr Packard reassured him.

'Well, suddenly Jack blurted out, "No one's allowed to be in the house New Year's Eve."

' "Why not?"

' "Oh, because the Bogey Man gets busy then. As a matter of fact, no one is supposed to have spent New Year's Eve at Gauntry for three hundred years. So as not to make it too conspicuous, we always clear out during the last week in November. Perhaps it's all bosh—I sometimes wonder. Anyway, I shouldn't be telling you this, but I'm slightly tight, and shall tell you some more."

'I was feeling rather ashamed of myself, and it was on the tip of my tongue to shut him up. But I didn't.

' "No one's allowed there on New Year's Eve, but early next morning old Carrow, the butler—the Carrows have been in our service for years and years—comes to the house and opens all the windows one after the other and shuts them again—the hell of a job. All but one, the one in the middle of the first floor of the south wing. And out of this one he has to hang a white silk banner which is in the Long Gallery and wave it three times very slowly, and then—shall I tell you what he has to do then?"

' "No," I said, for I knew I was hearing what I should not and that I should be bitterly repentant if I let him go on. "Shut up, and I'll forget what you've told me."

'This seemed to sober him up. "Yes, I hope you will," he replied, and got up and left the room. We never referred to the subject again.

'I spent half the summer vac. at Gauntry Hall for the four years I was "up". It was an exquisite house, gloriously placed, and the grounds were perfection. But you remember it, so I need not describe it. Sir John and Lady Gauntry were sweet survivals from an easier age—a type which began to disappear with the introduction of modern plumbing from America. They were rather slow and faded, their manners were a heritage, their benign suzerainty over the local serfs and villeins a sharp reminder that there was something in consonance with society in the Feudal System. Well, they are dust by now. I grew to love the old place. Its atmosphere seemed so placid, untroubled, unshakeable in those long, lovely summer days that I could hardly believe it was ever visited by a curious winter spell; that it ever could cease to drowse and become most malignantly awake. The subject was never alluded to within its walls, but I remember I used to find my eyes wandering up to that window in the middle of the south wing. Yes, I used to find myself looking up—that was all. At least, I think that was all, though one evening when I was taking a stroll after dinner I happened to glance up at this window, and for a second it seemed as if something white fluttered from it and disappeared. But it may have been a projection from my own mind.

'And then came the Boer War, and Jack went out with his Yeomanry and was killed on the Modder. The shock drove the old couple into complete seclusion, and they died within a few days of each other early in 1903. Meanwhile, I had completely lost touch with Gauntry Hall. And then one day I met Teller, the agent, in the street and he lunched with me. He told me the estate had been leased to people called Relf, *nouveaux riches*. Young Relf was the son of a millionaire multiple-shop owner in the North, and he had married some little vulgarian. Teller utterly despised these town-bred parvenus and considered their occupation of Gauntry defiling and almost intolerable.

' "But they may not be there much longer," he said, "for the damn fools are going to spend New Year's Eve in the house."

' "What!" I cried.

' "Oh, yes," he replied; "they are greatly looking forward to it. I felt it my duty to warn them, but I might have saved myself the trouble, for when I had said my piece, that little barmaid, Mrs Relf, who looks like a painted Pekinese, clapped her hands on her knees and declared she simply adored ghosts—didn't believe in them a bit, would have a house-party for the occasion, and wish a very Happy New Year to whoever or whatever came. I reminded her she was preparing to break a rule which had lasted for three hundred years. 'Quite time it *was* broken,' said she. So I shrugged my shoulders and gave it up. I wish them luck!"

' "All the same," I said, "it's one of the most interesting pieces of news I've heard for a long time."

' "Well, if you think that, why don't you make one of the party?" asked Teller, laughing.

' "How could I? I don't know them."

' "Oh, that doesn't matter. They're very partial to peers."

'I was about to say "No" most emphatically when I was seized by a most violent temptation. Here were these fools prepared to put this most ancient and vague and famous mystery to the test. It was a unique opportunity. Dangerous? Yes, probably, but the old house had always seemed friendly to me. Here was I a professed student of the occult, presented with a glorious opportunity for investigation. If I failed to take it I should never forgive myself nor have any respect for myself. I imagine you can sympathize with my feelings to some extent.'

'Oh, yes,' replied Mr Packard; 'no doubt I should have done as I infer you did.'

'Yes, I accepted.'

As the little man said this Mr Packard noticed the yokel glance across at him, and as their eyes met it seemed as though the fellow wished to convey a message of some sort. A warning, was it?

'Yes,' continued the little man. 'I accepted. Teller fixed up the invitation for me, and I reached Leicester Station about 5.30 on New Year's Eve twenty-three years ago. The moment I got into the trap and we began to drive eastward through rows of dingy villas, I began to feel a nervous irritation which steadily increased as we drove towards Gauntry. It was a foul night, blowing very hard, and sleeting, and every yard we travelled made me wish the more I hadn't come. I could feel the influence of Gauntry reaching out and attempting to repel me. I'd have gone straight back to the station but for one thing. Supposing I funked it and nothing happened. That story might get round, which wouldn't have been pleasant. All the same, when we reached the house, it took all my resolution to cross the threshold. The old place had always seemed so friendly and welcoming before; now it was sullen, and utterly hostile. I felt as if I were a traitor, as if I had been caught by my best friend in the act of forging his name. I was so seized by dread and nervously unstrung that I hardly noticed the rest of the party. I remember there were ten of us, five women and five men, and that they all appeared to be young, noisy and vulgar—so noisy that I was convinced they had had a good many of the primitive cocktails which they were drinking as I arrived, and presently I knew they were almost as full of dread and as unstrung as myself. The house seemed throbbing with a sinister rhythm. It seemed as if it had summoned the great wind which leaped at it in gigantic gusts. By coming there that day I had incurred its malignant enmity, and with cold austerity it was bidding me begone. I had my old room in the east wing, but when I went up to dress it was as though an almost materialized force was disputing my entry. I had to breast my way through it as through a hostile tide. I found they had decided to dine in the Great Hall instead of the dining-room—why, I don't know. Round it ran a balcony from which a door led through to the famous Long Gallery. When we sat down I knew them all to be suffering from an acute spiritual malaise, and that what they had drunk, far from lulling their sensitiveness to the power which menaced them, had but weakened their resistance to it. How soon will the storm break?'

'In ten minutes or so,' replied Mr Packard. 'I am surprised it has not broken before now. It is reserving all its venom for us.'

'Then I may have just time to finish. I do not remember whether I spoke a word throughout that meal, but I do know that I was under such a strain that I had to grip my chair to stop myself running from the room. The women were on the verge of hysteria, the men drank feverishly and, as time went on, a dreadful vague inane babble came from all of them. The woman on my right—she had a high, thin voice—suddenly gulped down a full glass of champagne, some of which swilled over her chin and neck, and shouted: "Well, when does it begin?" and then went off into peals of hysterical laughter. We did not move from the table, and from half-past ten onwards, Relf kept getting up to ring the bell, but no servant appeared. "Where are those bloody slaves?" he cried each time, and staggered back to the table and filled his glass again. From half-past eleven I was no longer master of myself. The room was thick with smoke which wreathed itself into fantastic patterns. The pressure grew unendurable, and suddenly my resistance broke, and I ran from the Great Hall up to my room and lay cowering on my bed. I could still hear the crazy, chaotic babble from those I had left, and then a great bell crashed out. *One-two-three*—and each mighty stroke followed so hard on its predecessor that the vile jangle almost seemed an undivided sound. It was as if a murderer was hammering in my brain. Suddenly it ceased, and I heard no sound from below, and then came one high, piercing scream from a woman: "Look up there!" and then every light in the house went out.

'Well, when that happened I groped around the room for my electric torch. At last I found it, and I think if I had not found it just then I should have suffered even more than I have suffered. I staggered downstairs and into the Great Hall, and flashed the lamp on the table. They were all sitting rigidly, their eyes looking up and focused on the door into the Long Gallery. I peered into their faces one by one. Their eyes were wide, yet drawn in, as though asquint; their heads were strained back on their shoulders; their mouths were open, and foam was on their lips. And then I flashed my torch up towards the door into the Long Gallery, and there—and there—'

The cloud army had advanced so far that it was looming down on them. Two striding horns of vapour preceded it. As the little man cried 'and there—and there—' a blinding flash leapt from one to the other, so that these enflamed and curled tentacles drove down at them, or so it seemed most terrifyingly to Mr Packard, and the rending crash of thunder which followed hard upon it hurled its echoes round the world. And then, with inchoate fury, the storm drove forward to the attack. And then, the little man leapt to his feet and flung his arms above his head and screamed out as though in agony: 'Look up there! Look up there!' Mr Packard moved towards him, but in a second the yokel had him by the shoulders. 'Leave him to me,' he shouted against the thunder, 'I know what to do.' And he began to propel the little man before him. Mr Packard, oblivious of the rain, stared after them. With a horrid regularity the little man flung up his arms and screamed: 'Look up there!' and presently they turned a corner and disappeared, and the screams grew fainter. For a moment Mr Packard stared upwards too, and then, as another flash speared down to the sea, he came to himself and turning up the collar of his coat, started to run through the blinding rain back to the hotel.

9

MARJORIE BOWEN

The Last Bouquet

I

Mme Marcelle Lesarge and Miss Kezia Faunce quarrelled violently in the private sitting-room of an expensive Parisian hotel. The interview had begun with embarrassment, but decorously, and had proceeded through stages of mutual exasperation to final outbursts of recrimination that were without restraint. The disgust, contempt, and fury which each had cherished in their hearts for years rose to their lips, and rage at being involved in such a humiliating quarrel added force to the energy with which they abused each other.

Mme Lesarge was a fashionable actress, beautifully dressed in a frilled, interchangeable crimson and blue silk, with dark red feathers in the small hat exquisitely poised on her glossy curls. The reticule that dangled from the wrist of her white kid pearl-buttoned gloves was of gold mesh, and the handle of her parasol was carved ivory. There were real diamonds at her ears and in the costly lace at her throat. All her movements were graceful and well trained, at once impetuous and languishing.

Miss Faunce wore an ugly brown travelling dress frogged with black braid. Her hair was grey and brushed into a chenille net. Her gestures were brusque and her voice was harsh.

These two women, who seemed in everything dissimilar, were twin sisters. They had not seen each other for ten years.

A spiteful curiosity that thinly masked hatred had brought Miss Faunce to Paris, and the same emotion had induced Mme Lesarge to call at her sister's hotel. Yet the first interchanges after this long silence had been civil enough. Miss Faunce had sent quite a friendly little note stating casually that she was in Paris for a few days, naming her hotel and adding how pleased she would be to see Martha again after so many years.

Mme Lesarge replied in a letter written on an impulse of kindness and had accepted, quite warmly, the invitation to renew the relationship broken off so early and for such a great while, as it seemed, completely forgotten.

But, when they met, the first friendly conventionalities had soon changed into this bitter quarrelling. Neither woman could forgive the appearance of the other. Miss Kezia Faunce saw in the actress the woman who had attained everything which she, in the name of Virtue, had denied herself. She admired, envied and loathed all the manifestations of this unblushing Vice which had made such a profitable use of its opportunities. In this successful wanton who was really her twin sister Kezia Faunce saw the woman she would have liked to have been, and the realization of this brought to a climax the smouldering anger of years. But, if she were enraged, no less deep was the fury of Martha who called herself Marcelle Lesarge, for in this plain woman with the grey hair, harsh voice, drab complexion, and clumsy clothes she saw herself, the woman who, without her affectations, her graces, her costly clothes, her paints and dyes, she really was.

It was true that she contrived to look thirty and that Kezia did not look a day less than fifty, but they were twins and their common age, forty-five, seemed to the actress to be written all over the red plush and gilt of the hotel sitting-room.

There was a pause in their fierce speech and they sat slack, exhausted by passion, staring at each other and each thought: 'It must never be known by any of my friends that that dreadful woman is my sister.'

'I should be ruined,' the actress said to herself. 'Everyone would think I am even older than I am. That hideous, middle-aged, dowdy *bourgeoise* my sister! I should be laughed out of Paris. Why did she come here? Why was I such a fool as to see her?'

And Kezia thought:

'If anyone at Stibbards were to see her I should be ruined and I should never be able to hold up my head again. A great, blousy, painted trollop! I must have been crazy to come.'

The actress was the first to recover herself. Her rage had resolved itself into a steady fear that someone in Paris should get to know that this miserable English provincial was her twin sister.

Mme Lesarge was not without rivals nor fears for the future. She had skilfully built up many legends about herself that even the whisper of the existence of Miss Faunce would destroy.

So, pulling at the large pearls that fastened her pale grey gloves she said, with some art:

'It is very stupid of us to quarrel. You should not have come and I should not have seen you. But now I suppose we have said all the unpleasant things we can think of. We had better try to forget each other again.'

'I wish I could forget, Martha, but you know perfectly well that one can't forget just because one wants to. . . . I've tried to forget you time and again for years, but it's no use. You keep coming up in my mind—between me and my duty, between me and my prayers, sometimes.'

Mme Lesarge laughed uneasily. The more she considered the situation the more she felt it imperative for her sister to leave Paris quietly and at once.

'Well, I can't help that, can I, Kezia? You must have got a morbid mind. I can't say I ever think of you, though I very well might. I might say that *you* got on *my* nerves.'

'That's impertinence,' put in Kezia sharply. Her lips were dry and trembling, and her flaccid cheeks quite pale.

'I don't see that it is impertinence. I ran away from home when I was sixteen, and I have had all manner of adventures since.'

'Pray don't relate any of them to me,' flung in Kezia.

'As if I should!' The actress smiled with a maddening self-complacency. 'You wouldn't understand them. They are quite out of the range of your experience. But, as I said, I left home when I was sixteen and I think it would be quite reasonable for me to feel that it was rather dreadful to think of you at Stibbards all that time—going on just the same, day in, day out. Doing everything exactly as mother used to do it. And grandmother before that, I suppose.'

'In other words,' interrupted Kezia, 'leading the life of a decent gentlewoman with a sense of honour and of duty.'

'How can you talk like that?' asked Mme Lesarge with a vicious smile. 'Don't you realize how really shocking that sounds to me? But I suppose I ought to be sorry for you. You never had the strength to break away.'

Miss Faunce rose and walked to the window and peered down through the stiff, white, starched lace curtains into the narrow noisy street below and watched a baker's boy putting the very long powdered loaves into a handcart. She wanted to say what she had to say with the deadly effect of perfect calm. She realized that it would, perhaps, be better to say nothing at all, but she could not attain to that amount of self-control.

She must, clearly, and once and for all, get out of her heart and soul all her thoughts about her twin sister.

Mme Lesarge was glad of this respite. She was sorry about the quarrel, which had been unbecoming and exhausting; she regretted that she had not had more power over herself. It had been a very long time since she had been in such a rage; she was, on the whole, a good-natured woman and not often crossed nor exasperated. Her life had been easy, full of facile success, light friendships and superficial adulation; she avoided everyone who disapproved of her, therefore this violent interview had been a detestable experience.

She rose also and went, not to the window, but to a mirror and there skilfully adjusted the smooth curls that should, perhaps, have been the same colour as the harsh locks of her sister, but which were very carefully tinted a glossy auburn. She took paint and powder from her reticule and made up her lips and her cheeks; she always looked at herself a little anxiously when she studied her face in the mirror, but never had she looked at herself so anxiously as she did now. For she seemed to see in her comely face, which had satisfied her well enough until the present moment, the ugly lines, the sour bilious tint, the creeping wrinkles, and the sagging folds that for the last half-hour she had been observing with fear and terror in the countenance of her twin sister.

She had thought, quite gaily, as she had come up the hotel stairs:

'I suppose Kezia will be looking a terrible frump by now.'

But she had been quite unprepared for what Kezia really did look like.

All the time they had been quarrelling she had been unable to take a terrified, fascinated gaze from the plain woman seated opposite her, and she had thought continuously, 'She is my age to the very minute.' Of course, no one would recognize that there was the least likeness between them; it was not only the dress and the paint and the dye and the acquired graces that disguised the actress. Although they were twin sisters their natures were absolutely different, always had been, but the fact remained that they *were* twin sisters, and Mme Lesarge knew that she would feel deeply uneasy until she was assured that Kezia had left Paris and was not likely to return.

So, when she had a little reassured herself by that nervous, anxious contemplation of her reflection in the mirror (her figure at least was very good, and her taste in clothes excellent), she turned and said, with an attempt at conciliation:

'Let us part with some civility at least, Kezia. I wish you no ill will. It was a stupid mistake for us to meet. When are you leaving Paris?'

Miss Faunce turned round from the window. She felt she had herself well in hand now, would be able to say exactly what she meant without allowing her passion to betray her into useless abuse.

'I don't know that it was a mistake for me to come to Paris,' she said deliberately. 'I felt it my duty to do so. As I said, I have been thinking of you continuously for years. I live alone, as you know, and of course, there is plenty to do, I am never idle. But there is no other person beside yourself nearly connected with me. Say and think what you like, Martha, we *are* twin sisters, and I suppose there is some sort of bond,' she paused and added, 'even if it be a bond of hatred.'

'Hatred,' repeated the actress, with an elegant shrug, 'that's an ugly word to use, isn't it? Why do you bother about me at all? I don't hate you, I assure you.'

'Oh, yes, I think you do,' said Miss Faunce. 'I think you do, Martha. I saw hatred in your eyes all the time we were talking together. You were thinking that I was old and ugly and your twin sister.'

'Did you read me as clearly as that?' smiled Mme Lesarge, rather pale under the careful tinting of powder and rouge. 'Well, perhaps some such thought did come into my mind. You've let yourself go, you see, terribly, Kezia. You look fifteen years older than you are. I suppose you rather revel in it.'

'I've let myself alone,' replied Miss Faunce. 'I am as God made me. My hair is the colour yours ought to be, my face looks as yours would look without all that stuff you've got on it.'

'Not quite, I think,' said Mme Lesarge. 'We have different thoughts, different minds. We live very differently. I don't suppose if we were stripped side by side we should look in the least alike.'

'Don't you? Well, I think that if we were stripped, people would know us for twins, but that's not what I want to argue about. And I don't want to hear about your life, which I am sure is vile and disgusting. It was thinking of your life and how horrible it was that brought me here. I felt it was my duty to try and save you.'

'Oh, for pity's sake,' murmured the actress. She picked up her gold-mesh bag and her ivory-handled parasol. 'You are really becoming absurd, ridiculous. Save me—from what?'

'You know quite well what I mean, and I really do want to save you. I dare say that, as you boast, I don't know as much of the world as you do, but I know what happens to women like you when they are not young. I suppose you haven't saved anything?'

'No, and I am in debt,' smiled the actress.

'I thought so. What are you going to do when you can't any longer get parts—when you can't find any friends?'

'That is many, many years ahead,' replied Mme Lesarge. 'You need not concern yourself about my future, my dear Kezia. Even if I do live to be old I shall——'

'Well, what will you do?'

Miss Faunce leaned forward eagerly.

'I shall repent, of course. Either marry some good man and go and live in the country or go into a convent. You know I am a Roman Catholic?'

Miss Faunce shuddered.

'You are the first of our family to become that,' she said with real distress.

Mme Lesarge laughed. She was uneasy and wanted to escape.

'Did you really come to Paris to say these silly things to me?' she said. 'You have wasted your time and your money.'

'I have plenty of both,' replied Kezia, 'you know Grandmother Tallis died last year. She left me all her fortune. Half of it would have been yours if you had been—a different sort of woman. I'd give you what would have been your share now, if you'd like to change your way of living.'

'Repent—I suppose, is what you wanted to say, Kezia. This is all so hopeless. We don't even talk the same language. I don't want Grandmother Tallis's money nor any of yours. Though you must admit,' she added, a little grimly, 'that it has been fortunate for you, from a practical point of view, that I did take—the primrose path, I suppose you'd call it, eh? You had everything, didn't you—the house, the lands, the money, father's fortune, mother's fortune, Grandmother Tallis's fortune. To whom are you going to leave it when you die?'

'To charities,' replied Kezia Faunce sternly. 'Every penny of that money will be left to do good to someone. I am quite prepared, as I said just now, to give you all you need, if you leave the stage—leave Paris.' Then, on another note, she added: 'Don't you ever feel homesick, Martha?'

Mme Lesarge reflected. The words did take her back to certain broken dreams and odd moments of nostalgia. She had run away from home when she was sixteen, a schoolgirl home for the holidays. She had eloped with a subaltern from the neighbouring garrison. They had gone to India and in three years she had been divorced ignominiously. There had been another marriage with a husband who drank and ill-treated her, and this time a separation without a divorce. Then, a long connection with Adrian Lesarge, the French actor, who had taught her his language and his art, given her the place which she had contrived to hold since. For she was industrious, clever, and talented, and had a rare charm and radiance in her personality.

It seemed a long time ago since she had fled from Stibbards, with a veil down over her bonnet and a small case in her hand. It was very early summer, she could recall the scent of the flowering currant bushes as she had hurried through the kitchen garden to let herself out by the back door in the red-brick wall where the apricots grew.

Homesick—for those sixteen years in an English village! She remembered it as always afternoon and always sunny, quiet, with the smell of hot jam coming from the kitchen.

Kezia was watching her keenly.

'You are homesick,' she said, 'you are. Martha, why don't you come back?'

Mme Lesarge looked up quickly, as if she wondered if these were the accents of love. Love? How could it be, or any touch of affection or any kindly feeling? Curiosity, envy, fused into hatred gazed out of Kezia's dull brown eyes. And Mme Lesarge knew that this expression was reflected in her own gaze. Yes, envy too. There was something about Kezia's life and character which she envied; when she looked at her sister she thought of things that she had missed, just as Kezia thought of lacks in her own existence when she looked at *her* sister.

Each woman hated and envied in the other what she might have been—it was a complex and terrible emotion.

The actress contrived to speak lightly.

'Return! Impossible! And you know it is. You would not wish to have me at Stibbards.'

'No, I suppose not,' agreed Miss Faunce. 'You're quite right, it would be a scandal—intolerable. Unless some story could be made up or you came as a penitent.'

Mme Lesarge laughed.

'I suppose you really are crazy enough to think that might happen—that I might come with a made-up story behind me, or as a penitent, and that you would be able to torture me day after day! We're both going crazy, I think. Let's try to talk of real things.'

She spoke with a good deal of resolution and with far fewer graces or affectations than she had used on her entry into this gilt and plush sitting-room. She was becoming indeed, though she did not know it, more like her sister in manner than she had been for years, more familiar with her own language that she had not spoken for so long, more like Kezia in abrupt gestures and straight looks.

'You know that I am not coming back. You know that I am not going to take any of Grandma Tallis's money. You know that I don't want ever to see you again. If you should come to Paris again, pray don't disturb me.'

She grasped the ivory-handled parasol so tightly that it seemed it might break. Kezia Faunce watched her very curiously.

'I daresay you think that I am completely degraded, but pray don't waste any such pity on me. I am successful—I always have been successful. I am, in a way, triumphant over everything, over the usual conventions, the traditions that bind women, over the usual stupid emotions that cause them to waste their hearts and lives; over all the pettifogging duties and obligations that wear away a woman like you. Yes,' she repeated, with a shrill note creeping into her voice, 'I am in every way successful and triumphant, and I beg that you will not think of me with any compassion or believe that I have or ever could have any regrets.'

Miss Faunce's contemptuous smile had deepened as she listened to this flaunting speech.

'And the end?' she asked. 'What is the end to be?'

'I beg you not to concern yourself about that, Kezia. I daresay my end will be as comfortable and as edifying as yours, and at least, it is a long way off.'

'You are not so secure as you think,' said Miss Faunce. 'I was in Paris two or three days before I let you know that I was here, and I made enquiries, and I read things for myself. You are not so popular as you were. Although you deliberately blind yourself, people do realize that you are getting old.'

The actress gave a painful smile.

'A woman like myself is never old.'

'Oh, that is very easy to say, Martha, and I have no doubt that it consoles you. You *are* forty-five. It will not be very long before you are fifty. There are younger women, and I know that you do not get such good parts as you did. And the men don't run after you like they used to. That you have lost one or two wealthy—protectors, don't you call them? That you go about now with very much younger men, quite young boys in fact.'

'So you have been spying on me!' cried Mme Lesarge, who looked quite livid. 'You who call yourself an honest, honourable woman!'

'No, I haven't been spying on you, Martha. It wasn't difficult to find out these things. Just a word here and there at the dressmakers, the perfumers, in the foyer of the theatre itself. Oh, I've been to see you two or three times. You act quite well, but you're getting tired, aren't you—very tired?'

'Your talk is ridiculous, inspired by envy. We are both of us in the prime of life. You need not look an old woman. If you had ever lived you would not do so, it is because everything has been dried up in you—always, you have faded without blooming.' Then, in desperation, almost with a note of appeal, Mme Lesarge added: 'Why could you not let me alone? I haven't thought of you for years. When your note came I did have an impulse of kindness.'

'Neither of those statements is true,' interrupted Kezia Faunce with a force that held the other woman utterly silent. 'You know that you have thought about me, again and again, and of Stibbards, and of the life I lead, of your own childhood and our own father and mother and all our neighbours and friends. Yes, we are twins, there is some affinity between us, and in a way we do know each other's thoughts, and I know you have thought of me—that I have haunted you like you have haunted me. That is the truth, is it not, Martha?'

With a half step threateningly forward the actress, with a shrug pulling at the pearls fastening her pale gloves, admitted sullenly:

'Yes, I suppose it is true. You have rather haunted me. And that is why I came. But what is there in it? Why do we talk about it or think of it?'

'And the other thing you said is not true, either,' continued Kezia, coming still closer to the other woman. 'You didn't come here in a fit of kindness. You hate me as much as I hate you. You can't endure to think that I am existing in Stibbards, any more than I can endure to think that you are existing in Paris.'

'It does get on my nerves, sometimes,' admitted Mme Lesarge, 'but I don't know why it should. It is a mere accident that we're sisters—twin sisters. We're quite different women.'

'I wonder,' said Kezia Faunce, with great bitterness. 'Perhaps we really are the same kind of woman, only in you one side, and in I the other, has got the uppermost. Well, it's no good talking about that. I, at least, have behaved myself, and you haven't. I've every right to scorn you, but you've no right at all to scorn me. You've been a bad woman since you were a young girl—bad daughter, bad wife. Not fulfilling a single duty or obligation, while I did everything that was expected of me.'

Mme Lesarge echoed these words with an accent of mockery.

'Everything that was expected of you—poor Kezia!'

'It's all very well to jeer, but I stayed behind. I nursed mother,

I nursed father, I didn't get married when I might have got married, because it meant leaving them. There were all kinds of things that I would have liked to have done, but I didn't even think about them. And when father and mother were dead I felt a duty towards Stibbards, to the name, the position we held.'

Mme Lesarge interrupted this with great gusts of laughter, half-hysterical laughter. She turned towards the door.

'I really think I shall go mad if I stay here and listen to you any longer. I do hope you will leave Paris soon. And please don't try to see me again.'

'No,' said Kezia sourly, 'I won't try to see you again, it's too horrible. The worst of it is that I shan't be able to avoid thinking about you.'

'I suppose not.'

Mme Lesarge had her hand on the doorknob. The two sisters were looking at each other very intently and in the utter unselfconsciousness of that moment of passion the likeness between them was quite strong. The dyed curls of the actress and the harsh grey hair of Kezia Faunce seemed mere details in the general resemblance, which was one of shape and structure.

'Are you going to act tonight?' asked Miss Faunce.

'Yes. I hope you won't be there to see me. It would make me nervous if I thought you were watching.'

'I've watched you twice, as I told you. I shan't come again. I suppose there'll be bouquets?'

'I suppose so. It is rather an especial occasion. Why did you ask?'

Kezia Faunce did not reply. She had grown flowers, profusion, multitudes of flowers all her life, she had given away flowers for village weddings and funerals, to the poor, the sick, to charity, to church festivals; she had plucked flowers by the armful, the basketful, to adorn her room, but she had never had as much as a single rose or lily given her, and all her life Martha had been receiving bouquets.

'Well,' she said, 'one kiss has got to be the last kiss, you know, and one bouquet the last bouquet. I wonder if you've ever thought of that?'

'Yes, I've thought of it,' replied the actress coolly. 'I daresay we have a good many thoughts in common. Never mind, my dear, I daresay I shall repent, as you call it, in time. I shall marry, as I said, some old respectable man, and keep house for him to the best of my ability. Or I shall go into a convent, or, I might die suddenly. In any of these cases there would be no more kisses nor bouquets, and I suppose you would be satisfied, Kezia?'

'Satisfied? I don't know. But I should like to think that the kind of life you are leading had come to an end. I shall watch the papers, Martha—the French papers.'

'Whatever I do won't be in the papers,' laughed Mme Lesarge. 'I shall keep it secret.'

'How am I to know then? I don't want you to write to me. I don't want a French letter to be seen at Stibbards.'

'Oh, I shan't write to you, but you'll know, somehow. I'll send you my last bouquet, Kezia.'

She pulled the door open, and with the swiftness of one well versed in dramatic effect was gone.

Kezia Faunce sat down, trembling; the palms of her hands and her forehead were damp. How hateful this interview had been! What a mistake—this hideous visit to Paris! She had certainly satisfied a curiosity that had haunted her for years; through all her monotonous, orderly, placid life had always run the question 'What is Martha like?' She had sometimes woken up in the middle of the night after a dream that had been of some other subject and sat up in bed and said to herself, half-aloud: 'What is Martha doing now? What is she wearing? Who is her present lover? What part is she playing? How many people are drinking her health or sending her presents? What does she look like and how much money has she got?'

And all these questions had been like so many arrows piercing her in the dark. She had felt that her own life was poor and mean before the opulence and splendour of Martha's life and yet at the same time, by a maddening paradox, she had felt intensely proud of her own virtue, supremely scornful of her twin sister's wickedness.

Nobody ever spoke of Martha in Stibbards. It was nearly thirty years since she had run away and Miss Faunce hoped that she had been forgotten through the sheer force of never being mentioned. Many people, surely, believed she was dead, and a great many more, even if they did occasionally read the newspapers and see the name therein of a certain famous actress, would not associate the name of Marcelle Lesarge with that of Martha Faunce. But always in her twin sister's mind she had been alive, vital, and exasperating, until this suppressed emotion had not been any longer endurable and Miss Faunce, under some excuse, more or less feasible, had left Stibbards and come to Paris and sought out and really seen Martha.

And now it was over, that momentous interview, and it had been nothing but recriminations, a bitter and humiliating quarrelling and an intensifying of her deep emotion of mingled contempt and envy. She sat stiffly in the red plush empire chair and rested her head on the back and closed her eyes and imagined herself in Martha's place.

She saw herself as Mme Marcelle Lesarge stepping out into her little phaeton with the smart groom in a smart livery on the box, and some comely, well-dressed gentleman beside her. She saw herself being swept over the cobbled Paris streets, laughing, chattering, bowing to acquaintances, and so to her sumptuous apartments.

Why hadn't Martha asked her to her apartment, why hadn't she, Kezia, insisted on going there? Merely through lack of courage. Because she had been ashamed of herself as much as of her sister. She would not have known how to behave to the people whom she might have met in Martha's bijou little house.

Ah, what was it like, that little house? Very different from Stibbards, Kezia was sure, full of gilded furniture, of pictures and statuary, all presents from her lovers, no doubt. And these lovers, who and what were they? Kezia Faunce had heard many rumours, many scandalous tales. She did not know which of them to credit. But what did that matter, the lovers were there, and she might imagine them as she pleased.

She opened her eyes and sat up. She found that this identification of herself with her twin sister was a dangerous pastime. Tomorrow she would return to England and to Stibbards. Everything would be as it was, outwardly, at least. She would not soon be able to forget, perhaps she would not be able to ever forget the interview in this hateful, gaudy room, with the vulgar, red plush and gilt furniture, the great mirrors, wreathed with coarse carvings that rose to the ceiling. Neither of the sisters would influence the other by one iota. Their tragedy was that neither could forget the other.

Her last bouquet!

What did she mean by that? How could she say anything so absurd?

'Send me her last bouquet'! Kezia Faunce could not get that out of her excited mind. She, who all her life had never had a posy sent her, to receive that bouquet which would mean that her sister's life of sin was over! The idea was as exasperating, as ridiculous as it was hateful.

Miss Faunce left Paris the next day. Her progress to the station was rendered hateful by constant glimpses of her sister, pretty, provoking, and elegant, smiling at her in red and black paint from the bill posters. In one of these she was depicted as holding an enormous cluster of scarlet roses in a stiff white paper frill, and Miss Faunce, staring at the vivid drawing which had in the set of the nose and chin a grotesque likeness to herself, repeated with bitter vexation:

'Her last bouquet! Her last bouquet!'

II

Kezia Faunce lived very well at Stibbards. She had power, money, position, activities, and leisure, and valued all these things exactly in that order.

There was no one to dispute her authority either in her own household or in the village; there was no fear of any contradiction either in her management of the Manor or in her general supervision of her poorer neighbours' affairs. She was charitable and even kind, for she felt these things to be virtuous and she had early set herself out to be virtuous. The fine Palladian Manor House, Tudor timber and bricks, re-fronted with eighteenth-century stone, classic portico and windows, was far too large for her, for she lived alone and seldom entertained. But she refused to shut up any of the rooms and the large staff of servants kept everything as precise and orderly as if the original number for which the house had been built still inhabited its spacious wings. And she filled her days that would otherwise have been sometimes empty and often lonely, by a minute supervision of all the details of her own household, by a close supervision of all the affairs of all her servants, tenants, and poorer neighbours.

For years she had led this active, authoritative life with no trouble save the annoying thought of Martha in Paris, and since she had been to Paris and seen Martha this thought had grown until it overspread all her days as a fungus will overspread a healthy tree, seizing on a speck of diseased wood and growing until there is no sap or vitality in root or branch, and, in the next Spring, no leaves are put forth.

There was no one to whom Kezia Faunce could speak of her sister, and therefore she brooded the more deeply day and night on that same personality that was at once so alien and so much part of herself, leading that other life so distant from her own, and yet very much a life that would have expressed something of herself that had never been expressed. It was not likely that she would ever see her again or that they would ever correspond. Some day she would read in the paper of the retirement or the death of Mme Marcelle Lesarge; possibly of her marriage or her disappearance into a convent. There was only one thing that Mme Lesarge, supposing that she ever looked at an English newspaper, could read of her, and that would be her death and her burial in the churchyard which was so near Stibbards and where every other Faunce lay and would lie, except Martha herself.

The estate would go to a distant cousin whose name was not Faunce, and Kezia's money would go to austere charities. And so the very existence of the two sisters would be, as it were, wiped off the earth. There would only be Kezia's name among all her ancestors in the English churchyard, and that assumed, false name of Marcelle Lesarge in some huge Parisian cemetery. And Kezia often wondered which of them would die first. Which would read the notice of the other's death in the paper? And what would it be like for her to realize that that other self of hers in Paris had ceased to exist, or for Martha to know that her second half which had stayed at home in Stibbards had left the familiar rooms empty?

Kezia Faunce tried, often enough, to analyse her feelings towards her sister, to get, as it were, to the very heart of this dull, envious hatred, but she could not. Whenever she tried to do so she became both confused and rebellious. She was quite sure that her scorn for Martha was sincere and that she despised the kind of woman that Martha was, and yet she was forced to admit that Martha had had a great deal that she would have liked to have had, experiences that she would have given much to have enjoyed, adventures that she would have delighted to have tested.

She believed that Martha felt much the same about her; surely she had seen regret and envy in those dark, painted eyes under the elegant little hat with the crimson ostrich feathers!

Martha had regretted, ah, surely, that she had forfeited her status as an English gentlewoman, that she had no part in Stibbards, and all that Stibbards meant. She had envied Kezia and the courage which had chosen the dull, monotonous way, the dignity that had clung to duty, the self-sacrifice, the austere decorum which would force even the most ribald and light-minded to respect Miss Kezia Faunce.

This obsession about Martha, which she had hoped a sight of her would efface, grew, on the contrary, from day to day, until it became almost unbearable.

'I suppose it will go on for years and years,' she thought, with a sense of panic, 'I used to think I saw her sitting at table with me, walking beside me in the garden, and even through the woods and the orchards; meeting me in the village and coming into my bedroom at night. But I always saw her as I remembered her—a young girl in a muslin frock, doeskin slippers, and long curls falling from under a chip straw bonnet. Well, I have got rid of that image, but it has been replaced by another. I see her now as I saw her in that detestable red plush and gilt drawing-room in the Paris hotel, in that vulgar interchangeable blue and red silk, in those diamonds—yes, I believe they were real—in that lace, I was sure it was genuine, on her bosom, with her hair dyed and her face painted, and the little hat with the crimson feathers placed so elegantly on her curls; looking, I must confess, no more than thirty-five, and yet I thought that towards the end of the interview she looked as old as I do. Yes, I see her like that, now. It is quite unescapable. I don't know what I shall do. It must be some kind of an illness.'

And she wondered passionately if Martha were haunted by her, if Martha, at the theatre, in her choice little apartment, in her tilbury, driving in the Bois in the midst of her little supper parties, saw her, Kezia Faunce, in her plain frock, cut by a provincial dressmaker, with her grey hair in the chenille net, with her uncared-for complexion and dull eyes, with her keys at her waist, and her account or receipt book in her hand, going from still-room to closet, from kitchen to dairy, through all the handsome well-kept, unused rooms of Stibbards.

'It is grotesque, it is absurd.' With all the force of her strong mind she endeavoured to shake off the obsession, and threw herself with suppressed and burning energy into good works.

Her charities, always considerable, became lavish; she gave away blankets and coals, medicines and foods, until the vicar protested that she was spoiling his parishioners. She bought a new organ for the church, although she cared nothing about music, and she spent many hours on her knees in her high pew with the green curtains though she knew nothing about prayer.

She began several letters to her sister, formal epistles, asking after her health, and the drama that she was appearing in, and asking, vaguely, for news.

But she sent none of these.

Towards September she felt much more at ease and she began to think with a great thankfulness that the haunting, as she secretly named it to herself, had ceased. She could not, of course, forget Martha, but the figure of the actress became vague and blurred in her mind, and for hours together, when she was absorbed in some task or in some outside interest she would not think at all of the woman in the full, be-ruffled, interchangeable blue and red taffeta, in the little hat and the crimson feathers.

She began to cease wondering how Martha was employing her time, to cease turning over in her mind, so ignorant of such affairs, the possible various episodes of that alien yet closely connected life. She ceased to wonder and to brood over these coquetries, the wickednesses, the successes of Martha. She was soothed by a sense of being more fairly treated than she had hitherto been, for it had always seemed to her grossly unjust that she, the virtuous, the spotless, the irreproachable, should have been troubled in the slightest by any thought of the worthless, the degraded, the contemptible.

Surely the reward for her noble life of complete self-sacrifice should, at least, have been complete peace of mind.

'God,' she thought, 'should have seen to that.'

And now she felt that He had done so, for when she did think of her sister it was in a vague, compassionate fashion. She would still wake up suddenly in the night, alert, and full of exasperation, expecting to be challenged by that thought of Martha. But now there would be emptiness, merely her large, handsome, silent bedroom with the harvest moon showing through the unshuttered windows, and a sense of security all about. She would think of Martha, certainly, but only of someone very far away who did not concern her in the least.

She would lie contentedly in the large bed considering her own possessions, Stibbards, full of her furniture, her silver, her pictures, her china; the stables, with her horses in them, the park full of her timber and sheep and cattle; her farms, well stocked, prosperous. All hers, glorifying her, supporting her, giving her honour, dignity and importance, while Martha had no part in any of them. Martha had run away from all this thirty years before, when she had gone through the garden perfumed by the early currants, and slipped away to her worthless young soldier, to whom she had not been for very long faithful.

In the first week of September, Miss Kezia Faunce superintended the making of pickles, sauces, and relishes from the early unripe fruit. Never yet, since as a girl of ten or so she began to help her mother in these domestic duties, had Miss Kezia missed the different picklings, preservings, jam and wine making as they came round at their several times of the year. The cupboards, closets, and presses of Stibbards were filled by the products of her industry; perfumes, lotions, preserves, balm, aromatics, sweet waters, washes, and confections, more than she would be able to use in the rest of her life, stood stocked in the darkness that they filled with a musty fragrance.

This year, when the last day of this work was over, Kezia Faunce felt suddenly tired, almost as if she were going to be ill. She walked out into the garden about the time of sunset in a lassitude that was too indifferent to seek rest. The evening was cloudless, overwhelming in spacious gold, the landscape was transfigured by the pure uninterrupted light of the western sun; the air was full of Autumn fragrances, and from the house came the mingled sour-sweet smell from the preserving-pans, still redolent of hot spices and sugared fruits.

The large house was silent, as if everyone rested after the day's labour. There was no one in the wide trim gardens but Miss Kezia Faunce herself. She wiped continually with a delicate handkerchief the last sparkles of sugar from her fingers. She felt a mingled sensation of excitement and apprehension, but she did not think of Martha at all. She went to the herb garden and noted how the various plants, hot and cold, moist and dry, were growing in the warm air. Everything grew well that year. It seemed as if there was going to be a splendid harvest of every kind of fruit, a thing that Miss Kezia Faunce could not remember having happened before—everything in fruitage at once. She found herself trembling and she sat down on the circular stone seat beside the great beds of thyme, rosemary, and lavender, all silver grey in that increasing golden light, for, as a lamp will flare up at the last before it goes out, so as the sun finally sank it seemed to give out a more powerful glow.

Miss Kezia Faunce thought that never before had she noted so much light. She sat there on the semicircular stone seat, between those high, silver-grey plants of rosemary, lavender, marjoram; she felt her senses becoming slightly confused and she had a sensation of light-headedness, as she had often experienced before a severe thunderstorm. Her glance fastened on a large rose bush in the bed opposite, which looked unnaturally tall and seemed to have uncommonly large red thorns. There were no flowers now on this bush, but she knew that it bore crimson blooms, the last of which had fallen about a week ago.

She thought then, not definitely of Martha, but of a bill poster that she had seen stuck up on an ugly brick wall in Paris as she drove to the station. An actress with a nose and mouth something like her own, holding a large bouquet of crimson roses with a white paper frill. The garden seemed too large and the sky too vast, and the bright light of the sunset too overwhelming for Miss Kezia Faunce's senses.

She turned and walked back towards the house as one seeking a refuge. She had not quite reached the large terrace when she saw Sarah, the new kitchen-maid, coming hurriedly towards her.

Miss Faunce frowned. It was not part of Sarah's duties to run errands or take messages to her mistress and she certainly had no business to be in the garden in the print dress and the white apron, now slightly sticky, which she had worn to help in the pickling and the preserving.

Miss Kezia Faunce hastened her step with a rebuke ready on her lips, but what Sarah had to say was so curious that Miss Faunce forbore her reproof.

The little kitchen-maid, who spoke rather breathlessly, had, she said, been standing at the kitchen door scouring out the last of Cook's pots when she had looked up and seen a lady standing just before the square of potherbs. She had stared at Sarah, smiled, turned away without a word, and gone through the gate in the privet hedge towards the house. Sarah had run after her, but lost sight of her. Then, seeing Miss Faunce in the distance, she had thought that she should tell her of this stranger.

'What was there strange in it?' asked Miss Kezia quickly. 'It was some visitor who had lost her way and come to the side kitchen door instead of to the front entrance. I can't see anything peculiar about it, Sarah.'

'But she was so odd, ma'am, and not like anyone round here.'

'What was she like, child? Don't make so many words about nothing. What was this lady like?'

'She was very finely dressed, ma'am, and had a queer look of you.'

'A look of me? What do you mean, child? Express yourself better. Do you mean that she was like me?'

The kitchen-maid became confused under this severity.

'She was something like you, ma'am. I don't know. She made me think of you. She had a big nosegay in her hand.'

Miss Kezia's lips pinched themselves together.

'Run away and finish your duties, Sarah. This lady has no doubt gone into the house, where she is waiting for me.'

Dismissing the kitchen-maid, Miss Faunce continued her slow walk towards the terrace.

So, Martha had come to Stibbards. Now, why? And in what devilish mood of mockery and spite? Was she going to be married or to enter a convent? Was she at last leaving the stage and her disgraceful manner of life? Miss Kezia felt her thin cheeks flush. Martha had come, bringing with her the bouquet.

The last bouquet?

'She means to disgrace me, I suppose. To make a scandal and a talk all over the place. Perhaps she has lost all her money and may be dependent on me, after all.'

Her thoughts full of hate, Miss Kezia Faunce entered the house which seemed to her more than usually quiet. If Martha had left the side kitchen door and gone through the gate in the privet hedge and then been lost sight of by Sarah, she must have entered the house by the front door. So Miss Kezia Faunce went directly to that and looked in the hall.

This was empty.

'I suppose that she would, even after all these years, remember the place very well. She has probably gone to the green parlour, where she used to sit and do her lessons with Mamma.'

So Miss Faunce opened the door of the green parlour, a room that, though kept spotlessly clean, swept and dusted, had been long since shut up and disused. The slatted dark-green shutters were closed now and the strong last sunlight beating on them filled the room with a subdued glow, almost as if it were under water.

The walls were painted an old-fashioned, dull green; the carpet was green and so were the rich curtains, the damask covered chairs. Everything was the same as it had been when Martha and Kezia used to have their lessons there with their mother.

There was the desk at which they had worked, the piano at which they had practised, and on the walls still hung some of the watercolours of moss roses, birds' eggs in nests, and white rabbits which they had drawn and painted together.

The room smelt slightly of musk and Miss Kezia, whose mind was not working very alertly and who felt some vagueness over all her senses, thought:

'I must have the shutters opened tomorrow and a little sun and air let in. I had forgotten quite how long it was since the room was used.'

And then she saw Martha standing up close against an inner door, looking at her over her shoulder, holding rather stiffly in both hands, a large bouquet of crimson roses, exactly as she had held them in the poster which Miss Kezia had seen the day she drove to the railway station in Paris.

'Martha,' said Miss Faunce stiffly, 'so you've come home at last. To give me the bouquet?'

Still smiling and still without speaking, Mme Marcelle Lesarge's delicately gloved hands held out the crimson bouquet.

Kezia Faunce took it, and as she did so all the roses turned to blood and emptied themselves into her bosom.

III

Miss Kezia Faunce was found dead in the green parlour where she and her twin sister Martha so often had lessons with their mother. She had fallen, and her head had struck the harp, an instrument that she used, in her girlhood, to play very well.

She had been dead several hours when she was found. The doctor said that her heart had always been weaker than he dared to tell her. She had, of late, been wearing herself out with good work and had been labouring in the kitchen on that particular day. She might have fallen, when unconscious, and killed herself by the blow given her by the harp.

There was no mystery about the affair and not much mourning.

Sarah, the kitchen-maid, did not dare to tell anyone about the lady who had come to the kitchen door with the bouquet. She feared that she would get into severe trouble for an untruthful romancing girl.

IV

Mme Marcelle Lesarge died in the same hour precisely as her twin sister, but not in so agreeable a manner.

She had lately become rather desperate in her choice of admirers, and on that September evening she had taken home to her apartments a worthless young rake who for some while had been flattering her.

What passed between them on this particular evening no one would ever exactly know, though it was not difficult to guess, for in the morning she was found murdered, her room robbed and rifled, all her jewellery stolen, and nothing left but the large bouquet of crimson roses, which were found flung down carelessly on her bosom, profaned, drooping, and dappled with her blood.

10

SIR ANDREW CALDECOTT

In Due Course

I

Fate, poaching as ever on preserves of human enterprise, had fired two barrels at young Alec Judeson. Malaria first got him down; dysentery prevented recovery. The board of doctors that yesterday examined him would, as they had warned him, in due course certify not merely that he must go home forthwith, but also that he must never return to the tropics. The days of his rubber planting in Malaya were numbered.

The medical examination had been at Penyabong, the chief town of Senantan, and Alec was now on his way back to the estate at Sungei Liat to pack up and to say goodbye. Tonight he would stay at the little resthouse on the summit of Bukit Kotak Pass, and leave the remaining forty-one miles to be driven in the cool of the early morning. Backing his two-seater car into the resthouse stable he suddenly realized how bitterly he would miss the touch of its steering-wheel and the feel of that patch on the driving seat where the stump of a fallen cheroot had burned through the leather. Nevertheless he must get out a quick advertisement for its sale if he was to scrape together enough dollars for his passage.

A zigzag of earthen steps led from the stable up to the small plateau on which the resthouse was perched. Empty beer bottles, sunk neck-downward into the soil for half their length, formed the vertical front of each step and so protected the stair from scour or detrition. On either side, amid the knee-deep lalang grass, sprawled straggly bushes of red shoe-flower or hibiscus. How weak he had become was brought home to Alec by painful inability to mount the steps without several stops and waits. 'Those damned doctors were just about right!' he muttered crossly, slashing with his cane at a stem of hibiscus that slanted across the path.

The action dislodged, and brought rustling and fluttering to the ground at his feet, a large green mantis. Uncannily swivelling its triangular head the insect fixed him with protuberant black eyes and challengingly crooked its long forelegs in the posture that has earned for the species the epithet of 'praying'. He flicked it distastefully with his stick into the gutter, climbed the few remaining steps to the rest-house verandah, and there sank heavily into one of the long rattan chairs.

A whisky and soda helped him regain his breath before, taking a packet of letters from his pocket, he drew out one from a bluish, crested envelope, unfolded it, and began to scan its contents attentively. The embossed address was: 'Saintsend, Dedmans Reach, Tillingford', and the manuscript below it ran as follows:

My dear Alec,—I am greatly distressed by the news of your breakdown in health. You will remember my dubiety as to your physical fitness for work in a tropical climate and my unavailing attempts to dissuade you therefrom. This letter, however, is written in no spirit of 'I told you so,' but repeats my former invitation to come and live with me here at Tillingford. Your father (and I state this with certainty, as he told me so only ten days before he died) would have approved. It is indeed obviously right that you should get to know, and to regard as 'home', the property that you will come into sooner rather than later; for I am now 67 and do not need a medico to tell me that I've got a dicky heart. So do come along, and if you want to bring with you any of your oriental paraphernalia, there's plenty of room here for its exposition or stowage. Yours avuncularly,—MATTHEW JUDESON.

P.S.—You will find several improvements at Saintsend. The Conservancy people refused to let me root out those pollarded willows from the river bank; so I have blotted out all view of them by continuing the garden wall round to where the boathouse used to be. This I have pulled down, filled in the dyke, and built instead a decent-sized studio, music-room and library— my 'Athenaeum', I call it.

'Yours avuncularly!' 'Exposition or stowage of oriental paraphernalia!' 'Athenaeum', indeed! Alec winced as these phrases stung him into remembrance of Uncle Matthew's pomposity and humourless affectation. And why, in heaven's name, wall off the old willows and thereby lose those lovely glimpses of river? Well, in due course (a half-conscious euphemism, this, on Alec's part for after his uncle's death), in due course the wall could be pulled down again; and a temporary circumvallation would only in small degree detract from the amenities of an exceedingly comfortable and commodious residence. Amused that his thoughts should thus run in terms of a house agent's advertisement Alec mentally registered acceptance of his uncle's offer. He would telegraph to the old man as soon as his sailing date was fixed; but, for the moment, he felt it sufficient to clinch his decision with another whisky and soda.

As he lay in the long chair, sipping it, there clumsily alighted on the verandah rail beside him another mantis; or, maybe, the same one as before, for the beady stare and aggressive genuflexion were identical. Making a trigger of right forefinger and thumb, he flipped the creature off its perch into the garden and, in doing so, turned his eyes towards the sunset. This was of that jaundiced kind for which Malays have the ugly word *mambang*. Not merely the western sky but the whole vault was dyed an ugly stagnant yellow. Hills and jungle seemed to soak in it, and Alec remembered that, on such an evening, Malay children would be kept indoors: an understandable, albeit superstitious, precaution.

Five minutes or so later, the yellow glare having dimmed with a suddenness reminiscent of opera, the resthouse-keeper lit the lamp which hung above the dry-rotten table whereon he would shortly lay supper. Numerous patches of iron-mould gave the badly laundered cloth a resemblance to maps of an archipelago, and so turned Alec's thoughts to Java and to the set of shadow-show silhouettes which he had bought on holiday there eighteen months ago. He had, indeed, already been twice reminded of them this evening by the praying mantis, the disproportion of whose neck and arms to the rest of its body was as great as in the case of the shadow puppets. In their case this disproportion was of course necessary in order that the jointed arms should be long enough for the showman to jerk them by their slender rods into the attitudes and gesticulations demanded by his miniature drama. A marionette is manipulated by strings from above, a shadow silhouette by spindles from below; the one being pulled and the other pushed much in the same way, Alec cynically reflected, as weak or obstinate characters need pulling or pushing in real life. He would certainly take these shadow figures home with him, as being the only 'oriental paraphernalia', to use his uncle's expression, that he possessed. They had been cut in thick buffalo hide and elaborately painted in gold, silver, crimson, saffron, brown, and indigo; but on one side alone, the other being left polished but bare: for a shadow drama is watched from both sides of a stretched sheet—on one side, spectators see the painted surfaces of the figures against the white cloth and in the full glare of footlights; on the other, the clear-cut shadows of them projected through the cloth. From neither side is the showman visible, for he operates between two parallel screens of palm-leaf immediately beneath the sheet.

The meal, over which Alec Judeson indulged in these Javan memories, was not, for dietetic reasons, that prepared for him by the resthouse-keeper, whose menus depended for edibility on liberal libations of Worcestershire sauce. His hostess at Penyabong had prudently provided him with a hamper of more palatable, and less dangerous, fare. Nevertheless he was too tired to eat more than a few mouthfuls of each dish; and, before many minutes passed, he gave up the effort and went straight from table to bed.

As he undressed a slight movement of the mosquito-net aroused his curiosity; so, before taking off his shoes, he got up from the chair to investigate. To his annoyance he discovered, for the third time that evening, a mantis. So strong was the grip of its hind legs on the curtain that its head and neck were thrust toward him, at right-angles to the body. Neglectful of their sharp spurs Alec seized the waving forelegs and was sharply pricked for his rashness. This angered him. Savagely grabbing it by its back and wing-cases, he tore the creature roughly from the net and held its head over the smoking chimney of the lamp. As the black, starting eyes became incinerated into opaque grey, he heard a sizzle and a crackle before he threw the still-wriggling insect to the floor and crushed it under foot. Next moment he was hating himself for this cruelty. Walking to the window he stood for some seconds listening to the stridulation of cicadas in the jungle; then spat into the darkness and returned to his undressing. A few minutes later he parted the mosquito curtains and crept into bed.

Out of weakness and exhaustion he was soon in the indeterminate borderland between waking and sleeping. Pictures passed before his closed eyes of Saintsend garden and he found himself wondering whether, after all, Uncle Matthew had not been right about those pollarded willows at the river edge. Were they not, perhaps, a little too like those gruesomely vitalized trees in Arthur Rackham's illustrations to *Peter Pan*? There certainly seemed to be a group of shadow-show figures in the tree to the left of the sundial, and there appeared, too, to be something waving at him from among the spindly boughs of the one on the right. Then of a sudden they parted, and the thing looked out at him. 'O hell! That bloody mantis again!' He had cried this aloud and thereby woken himself out of his half-sleep. Was the wretched fever on him again? Having lit the bedside candle and rummaged in a suitcase for his thermometer, he took his temperature. Normal. Nerves, then, must have caused his dream, and small wonder after that episode of the mantis! To guard against further nightmare by forcing all nonsensical fancies out of his brain, he now set it to visualize Saintsend with all the accuracy and detail of which his memory was capable. This stern mental exercise, which within half an hour induced a sound sleep, enabled him also to contemplate, with pleasurable anticipation, various improvements to house and garden which it would be possible to make—in due course.

II

Nine weeks later a taxi from Tillingford pulled up at the steps of Saintsend. Young Judeson had scarcely opened its door before he heard the voice of his uncle raised in ponderous salutation.

'Alec, my dear boy, how splendid to see you again! You must excuse a rising septuagenarian for not coming down the steps to greet you. The legs are willing but the heart is weak! Come along up and let Larkin attend to your impedimenta. What? Only two cabin trunks? I thought you Eastern nabobs travelled with more than that!'

'Nabobs may do so, but not a broken-down planter!' frowned the nephew as he paid off the taxi-man and turned to mount the steps. 'Why, uncle, how fit and young you're looking!'

'Looks are liars, I'm afraid, my dear boy. Soon falls the rotting leaf that autumn gilds: that's from one of my own poems. Now, if you hand over your keys to Larkin, he'll show you upstairs and help you unpack. They're putting you in the south wing, where you'll enjoy a safe refuge from avuncular intrusion. No more going up and down stairs for the victim of myocarditis! Come and see the athenaeum as soon as you've tidied yourself up, and don't take too long about it, because our new neighbour at Sennetts, Miss Scettall, has promised to drop in to tea, and you will like to have a look round before she comes.'

Alec highly approved the bedroom and adjoining sitting-room assigned to him. The windows of both gave on to the riverside, and he could look over the new wall and the willow-tops on to the marshland and wood beyond. In the right foreground rose a whitewashed gable of the new studio or music-room, which looked far too nice and unpretentious to be dubbed an athenaeum. In order that it might be above flood-level, it had been built on a raised terrace and was approached by a ramp of masonry leading from a french window in the library. Steps had thus been avoided at either end, and the rough stonework was already ornamentally studded with patches of saxifrage and wall-rue. It would be a dangerous passage to fall from, and Alec found himself considering whether the addition of a rail or low parapet might not be an improvement—in due course.

A deferential cough woke him from this reverie, and, turning round, he saw Larkin standing in the doorway.

'Pardon me asking, sir, but would you be wanting them two parcels as is atop of the brown trunk to be undone? Both of 'em seems to be stuck up with sealing-wax, like.'

'Oh no, thank you, Larkin; just put them, as they are, into that big drawer below the cupboard. Be careful not to shake the square cardboard box: it's got some rather rare and valuable insects inside it.'

Larkin seemed greatly interested at this. 'Then who'll be attending to their feeding, sir; if I may ask it? My young Tom, now, 'e's fair nuts on caterpillars. Hentomolology, the master names it in 'is school report; but, "Tom," I says, "don't you never be putting them bug-'utches again in my pantry, for they ain't 'ealthy; not about the 'ouse."'

'No; but mine aren't alive, Larkin! They're stuffed specimens, like you see in a museum. The fellow in the dispensary on our rubber estate gave them to me when I was saying goodbye. I had been telling him about an experience with what they call a praying mantis. You tell young Tom, next time he has a half-holiday to pop in here, and I'll show him all sorts of queer things—scorpions, centipedes, mantises, and what not. A bit of a surprise for him after butterflies and moths!'

Having dismissed Larkin with this invitation for Tom, Alec brushed his hair with unusual attention, for the benefit of Miss Scettall, and started to go downstairs. He walked slowly and musingly. His uncle's appearance had very greatly shocked him by its promise of longevity. The cheeks were fuller than he remembered them and positively ruddy. The hair too was but little greyer, if at all, and the eyes gave no hint of weakening. Matthew, in short, looked good for another ten years at least; whereas during the voyage home from Malaya Alec had been nursing the prospect of a brief spell of nepotal attention being speedily rewarded by grateful benedictions from an early deathbed. After all, had not his uncle indicated as much in his letter of invitation? But not only did he now appear in deplorably rude health, but in five minutes of conversation had paraded all those exasperating affectations that would render any long companionship with him intolerable. Those bleats of 'my dear boy' and 'your poor old uncle'! That periphrastic avoidance of the first person singular; a maddening habit copied, perhaps, from those among the Anglican hierarchy who address their children in God as 'your Bishop'!

Alec was by now at the foot of the staircase and in the long corridor leading to the library. On either side hung paintings in oils of his grandfather's hunters and dogs, heavily and gaudily framed. The names were on plaques beneath: Cæsar, Hornet, Buster, Ponto, and the rest. Alec made a mental note for their removal in due course; and then he suddenly frowned. With his uncle in such good trim, how could his promised inheritance be expected any longer to eventuate in due course. It was bound to be overdue: damnably overdue!

As if to corroborate this anticipation, Matthew Judeson emerged at this moment from the library door, and in full bleat. 'What, down again already? Good on you, my boy; quick work! Now be careful of this rug; it's apt to slip on the marble floor and have you over. Now one goes out through the french window and here we are, you see, on a ramp or isthmus; no steps to negotiate, just a gradual incline. And this is the door of the *Sanctum Sanctorum*! Open it, Alec; and please not to say that you are disappointed!'

Alec certainly was not. He was wondering in fact how so fussy and finical a man could have evolved so restful a room. The plain large open fireplace, the unstained panelling, unceiled barrel roof, grand piano in unpolished oak, red Dutch tiles and rough cord carpets, deep broad leathered chairs—all were right and pleasing.

'One tries,' his uncle resumed, 'to do a good turn to friends whenever occasion offers. The Scettalls are poorly off, so I called in young Alfred for a fee to help with the designs and furnishing. He would already have set up as an architect by now, but for his having got mixed up in a business of which his sister is best left in ignorance. He can rely on his present benefactor, of course, not to tell her.'

'What do you mean by his present benefactor?'

'Why, this old uncle of yours: who else?'

'Well, this unfortunate young nephew of yours. . . .' Alec had thus begun in bantering imitation of the old man's circumlocution when Larkin appeared, not obtrusively but withal importantly, in the doorway and announced: 'Miss Scettall.'

At her finishing school the lady who now entered had been known among the other girls as 'Mona Lisa'. Her likeness to Leonardo's famous picture had grown rather than lessened with her years, and renders any detailed description of her appearance unnecessary. It need only be said that she was fully conscious of the likeness, dressed to the part, and expected all the attention that it demanded. During the conversation that followed her introduction to Alec, although politeness required her to address her remarks mainly to her host, she held the younger man's interest and attention by beck or smile and was gratified to find him all eyes and ears. The tea talk was suitably trivial, but two bits of it must be recounted as bearing upon later developments. The first related to a review in the *Tillingford Gazette* of Matthew Judeson's locally printed *Second Posy of Poesy*, wherein it was opined that the best compliment payable to the second posy was that nobody could have suspected its authorship to be identical with that of the first.

'Now tell us, Mr Judeson,' Mona Lisa commanded with a shake of the forefinger, 'just how you feel about that criticism. Are you conscious of having changed, or shall we say "developed," so greatly? Does your old self know your new self? Or vice versa?'

The question was clearly distasteful to Uncle Matthew; for he answered with a certain acidity that he would ask his nephew to read the books, of which Larkin had already been instructed to place author's presentation copies by his bedside, and to pass judgement. He could not help feeling that his first 'posy' had been much underrated. Only forty-three copies had in fact been sold.

That ended discussion on this topic; but after desultory talk of weather, crops, and the new vicar at Fenfield the conversation took its second turn of relevance to our story.

'By the way, Mr Judeson,' said Miss Scettall in low confidential tones, 'your friend spoke to us again last night.'

'Which? Saint or the corpse?'

'Well—both or either; you see, our saint *was* the corpse!'

After this enigmatic utterance Miss Scettall turned to Alec and, raising her voice, continued: 'Now let me warn you before it is too late, Mr Alec, not to allow your uncle to interest you too much in his spiritualism. It isn't always quite comfortable, and I'm glad that he's got your company now in this old house. Good gracious, six o'clock! I must be off at once or Alfred will go without his supper, for we've no cook these days.'

As they escorted her to the front door, Alec wondered how earlier in the day he could have thought his uncle looking well. Perhaps it was the gloom of the corridor, but his face now appeared drawn and grey.

'Alec, my dear boy,' he said as soon as the guest was gone, 'the excitement of your arrival has quite knocked me over. (Alec noted this first allusion to himself as 'me'.) I shall need to take dinner in bed if you will excuse me. Please make yourself thoroughly at home. You can't think how eagerly I have awaited your coming. Tomorrow we'll inspect the gardens together and the fields. There's lots to show you. Goodnight, my dear boy, and God bless you!'

Alec, too, was tired and went early to bed. He woke but once in the night when he heard the stable clock strike four. A patch of light which he had vaguely noticed before falling asleep still showed on the ceiling. One of the curtains, he now saw, had been only half drawn and, going to the window to adjust it, he found that the light came from a chink in the shutters of his uncle's downstair bedroom. Was the old fellow then afraid to sleep in the dark?

III

Of Alec's first days at Saintsend it is necessary only to record his growing affection for the place and increasing dislike of his uncle. This dislike was only slightly relieved by curiosity in regard to his character and behaviour. The two books of verse, which Alec found duly placed by Larkin at his bedside, certainly presented an enigma. *A Posy of Poesy*, published six years ago, was a collection of what might be described as period pieces; metrical exercises of classical artificiality. The first to catch Alec's eye as he opened the volume ran as follows:

> *Time was when I with heart intact*
> *Would mock the poet's fancy*
> *Whose heart, he quoth, was well nigh crackt*
> *For love of pretty Nancy.*

> *But, now I know, he stated truth:*
> *Of me the same were spoken*
> *Save that my dearling's name is Ruth,*
> *My heart completely broken!*

And so on, page after page, until Alec, nauseated by the banality of

> *My heart is locked and, woe is me,*
> *Cressida doth keep the key*
> *And will not unlock it!*

closed the book with a vicious snap and picked up its newly published successor. In order not to waste time over it he would read the first poem, then the last, and then one taken at random from the middle.

The first was headed 'Red Idyll' and, as it seemed rather long, he looked at the last two verses only:

> *He smelt the hot blood spurting; then*
> *Pressed the red blade to his own heart:*
> *Oh throbbing wild embrace! Next morn*
> *They two were difficult to part.*

> *The dayspring crimsoned overhead,*
> *But grey and cold they lay beneath;*
> *Starkly protesting to the skies*
> *Swift tragedy of love and death.*

Good heavens! Uncle Matthew trying to be passionate and modern! What about the end piece? Here it was, written in a loose hexametrical form and entitled 'On My Portrait by N. . . .'

> *How can you bid me, sir, accept the* ME *of this portrait?*
> *Does it not lie by its truth, a truth that is irreligious?*
> *Secrets are blabbed by those lips that my will had sealed for ever,*
> *While from the eye peeps hunger for things that I live to dissemble:*
> *The nose, too, is tendentious, sniffing up self-approval,*
> *And a smug ear sits tuned for flattering insincerities.*
> *Take it away, I beg: I cannot conspire betrayal*
> *Of the poor Jekyll who gives to Hyde, out of decency, hiding.*

Uncle Matthew turning autopsychoanalytic! Good gracious me! And now for a piece from the middle. Here we are—'Firewatching'.

> *What seest thou in the caves of fire?*
> *I see red avenues of desire*
> *Slope to a fen of molten mire.*

> *What hearest thou in the caves of fire?*
> *I hear the hiss of a hellish quire,*
> *The knell of a bell in a falling spire.*

> *What smellest thou in the caves of fire?*
> *I smell the reek of a funeral pyre,*
> *Foul incense raised to Moloch's ire.*

> *What tastest thou in the caves of fire?*
> *The gust of rouge when cheeks perspire,*
> *The acrid lips of a wench on hire.*

> *What touchest thou in the caves of fire?*
> *The dead grey ash of lust's empire*
> *Cold or ever the red flames tire.*

'Really, Uncle Matthew!' murmured Alec, and then hastily corrected himself. 'No, *not* really, Uncle Matthew. It just can't be; it's the sort of stuff he won't allow himself even to read. It's quite beyond or, he would say, below him.'

The next poem, in three cantos headed 'addenda', 'corrigenda', and 'delenda', repudiated his authorship even more loudly; but Alec was prevented from trying to guess any solution to the puzzle by a knock at the door and the entry of Larkin. Young Tom was going to be at home that morning and would Mr Alec be so good as to show him them insects? Yes, Mr Alec would, and at half-past eleven if convenient. At that hour consequently we find young Tom in a transport of delight and his father performing the role of commentator.

'Coo! Weren't that stinging crab a fair caution? Beg pardon, sir, did you say scorpion or scorpicle? And 'ooever seed the likes of this 'ere? A prying mantis? What, sir, prying like what they pries in church? Well, fancy that! 'E don't look much of a church-goer to me. But now, Mr Alec, if I may make so bold, please don't let Tom 'ere waste any more of your time. If you'll let me take the box downstairs 'e can make some drorins of the creeturs in the pantry for 'is Natural 'Istory master and I'll mind 'e keeps it careful as gold.'

'Very well, take it by all means: and when Tom has finished his drawings you can place it on the hall table where you put the letters.'

Who could have foretold that this simple and reasonable request was a first link in the chain of destiny that was to drag two masters of Saintsend to their deaths? Yet so it was to prove; and with speed.

On return from a walk down-river that afternoon Alec found a car at the front door and a sadly worried Larkin to greet him. His uncle, so Larkin said, had been took very poorly, not to speak of a fit, and the doctor was with him now. It had all happened along of them insects, for Mr Judeson must have seen the box on the hall table and had opened it. Talk of a shock, why in all his life Larkin had never seen anyone took worse. Matthew Judeson was indeed in serious case. Not a stroke, luckily, said the doctor, but nevertheless a cardiac upset of grave omen for the future. Of his surviving the present collapse the doctor was very hopeful, but he must lie in bed until further notice and receive no outside visitors. With the aid of a draught sent posthaste from the Tillingford dispensary the patient fell into a restful sleep and it was Alec, not he, who lay awake into the early hours of the morrow, thinking of the many things which he would venture upon in due course and congratulating himself on a probable acceleration in the time schedule.

His uncle's salutation when he went to see him next morning was unusual. 'I suppose, Alec,' he said, 'you don't believe in witches? No, I thought not. Nor had your old sceptic of an uncle ever done so until he met Miss Scettall. Now, however, he has his doubts, and perhaps you would be interested to hear the reason.'

'Look here, uncle,' Alec interrupted at this point, 'the doctor says that you're not to tire yourself. So please cut out all this roundabout talk of "your old uncle" and try to speak of yourself as "me" or "I". Yes, I would like to hear about that Mona Lisa woman if only you will speak naturally.'

Matthew contrived to turn a wince into a smile with some difficulty, because his conversion of first into third person was a trick that enabled him, as it were, to sit with the audience and admire his own play-acting. However, he affected to take the request in good part and continued, 'Anything to please you, my dear Alec! Well, when Miss Scettall came to Sennetts last year she somehow took to me and I to her. We were excellent neighbours. But as the months passed by I noticed her becoming increasingly possessive, and on New Year's Day I got a card from her with the message, 'May this Leap Year bring you happiness!' That put me on my guard, and when she suggested a walk on the afternoon of 29th February I was ready for her. After effervescing about her love for the river country, she began to enthuse over Saintsend and said that all the dear old house needed was an understanding chatelaine. It was then that I quoted two lines from my first book:

> *Ah! hapless nymph, what boots it him to harry*
> *If Strephon is resolvèd not to marry?*

She gave a laugh, but the sound of it was unpleasant. 'Surely,' she said, 'you don't imagine that I'm the sort to angle for superannuated fish? Come along to Sennetts and I'll give you a cup of tea.' I had to go, of course, and when tea was over and Alfred had joined us, she began the séance business that has been the curse of my life ever since.'

The doctor's arrival at this point gave his patient a respite from completing the story. This was just as well perhaps, for he was becoming exhausted.

IV

Three or four days were to pass before, at Alec's prompting, his uncle took up the unfinished tale. Once again he started with a question.

'You know perhaps the origin of the name Saintsend?'

'Why, yes: I've read it in Bennet's *Tillingford*.'

'And what does Bennet say?'

'That before the big house at Sennetts was burned down in 1747 and the estate broken up, the farm we now call Santry was known as Sennett's Entry and Saintsend as Sennett's End. The present names are just contractions.'

'Then what does he say of Dedman's Reach?'

'Oh, that's a much more modern name. The land belonged not so long ago to a Sir Ulric Dedman.'

'I wish, my dear boy, that what Bennet wrote were true. Unfortunately, I know better, or perhaps I should say, worse. I learned the real truth during those séances I have told you of. The first spirit we got into touch with gave his name as Saynt; Lemuel Saynt. He said that he wanted to warn me about evil existences in the riverside willows that had brought about his drowning (Saintsend, you see, means Saynt's end) in 1703. That he was right about the willows I found out soon after, for I very nearly fell into the stream myself. I distinctly felt a push from behind, and there was a sort of gurgling grunt as my left leg slipped in. It was a horribly near thing. I have seen them too sometimes—or rather their arms and legs. That was why your mantis and stick-insects gave me such a shock last Friday. Luckily, I cannot see the willows any more now that the wall is finished and I sleep downstairs. You can still see them from your room of course, and I advise you to keep the curtains drawn on moonlit nights. We never managed to get a clear account from Saynt of the dead man in the reach. You heard Miss Scettall say the other afternoon that it was Saynt himself. I suspect her and Alfred, however, of inventing things when I am not there, and I've caught Alfred trying to guide the planchette. I'm certain, too, that both of them try to incite the willow Things against me. On quite windless nights I sometimes hear them scraping and scratching at my new wall. Who was it, Alec, who said that Hell holds no fury like a woman scorned? It's true enough of Adeline Scettall. She's playing the witch on me night and day. Your coming here, my dear boy, made me feel safer until I opened that box of yours. Magnify that mantis a dozen times and you'll have some idea of what's in the willows. You believe me, don't you? It's all perfectly true, and I simply had to tell you.'

Alec sat thinking for some moments, and then he drew his bow at a venture. 'Uncle,' he said, 'you spoke just now of Alfred guiding the planchette. Does that by any chance account for your second posy of poesy?'

'It certainly came from the planchette,' was the answer, 'and there was a spirit's order to publish it in my name. I hope that it was not Alfred: if so, he's as bad as his sister. All my nice friends are offended by the verses, and the vicar at Fenfield has even asked me to give up taking round the bag. From being a sidesman I've become an untouchable! I can't blame him either.'

Unable to repress a slight smile at this ecclesiastical deprivation, Alec told his uncle not to take such things too seriously. Everything would be right and normal again so soon as the séances were stopped. Then, bidding the old man calm himself and take a nap, the nephew went out into the garden to think things over. For an hour or more he paced slowly to and fro, his eyes upon the ground. Finally, with the air of one who has laid his plan, he walked briskly across the stable-yard, through the coach-house (now used as a garage) and into the little harness-room. On a shelf stood two old acetylene car-lamps, one of which he took down and filled with carbide. He had promised to show Larkin how the shadow puppets worked and now he needed only a dust-sheet, which was soon got, for a practical demonstration. This he gave in his bedroom after dark and, when Larkin left to lay the table for dinner, he switched the beam of the lamp for a brief moment on to the white gable of the athenæum. '*Jadi!*' he said; which is Malay for 'it'll do'.

Next morning, as though to assure his uncle that he had seen nothing incredible in the previous day's narration, he remarked that, having had to get up just after midnight to open the window, he had made the mistake of looking at the willows. There was certainly something there which he could not associate with the vegetable or animal creation. He felt that his uncle must shake himself and Saintsend free from this ugly tangle of spiritualism without a day's delay. It was getting on his own nerves too.

This speech had the desired effect. 'I'll write at once,' the uncle replied, 'to Miss Scettall and tell her to arrange a final séance at Sennetts tonight. A final séance is necessary because Saynt has hinted before now of other and more direct methods of approach to me and I must avoid that at all costs. We must pension him off decently, so to speak. The doctor won't like my going out to dinner, but to be quit of this wretched business will be better medicine than any he has ever prescribed. Anyhow, I have made up my mind to go.'

After lunch Alec heard Larkin being told that his master would be out to dinner at Sennetts and that brandy, whisky, and two glasses were to be put on the small table in the athenæum against his return. Larkin need not sit up; he would close the house himself.

'If the whisky and the second glass are meant for me,' interposed Alec, 'I must ask to be excused. I feel a bout of malaria coming on and shall go early to bed with a couple of quinine tablets. You can tell me all about your evening at Sennetts after breakfast tomorrow.'

'Very well, Larkin; the brandy and one glass only. Be careful not to forget, for after my recent collapse I may need it.'

Thus came it about that, when at nearly midnight he heard the sound of his uncle's car returning down the drive from Sennetts, Alec was in his bedroom. But not in bed. He sat on a stool by the window. On a small table behind him stood an acetylene car-lamp with a sheet of heavy cardboard pressed against the glass to block its rays. In his right hand he held a shadow puppet ready for manipulation. Through the window he could now see the figure of his uncle moving up the ramp towards the athenæum. Just as the figure reached the highest point Alec suddenly whipped away the sheet of cardboard and manipulated his puppet. Simultaneously, on the white gable above his uncle, loomed a long-armed, narrow-bodied, spindly shadow, beckoning and waving.

There was no cry nor sound of any sort save a dull dead thud on the gravel path beneath the ramp. Within five seconds the acetylene lamp was in a cupboard, the puppet back in its box, and Alec's head on its pillow. Nothing occurred to disturb the remaining hours of night, but early next morning Larkin found the lights in the athenæum still burning. A moment later he knew the cause. Another light, and one that could not be relit, had been extinguished.

V

The interval between the inquests on uncle and nephew was almost exactly four months. Certain events during this period are worthy of brief record for the purposes of rounding off our tale.

Nobody knows whether Leonardo da Vinci liked or disliked the smile on his Mona Lisa. Worn by Miss Scettall on a call of condolence it infuriated the new master of Saintsend. So also did her remark that all of us must come to the grave *in due course*. What the hell did she mean by that? Had she any suspicions? Anyhow, he wasn't going to have her poking her nose into his affairs: so he told her bluntly that he attributed his uncle's death to her spook-raising and that she would not be welcomed at Saintsend again so long as he was there. 'No doubt you'll have company enough without me,' she had replied: and what exactly did she mean by that?

Larkin always said that his new young master's heavy drinking began on the night of the old one's funeral. A tile had been blown off the bedroom roof and while dressing for dinner Alec heard the drip-drip of a leak from the ceiling. The drops were falling on the puppet box, and removing the top ones he carefully wiped each before putting the box into a drier place. He did not trouble to wash his hands thereafter and Larkin said to him as he sat at table, 'Why, sir, your fingers is all bloody!' The crimson veneer from a damp puppet had in fact come off on them, but there seemed no sufficient reason in this for Alec's extreme concern and annoyance. His face turned scarlet and then suddenly white; he swore at Larkin and bade him bring a neat brandy.

On the following morning he threw the whole collection of shadow figures, box and all, into the river. Revisiting the place that evening he cursed himself for not having corded the box. As a result of

165

the omission one of the figures suddenly protruded itself at him from the swirl of an eddy. It seemed to him to have expanded in the water and to be now nearly life-size. That, of course, must have been an optical illusion; but Alec never cared to walk on the river-bank again and when the masons arrived by his order to pull down the garden wall he abruptly told them to leave it alone and get out. The same day he had his bed moved downstairs to a room at the opposite end of the corridor to where his uncle had slept. He was suffering, he said, from insomnia. A week or so later he ordered all windows on the river side of the house to be kept closed and shuttered by day as well as night.

The effects of heavy drinking had indeed begun to exact a heavy toll on mind and body. Larkin was accused of allowing young Tom to put scorpions and centipedes into Alec's boots and shoes and a scarlet mantis into his bed. All patterned carpets and rugs had soon to be taken up and stowed in the box-room, for Alec felt that in some strange way insects and shadow figures had got woven into the designs. Curtains were next taken down because of what he believed to lurk in their folds, and pictures because of what might hide behind them. No window might now be opened, even on the landward side, and bath plugs must be kept firmly in their sockets for fear of what might otherwise crawl out on him.

The faithful Larkin at last gave notice. Before its term was up, however, the end had come, and from a trivial causation. The Tillingford Grammar School was about to stage a speech-day pageant, of which one item would be a 'grasshopper parade' performed by the smaller boys. Their costumes, cheap but effective, were of green-dyed sacking with long thin osier shoots for antennæ and legs. After rehearsal one evening Tom, thus clad, ran up to Saintsend to show his father. In an end-of-term exuberance he jumped the little clipped yew hedge below the rose garden and landed nimbly on the lower lawn. Alec at this moment, perhaps in maudlin remorse, was gazing down from the stone ramp onto the spot in the gravel path below where his uncle had fallen to his death. Out of the corner of a bloodshot eye he caught a sudden glimpse of the boy-grasshopper. With a hysterical cry of 'Good God! That mantis again!' he stumbled, pitched forward and fell.

Larkin, who was tidying up inside the athenæum, heard both cry and thudding crunch. Quick though he ran to his master's assistance, it was to no use; for the neck was broken.

Saintsend thus passed into possession of a distant and wealthy cousin, John Fenderby-Judeson. Within a year or so he had made many improvements, including the removal of Matthew Judeson's wall. Later he married a neighbouring lady whose Christian name was seldom spoken, for he chose to call her 'Mona Lisa'. The most recent accounts from Tillingford and Fenfield suggest that the riverine air of Saintsend is not suiting her too well and that she would like the dividing wall to be rebuilt. She complains, too, of bad nights, but her husband assures her that, if only she will exercise patience, an end will surely come to them in due course.

11

A. N. L. MUNBY

A Christmas Game

The old country doctor who told me these strange events has died during the late war at the age of about eighty-five. He was a medical student at the time of the incidents which he related, so they can be assigned to the late seventies of the last century. I made profuse notes of his narrative, and I give it, as far as possible, in his own words.

I was spending Christmas with my family in Dorset—my father was a solicitor in Dorchester, and we lived in a comfortable Victorian house about three miles south of the town. The party in the house was a large one. It included my mother and her two unmarried sisters—my Aunts Emily and Gertrude—my younger brother Edward, who was then a schoolboy at Blundell's, and my two small sisters, Bella and Felicity, aged sixteen and ten respectively. In addition, we had staying with us our young cousin Giles; and a number of young people in the neighbourhood were constantly coming to see us, so everything indicated that we should have a festive Christmas holiday. I myself, the eldest son, was a medical student in London, and I arrived home on the afternoon of December the 22nd. Rather to my surprise my father was away when I got there, for he led a fairly leisurely existence, and normally took a clear week off for Christmas. I was told, however, that he had had to go to Exeter on business and would be returning that night.

It was about nine o'clock when I heard the wheels of our dogcart on the drive and I ran out to greet my father. I was astonished to see that he was not alone; for nothing had been said about his returning with a guest. However, a tall, elderly man dismounted with him, very much muffled up, who was introduced to me as Mr Fenton. My father asked me to take the dogcart round to the yard and to see to the horse, and he passed into the house with the stranger. When I returned, I met my mother in the hall. She seemed to have lost some of her normal placidity.

'Really,' she said, 'your dear father is the most impulsive man. He met Mr Fenton in Exeter, and apparently he knew him years and years ago. On hearing that he had nowhere to go for Christmas, he asked him to come and stay with us. He *is* so hospitable, and says that he couldn't bear the thought of anyone spending Christmas alone at an inn. I know that I ought to feel the same, but I *had* been looking forward so much to having just the family round me, and however nice Mr Fenton may be, he will still be a stranger. However, we must just make the best of it. Giles will have to move into Edward's room. . . .' And she digressed into domestic affairs.

In the drawing-room I was first able to get a proper view of our guest. He was old, I should think sixty-five, but he carried himself well. His face was bronzed and he had a high colour; his nose was aquiline and he had a patrician air about him. His expression was not a kindly one—it was hard, even forbidding in repose, and I could picture him as being given to fits of imperious anger. Altogether I fully shared my mother's regrets that such a stranger should have been introduced into our family circle at the Christmas season. Nevertheless, he greeted me politely and expressed his gratitude that my father had taken pity on his solitary condition, and he said that he hoped his presence would not in any way interfere with our plans. As a matter of fact, he proved a singularly unobtrusive guest, and seemed quite content to withdraw to my father's study with his book and his cigar, or to take long, solitary walks. At meals he took his share in the family small talk and made himself quite a favourite with my aunts.

It was at a meal—dinner on Christmas eve—that I committed inadvertently what seemed to be a *faux pas*. Something in our guest's conversation had given me the idea that he had travelled extensively. In some way or other discussion at table had turned itself to the topic of New Zealand, and in order to bring Mr Fenton into the conversation, I asked him if he had ever been there. He replied with the curt monosyllable 'Yes' and at once changed the subject. I caught a warning glance from my father's eye at the top of the table, and he gave an almost imperceptible shake of the head. After dinner he drew me to one side.

'I shouldn't raise the topic of New Zealand with Mr Fenton,' he said. 'I have done so myself on one occasion and he obviously found it distasteful. I know that he spent some years as a young man in the Colonial service, and I believe now that I remember hearing that some sort of scandal was circulating at the time of his retirement. I never knew the details—it was the merest rumour and nearly thirty years ago now.'

'When did you know him before?' I asked.

'As a boy,' he replied. 'His father owned considerable property in these parts, but he made a number of unwise speculations in railway stocks and died a comparatively poor man. That was no doubt the reason why his son went into the Colonial service. He has really changed very little since I first knew him. I recognized him at once.'

Christmas Day passed pleasantly enough. No doubt modern children would have found it intolerably dull, but we were content with simpler pleasures. The whole household went to church in the morning, and after luncheon the young people went for a walk with the dogs. It was not until we'd had our tea that the serious business of the day began. We all went into the drawing-room, where the Christmas tree had been set up; the servants filed in under the watchful eye of Watkins, our old butler, and we all received our presents. I was gratified to get a sovereign, neatly wrapped in tissue paper, from Mr Fenton, and my younger brother and two sisters received half a sovereign apiece from the same source. He seemed to be entering into the spirit of the occasion, and was quite genial at dinner, which followed at six. After the meal my smallest sister, Felicity, was sent up to bed, which occasioned a few tears, and the rest of us proceeded to play various games, such as Dumb Crambo and Forfeits, and the evening passed merrily.

At half-past eleven we started to play a game which had become almost a family institution. It was simple in the extreme. The lights were extinguished and a screen was drawn in front of the fire; then my father began to tell us a horrid tale, which gave rise to many delicious shudders. We children knew it almost by heart, but it never lost its appeal. It was my role to assist him in this, by passing round in the darkness certain objects which illustrated the story. I expect our modern psychoanalysts would say that it was harmful to the young, but in those days, thank God, we weren't burdened with that sort of moonshine. I still recall the plot of my father's tale. It described how a lonely traveller in North America had to pass through a dark, almost impenetrable forest. Night overtook him before he had reached his destination, and he became aware that stealthy footsteps were following him. Suddenly he heard the dreaded sound of the Indian's war-whoop, and he was surrounded by a band of yelling savages who dispatched him with their tomahawks. The abandoned wretches proceeded to dismember the corpse—first the scalp was removed. This was my cue to pass round the circle an old strip of a fur rug, which was greeted with much giggling and with exclamations of disgust from my aunts. Then my father described how the tongue of the victim was cut out, and I sent passing from hand to hand a small padded wash-leather bag, which I had carefully damped with glycerine. Finally the unfortunate man's eyes were gouged out, and this was the signal for my *pièce de résistance*. Two large muscatelle grapes had been peeled and I picked them up to hand them to my neighbour. This was Mr Fenton. He seemed unwilling to receive them, but I found his left hand in the darkness and thrust into it the slimy horrors. To my astonishment he gave an inarticulate half-strangled cry of disgust, and rising from his seat he snatched aside the firescreen and hurled the grapes into the flames. Then he took a step back and slumped into his chair, breathing heavily. An embarrassed silence fell upon the room, broken by my father's anxious query of 'Are you all right, Fenton?' There was no reply. In the flickering firelight I could see my father fumbling with a lamp. As the light came up we could see that our guest was lolling back in his chair with his head drooping at an unnatural angle. He was very pale and his eyes were closed. I expect you can imagine the confusion that broke out. My sister burst into tears, and one of my aunts started to scream hysterically, until my mother led her from the room. My father sent my cousin Giles post-haste for the doctor, and in the meantime he tried to revive Fenton with brandy. In the midst of all this, I was the only one present who looked into the fire. I suppose I wondered subconsciously why our guest had reacted so strangely to the grapes I had passed him. Anyhow I bent down to look into the grate for them. You won't believe me when I say what I saw. I swear that instead of grapes there was a pair of eyes, sizzling and sputtering in the flames. I know I wasn't mistaken, and I know they were human eyes. I'd seen enough in the dissecting-room to make no error about that. I was dreadfully shocked, but in some curious way I didn't question the evidence of my senses. I realized that I had come face to face with something outside the scope of my comprehension—something in which all my scientific training would be of no avail. I resolved to keep my discovery to myself—for I could visualize the effect that any disclosure on my part would have upon that overwrought room. So I seized the poker and brought the flaming logs tumbling down, and those dreadful relics were buried from sight.

All this took only a few seconds, and I was quickly helping my father to revive the prostrate man. A cursory examination showed that he was the victim of some sort of stroke—a condition beyond the range of my elementary medical knowledge. I was therefore relieved when Giles returned in a few minutes with the doctor, who was a near neighbour. He seemed to take a grave view of our guest's appearance. Under his direction we carried the unconscious figure up to his bedroom and undressed him, leaving him alone in the doctor's care.

By this time it was very late. The other members of the household had gone quickly off to their beds, and I went to my room, where I sat down for a few minutes to try to collect my thoughts. The house was now almost silent, and I was oppressed by my extraordinary experience. I tried to persuade myself that I'd been the victim of some sort of optical illusion—that the eyes had existed only in my imagination; but I had seen them so distinctly—the pupil, the iris, every detail. They had been dark brown, almost black. The more I thought about it, the more I was appalled and dismayed. The transition from the cheerful atmosphere of the Christmas party had been terrifyingly abrupt. It was as though a curtain had been lifted for a moment, and beyond it I had glimpsed another world, exempted from the laws of Nature. I recalled an old piece of ecclesiastical dogma that I'd heard quoted, 'God may work above Nature, but never contrary to Nature.' If I had observed a miracle, it had certainly no Divine origin.

My meditations were interrupted by a noise from downstairs, the intermittent scratching and whining of a dog, and I recollected that in the excitement of the evening, no one had put our spaniel, Danny, outside before locking up. I went down and let him out through the door in the drawing-room, which led on to the terrace. Then, as I had a few moments to wait I lit the lamp and seated myself on the sofa. The idea of waiting in that room without a light did not appeal to me. The fire had died to a few glowing embers, and whatever had been put there had been utterly consumed.

The minutes passed and I became impatient. I went to the door and whistled, but Danny did not come. He was normally a most obedient dog, and his behaviour seemed quite unaccountable. Suddenly he began to howl, low at first but increasing in mournful intensity, making an eerie sound that sent shivers down my spine. I realized that he had gone down the drive into the shrubbery, and I called him again sharply, but again with no result. Seriously irritated, I went out to find him and after some difficulty I located him in the laurels. He was still whining and whimpering when I came upon him, and as he paid no attention to my command to follow me back to the house, I stooped and picked him up. I was surprised to find that he was trembling violently, and as soon as he was in my arms he pushed his head inside my jacket and kept it there, while his body twitched and quaked. I turned towards the house and took a few steps up the drive. Then I stopped as though transfixed.

I had left the garden door of the drawing-room open, and through it the light was streaming out on to the terrace. Into this ray of light a figure was moving, approaching the open door with faltering steps. It became silhouetted in the doorway, and I was able to see its outlines clearly. It was a fantastic, incredible form to see in the familiar setting of my Dorset home. It was not a white man. I could see the gleam of a golden-brown body and a head covered with glossy black hair. One side of the face was visible and it was heavily tattooed. A short skirt of rush or flax was its sole covering, and its feet were bare. In one hand it held a stick, and I realized that it was blind, for it tapped gently upon the paving-stones and felt its way towards the door. In another moment it had passed into the room and was lost to my view.

173

I silently changed my position in order to see more, and in doing so I came nearer to the house. The figure came once more into my range of vision, and I saw that it was on its knees before the chair in which our guest had been sitting, and that it was searching feverishly upon the floor, groping blindly round the chairlegs with clawlike hands. I was near enough to hear it give a deep sigh of vexation as it found nothing. Then it turned to the remains of the fire and with fascinated horror I watched it plunge its hands into the still glowing embers and pull them out on to the hearth. It scrabbled in the red-hot ashes for a moment or two, then it gave a low cry, almost heart-rending in its bitterness and despair. No soul in limbo could have given vent to a sound more fraught with desolation. As I stood watching, it rose silently to its feet and moved across the room, out of my sight once more.

For some reason I was no longer afraid, just amazed and curious. I take no particular credit for this; I divined in some obscure way that the apparition, or whatever it may have been, was not malevolent to myself. So you need not think that I was exceptionally brave when I tell you that I strode quickly across the terrace and in through the door. The room was deserted; a second's glance told me this, and as I stood there the inner door of the room opened and my father came in. If the strange visitant had left, it could only have done so by the door at which he entered, and he must surely have passed it in the passage.

'Did you see anyone as you came in here?' I asked.

My father frowned and replied sharply. 'What are you talking about? Why on earth don't you go to bed? Shut the door and go upstairs at once. It's nearly two o'clock.'

I glanced at the fireplace before replying. There were the embers, scattered about the hearth—unshatterable testimony that my eyes had not deceived me. But I didn't say anything to my father about it. I went somewhat in awe of him, as did many sons at that date, and there was no very complete and frank understanding between us. I feared his anger and I feared his ridicule: I knew that any revelation on my part must bring both upon my head. So I stammered out some-thing about having let the dog out, holding out the now quiescent Danny as evidence for my words. Then I quickly locked up. My father waited until I'd finished.

'Fenton's pretty bad, I'm afraid,' he said; 'but the doctor says that there's a chance of recovery. I'm glad I asked him here. I wouldn't like to think of any friend of mine being taken ill staying alone at some inn. I'm sorry that it has spoilt our Christmas, though.'

We went up the stairs together, and on the landing my father wished me goodnight. As he did so, we heard a confused noise from Fenton's room. The old man must have recovered consciousness, for we could perceive quite distinctly his rather high, querulous tones intermingled with the quieter phrases of the doctor. As we listened the patient's voice became louder and we caught his words.

'Keep him off—keep him away,' he was shouting, 'for God's sake, don't let him come near me.'

Some reassuring remarks of the doctor's followed, but Fenton didn't seem to be pacified.

'Can't you see him?' he cried. 'Over there by the window!' His voice became shriller and he lapsed into some foreign language that I did not understand. The doctor's tones became louder and more authoritative as he said:

'Lie down, sir, lie down. I tell you there's nothing there. I assure you that there's no one in the room but you and myself.'

I looked questioningly at my father for direction, but he shook his head and said:

'I don't think we'd better go in. There's nothing we can do. Leave it to the doctor.'

He was interrupted by another series of cries, culminating in the sound of a struggle, as though Fenton were being forcibly held down upon his bed. Then, quite suddenly, there was utter silence for a period of perhaps two minutes. We waited, straining our ears. Our vigil was broken by the door being opened; the doctor stood upon the threshold, looking pale and tired.

'I'm afraid he's gone,' he said simply. Then, as my father stepped forward, he held up his hand and added:

'I should not go inside. The poor devil was in the grip of some terrifying hallucination at the end, and he didn't have a very peaceful passage. His appearance would only upset you. You go off to bed. I'll make all the necessary arrangements.'

We obeyed and tiptoed quietly away. When I got to my room I found that I still had Danny in my arms, and very glad I was of his company for the remainder of that night.

It must have been quite ten years later, when I was qualified and in practice at Cheltenham, that I met a man who knew Fenton's name. He was a retired sheep farmer who had spent twenty-five years in New Zealand, and though he was too young to have known Fenton personally, he knew him by repute. It was from him that I learned some details of the scandal that surrounded Fenton's retirement from the Colonial service. Dark stories of his ruthlessness and brutality as an administrator had for a time been circulating, but finally there had been an incident which the authorities could not ignore. Under Fenton's direction an alleged malefactor had been subjected to torture, in order to wring a confession from him. When other methods had failed, he had been threatened with blinding, and upon his still remaining obdurate, this dire threat had been carried out. A subsequent inquiry had established the native's innocence, but for the sake of British prestige there had been no public denunciation of the public servant, who had so grossly exceeded his powers. Fenton's only punishment was to be sent home. But though his retribution was light at the hands of men, it would seem that finally he was called to account before a different and a higher court.

12

SHAMUS FRAZER

Florinda

'Did you and Miss Reeve have a lovely walk, darling?' Clare asked of the child in the tarnished depths of glass before her.

'Well, it was lovely for me but not for Miss Reeve, because she tore her stocking on a bramble, and it bled.'

'The stocking?'

'No, that ran a beautiful ladder,' said Jane very solemnly. 'But there were two long tears on her leg as if a cat had scratched her. We were going along by the path by the lake when the brambles caught her. She almost fell in. She *did* look funny, Mummy, hopping on the bank like a hen blackbird a cat's playing with—and squawking.'

'*Poor* Miss Reeve! . . . Your father's going to have that path cleared soon; it's quite overgrown.'

'Oh, I hope not soon, Mummy. I love the brambly places, and what the birds and rabbits'll do if they're cut down I can't imagine. The thickety bushes are all hopping and fluttering with them when you walk. And the path wriggles as if it were living, too—so you must lift your feet high and stamp on it, the way Florinda does . . .'

But Clare was not listening any more. She had withdrawn her glance from Jane's grave elfin features in the shadowed recesses of the glass to fix it on her own image, spread as elegantly upon its surface as a swan.

'And if Daddy has the bushes cut down,' Jane went on, 'what will poor Florinda do? Where will she play? There will be no place at all for the little traps and snares she sets; no place for her to creep and whistle in, and tinkle into laughter when something funny happens— like Miss Reeve caught by the leg and hopping.' This was the time, when her mother was not listening, that Jane could talk most easily about Florinda. She looked at her mother's image, wrapt in the dull mysteries of grown-up thought within the oval Chippendale glass—and thence to the rococo frame of gilded wood in whose interlacing design two birds of faded gilt, a bat with a chipped wing and flowers whose golden petals and leaves showed here and there little spots and tips of white plaster like a disease, were all caught for ever.

'That's how I met Florinda.' She was chattering quite confidently, now that she knew that it was only to herself. 'I had been down to the edge of the lake where there are no brambles—you know, the *lawn* side; and I knelt down to look at myself in the water, *and there were two of me*. That's what I thought at first—two of me. And then I saw one was someone else—it was Florinda, smiling at me; but I couldn't smile back, not for anything. There we were like you and me in the glass—one smiling and one very solemn. Then Miss Reeve called and Florinda just *went*—and my face was alone and astonished in the water. She's shy, Florinda is—and sly, too. Shy and sly—that's Florinda for you.'

The repeated name stirred Clare to a vague consciousness: she had heard it on Jane's lips before.

'Who is Florinda?' she asked.

'Mummy, I've told you. She's a doll, I think, only large, large as me. And she never talks—not with words, anyway. And her eyes can't shut even when she lies down.'

'I thought she was called Arabella.'

'That's the doll Uncle Richard gave me last Christmas. Arabella *does* close her eyes when *she* lies down, and she says "Good night, Mamma," too, because of the gramophone record inside her. But Florinda's different. She's not a house doll. She belongs outside—though I *have* asked her to come to tea on Christmas Eve.'

'Well, darling, I've lots of letters to write, so just you run along to the nursery and have a lovely tea.'

So Florinda was a doll—an ideal doll, it seemed, that Jane had invented in anticipation of Christmas. Nine in the New Year, Jane was growing perhaps a little old for dolls. A strange child, thought Clare, difficult to understand. In that she took after her mother—though in looks it was her father she resembled. With a sigh Clare slid out the drawer of the mahogany writing-desk. She distributed writing-paper and envelopes, the Christmas cards (reproductions of Alken prints), in neat piles over the red leather—and, opening her address-book, set herself to write.

Roger came in with the early December dusk. He had been tramping round the estate with Wakefield the agent, and the cold had painted his cheeks blue and nipped his nose red so that he looked like a large, clumsy gnome. He kissed Clare on the nape, and the icy touch of his nose spread gooseflesh over her shoulders.

'You go and pour yourself some whisky,' she said, 'and thaw yourself out by the fire. I'll be with you in a minute.' She addressed two more envelopes in her large clear hand, and then, without looking round, said: 'Have we bitten off rather more than we can chew?'

'There's an awful lot to be done,' said her husband from the fire, 'so much one hardly knows where to begin. The woods are a shambles—Nissen huts, nastiness and barbed wire. One would have thought Uncle Eustace would have made some effort to clear up the mess after the army moved out . . .'

'But, darling, he never came back to live here. He was too wise.'

'Too ill and too old—and he never gave a thought to those who'd inherit the place, I suppose.'

'He never thought we'd be foolish enough to come and live here, anyway.'

Roger's uncle had died in a nursing-home in Bournemouth earlier in the year, and Roger had come into these acres of Darkshire park and woodland, and the sombre peeling house, Fowling Hall, set among them. At Clare's urging he had tried to sell the place, but there were no offers. And now Roger had the obstinate notion of settling here, and trying to make pigs and chickens pay for the upkeep of the estate. Of course, Clare knew, there was something else behind this recent interest in the country life. Nothing had been said, but she knew what Roger wanted, and she knew, too, that he would hint at it again before long—the forbidden subject. She stacked her letters on the desk and went to join him by the fire.

'There's one thing you *can* do,' she said. 'Clear that path that goes round the lake. Poor Miss Reeve tore herself quite nastily on a bramble this afternoon, walking there.'

179

'I'll remind Wakefield to get the men on the job tomorrow. And what was Jane doing down by the lake just now as I came in? I called her and she ran off into the bushes.'

'My dear, Jane's been up in the nursery for the last hour or more. Miss Reeve's reading to her. You know, she's not allowed out this raw weather except when the sun's up. The doctor said—'

'Well, I wondered . . . I only glimpsed her—a little girl in the dusk. She ran off when I called.'

'One of the workmen's children, I expect.'

'Perhaps . . . Strange, I didn't think of that.'

He took a gulp of whisky, and changed the subject: 'Clare, it's going to cost the earth to put this place properly in order. It would be worth it if . . . if . . .' He added with an effort, 'I mean, if one thought it was leading anywhere . . .'

So it had come out, the first hint.

'You mean if we had a son, don't you? . . . Don't you, Roger?' She spoke accusingly.

'I merely meant . . . Well, yes—though, of course—'

She didn't let him finish. 'But you know what the doctor said after Jane. You know how delicate she is . . . You can't want—?'

'If she had a brother—' Roger began.

Clare laughed, a sudden shiver of laughter, and held her hands to the fire.

'Roger, what an open hypocrite you are! "If she had a brother," when all the time you mean "if I had a son". And how could you be certain it wouldn't be a sister? No, Roger, we've had this out a thousand times in the past. It can't be done.' She shook her head and blinked at the fire. 'It wouldn't work out.'

Roger went into the nursery, as was his too irregular custom, to say good night to Jane. She was in her pink fleecy dressing-gown, slippered toes resting on the wire fender, a bowl emptied of bread and milk on her knees. Miss Reeve was reading her a story about a princess who was turned by enchantment into a fox.

'Don't let me interrupt, Miss Reeve. I'll look in again later.'

'Oh, do come in, Mr Waley. We're almost ready for bed.'

'I was sorry to hear about your accident this afternoon.'

'It was such a silly thing, really. I caught my foot in a slipnoose of bramble. It was as if somebody had set it on the path on purpose, only that would be too ridiculous for words. But it was a shock—and I tore myself painfully, trying to get free.'

There was still the ghost of that panic, Roger noticed, in Miss Reeve's pasty, pudgy features, and signalling behind the round lenses of her spectacles. 'It's not a very nice path for a walk,' she added, 'but one can't keep Jane away from the lake.'

'I'm having all the undergrowth cleared away from the banks,' said Roger; 'that should make it easier walking.'

'Oh, that'll be ever so much nicer, Mr Waley.'

'Florinda won't like it,' thought Jane, sitting stiffly in her wicker chair by the fire. 'She won't like it at all. She'll be in a wicked temper will Florinda.' But she said aloud in a voice of small protest—for what was the use of speaking about Florinda to grown-ups—'It won't be nice at all. It will be quite horribly beastly.'

The men didn't care for the work they had been set to do. It was the skeletons, they said—and they prodded suspiciously with their implements at the little lumps of bone and feather and fur that their cutting and scything had revealed. There was a killer somewhere in the woods; owls said one, stoats said another, but old Renshawe said glumly it was neither bird nor beast, that it was Something-that-walked-that-shouldn't, and this infected the others with a derisive disquiet. All the same, fifty yards of path were cleared during the morning, which took them beyond the small Doric pavilion that once served as boathouse and was reflected by a stone twin housing the loch mechanism on the eastern side of the lake.

Miss Reeve took Jane out in the afternoon to watch the men's progress. Jane ran ahead down the cleared path; paused at the pavilion to hang over the flaking balustrade and gaze down into the water: whispered something, shook her head and ran on.

'Hullo, Mr Renshawe—*alone*?' she cried, as rounding a sudden twist in the path she came upon the old man hacking at the undergrowth. Renshawe started and cut short, and the blade bit into his foot. This accident stopped work for the day.

'It wasn't right, Miss Jane, to come on me like that,' he said, as they were helping him up to the house. 'You gave me a real turn. I thought—'

'I know,' said Jane, fixing him with her serious, puzzled eyes. 'And she *was* there, too, watching all the time.'

Whatever the killer was, it moved its hunting-ground that night. Two White Orpingtons were found dead beside the arks next morning, their feathers scattered like snow over the bare ground.

'And it's not an animal, neither,' said Ron, the boy who carried the mash into the runs and had discovered the kill.

'What do you mean, it's not an animal?' asked Wakefield.

'I mean that their necks is wrung, Mr Wakefield.'

'Oh, get away!' said Wakefield.

But the following morning another hen was found lying in a mess of feathers and blood, and Wakefield reported to his master.

'It can't be it's a fox, sir. That head's not been bitten off. It's been pulled off, sir . . . And there was this, sir, was found by the arks.' It was a child's bracelet of blackened silver.

The path was cleared, but on the further side of the lake the shrubberies that melted imperceptibly into the tall woods bordered it closely. Here Jane dawdled on her afternoon walk. At the bend in the path near the boathouse she waited until her governess was out of sight—and then called softly into the gloom of yew and rhododendron and laurel, 'I think you're a beast, a *beast*! And I'm not going to be your friend any more, d'you hear? And you're *not* to come on Christmas Eve, even if you're starving.'

There was movement in the shadows, and she glimpsed the staring blue eyes and pinched face and the tattered satin finery. 'And it's no use following us, so there!' Jane stuck her tongue out as a gesture of defiance, and ran away along the path.

'Are you all right?' asked Miss Reeve, who had turned back to look for her. 'I thought I heard someone crying.'

'Oh, it's only Florinda,' said Jane, 'and she can sob her eyes out now for all I care.'

'Jane,' said Miss Reeve severely, 'how many more times have I to tell you Florinda is a naughty fib, and we shouldn't tell naughty fibs even in fun?'

'It's no fun,' said Jane, so low that Miss Reeve could hardly catch a word, 'no fun at all being Florinda.'

A hard frost set in overnight. It made a moon landscape of the park and woods, and engraved on the nursery window-panes, sharply as with a diamond, intricate traceries of silver fern. The bark of the trees was patterned with frost like chain-mail, and from the gaunt branches icicle daggers glinted in the sun. Each twig of the bare shrubs had budded its tear-drops of ice. The surface of the lake was wrinkled and grey like the face of an old woman. 'And Wakefield says if it keeps up we may be able to skate on it on Boxing Day . . .' But by mid-day the temperature rose and all out-of-doors was filled with a mournful pattering and dripping.

Towards evening a dirty yellow glow showed in the sky, and furry black clouds moved up over the woods, bringing snow. It snowed after that for two days, and then it was Christmas Eve.

'You *look* like the Snow Queen, but you *smell* like the Queen of Sheba. Must you go out tonight, Mummy?'

'Darling, it's a bore. We promised Lady Graves, so we have to.'

'You should have kept your fingers crossed. But you'll be back soon?'

'In time to catch Father Christmas climbing down the chimneys, I expect.'

'But earlier than that—promise . . .?'

'Much earlier than that. Daddy wants to get back early, anyway. He and Wakefield had a tiring night sitting up with a gun to guard their precious hens . . .'

'But she . . . it never came, did it?'

'Not *last* night. And now you go to lovely sleeps, and when you wake perhaps Father Christmas will have brought you Florinda in his—'

'No,' cried the child, 'not Florinda, Mummy, *please*.'

'What a funny thing you are,' said Clare, stooping to kiss her; 'you were quite silly about her a few days ago . . .'

183

Jane shivered and snuggled down in the warm bed.

'I've changed,' she said. 'We're not friends any more.'

After the lights were out, Jane imagined she was walking in the snow. The snowflakes fell as lightly as kisses, and soon they had covered her with a white, soft down. Now she knew herself to be a swan, and she tucked her head under a wing and so fell asleep on the dark rocking water.

But in the next room Miss Reeve, who had gone to bed early, could not sleep because of the wind that sobbed so disquietingly around the angles of the house. At last she put out a hand to the bedside table, poured herself water, groped for the aspirin bottle and swallowed down three tablets at a gulp. It was as she rescrewed the top, she noticed that it was not the aspirin bottle she was holding. She could have sworn that the sleeping-tablets had been in her dressing-table drawer. Her first thought was that someone had changed the bottles on purpose, but that, she told herself, would be too absurd. There was nothing she could do about it. The crying of the wind mounted to shrill broken fluting that sounded oddly like children's laughter.

The first thing they noticed when the car drew up, its chained tyres grinding and clanking under the dark porch, was that the front door was ajar. 'Wait here,' said Roger to the chauffeur, 'there seem to have been visitors while we were away.'

Clare switched on the drawing-room lights, and screamed at the demoniac havoc they revealed, the chairs and tables overturned, the carpet a litter of broken porcelain, feathers from the torn cushions, and melting snow. Someone had thrown the heavy silver inkwell at the wall glass, which hung askew, its surface cracked and starred, and the delicate frame broken.

'No sane person—' Roger began.

But already Clare was running up the stairs to the nursery and screaming, 'Jane! . . . Jane!' as she ran.

The nursery was wrecked, too—the sheets clawed in strips, the floor a drift of feathers from the ripped pillows. Only the doll Arabella, with a shattered head, was propped up in the empty bed. When Clare touched her she fell backwards and began to repeat, 'Good night, Mamma!' as the mechanism inside her worked.

They found Jane's footsteps in the snow, leading over the lawn in the direction of the lake. Once they thought they saw her ahead of them, but it was only the snowman Roger had helped her to build during the afternoon. There was a misty moon, and by its light they followed the small naked footprints to the edge of the lake—but their eyes could make out nothing beyond the snow-fringed ice.

Roger had sent on the chauffeur to a bend in the drive where the car headlights could illuminate the further bank. And now, in the sudden glare, they saw in the dark centre of ice the two small figures, Jane in her nightdress, and beside her a little girl in old-fashioned blue satin who walked oddly and jerkily, lifting her feet and stamping them on the ice.

They called together, 'Jane! . . . Jane! Come back!'

She seemed to have heard, and she turned, groping towards the light. The other caught at her arm, and the two struggled together on the black, glassy surface. Then from the stars it seemed, and into their cold hearts, fell a sound like the snapping of a giant lute-string. The two tiny interlocked figures had disappeared, and the ice moaned and tinkled at the edges of the lake.

NOTES

1

'Wicked Captain Walshawe, of Wauling' by J[oseph] S[heridan] Le Fanu (1814–73). First published in the *Dublin University Magazine* (Apr. 1864); first reprinted in M. R. James's selection of previously uncollected stories, *Madam Crowl's Ghost, and Other Tales of Mystery* (1923). Le Fanu, one of the first writers to explore the psychological dimensions of the ghost story, was the son of an Anglo-Irish Protestant clergyman. He was educated at Trinity College, Dublin, and published his first novel, *The Cock and Anchor*, a costume romance in the style of W. H. Ainsworth and G. W. M. Reynolds, in 1845 at the age of 31, though his first short story had appeared in 1838. In 1861 he purchased the *Dublin University Magazine*, in which many of his stories and novels were first published. Le Fanu was placed by M. R. James 'absolutely in the first rank as a writer of ghost stories'.

2

'A Terrible Vengeance' by Mrs J. H. [Charlotte Elizabeth Lawson] Riddell, *née* Cowan (1832–1906). From *Princess Sunshine, and Other Stories* (2 vols., 1889). Born at Carrickfergus, County Antrim, Charlotte Riddell was a prolific and industrious writer of fiction and short stories. Known especially for her novels set in the City of London, she struggled in later life to pay off huge debts left behind at the death of her husband, Joseph Riddell. Her most successful novel was *George Geith of Fen Court* (1864), which transferred with equal success to the stage. Six of her best supernatural tales were collected in *Weird Stories* (1884).

3

'Number 13' by M[ontague] R[hodes] James (1862–1936). From *Ghost Stories of an Antiquary* (1904). James was, by common consent, one of the most original and influential ghost-story writers of the early twentieth century. Successively Provost of King's College, Cambridge, and of Eton, he used his immense erudition to create a distinct species of supernatural fiction, the antiquarian ghost story, which has spawned a host of imitators. The setting of 'Number 13' was inspired by holidays taken by James in Denmark in 1899 and 1900. James was proficient in Danish and later translated forty stories by Hans Christian Andersen (published 1930).

4

'Railhead' by Perceval Landon (1869–1927). From *Raw Edges: Studies and Stories of These Days* (1908). Landon, a barrister and journalist, was the author of one of the most powerful and frequently anthologized ghost stories in English, 'Thurnley Abbey'. *Raw Edges* was his only collection of stories.

5

'The Toll-House' by W[illiam] W[ymark] Jacobs (1863–1943). From *Sailors' Knots* (1909). Journalist, dramatist, and humorist, Jacobs is mainly remembered as the author of 'The Monkey's Paw' (1902), probably the best-known ghost story of the twentieth century and subsequently dramatized for both the stage and for radio. Amongst contemporary readers he achieved great popularity through his short stories about seafaring characters on shore and at sea. His collections in this vein included *Many Cargoes* (1896) and *Light Freights* (1901).

6

'The Face' by E[dward] F[rederic] Benson (1867–1940). From *Spook Stories* (1928). Fred Benson—son of Edward White Benson, Archbishop of Canterbury, and brother of A. C. and R. H. Benson—came to prominence as a writer with his successful society novel *Dodo* (1893) but is now remembered chiefly for his comic tales featuring Mapp and Lucia. All three Benson brothers wrote supernatural fiction, but Fred was the most prolific and his stories continue to be savoured by enthusiasts. They are mainly collected in *The Room in the Tower* (1912), *Visible and Invisible* (1923), *Spook Stories* (1928), and *More Spook Stories* (1934). A further volume of mostly uncollected stories, edited by Jack Adrian, was published in 1988 as *The Flint Knife: Further Spook Stories*.

7

'The Tool' by W[illiam] F[ryer] Harvey (1885–1937). From *The Beast With Five Fingers* (1928). A Yorkshireman by birth and educated at Balliol College, Oxford, Harvey went on to study medicine and served as a Surgeon-Lieutenant in the Royal Navy during the First World War. His supernatural stories are consistently well written and he excels at describing characters who find themselves being controlled by forces and processes that they cannot understand.

8

'Look Up There' by H[erbert] Russell Wakefield (1888–1964). From *Old Man's Beard: Fifteen Disturbing Tales* (1929). Little is known of Wakefield's life. He was educated at Marlborough and at University College, Oxford. In 1911 he became personal private secretary to Lord Northcliffe and during the First World War served with the Royal Scots Fusiliers. Though admired by devotees of supernatural fiction, he has never achieved the wider fame enjoyed by contemporaries such as M. R. James. His other collections include *They Return at Evening* (1928) and *Imagine a Man in a Box* (1931).

9

'The Last Bouquet' by Marjorie Bowen (i.e. Gabrielle Margaret Vere Campbell Long, 1886–1952). From *The Last Bouquet* (1933). It was after reading Marjorie Bowen's novel *The Viper of Milan* at the age of 14 that Graham Greene decided he would become a writer: 'One could not read her', he said later, 'without believing that to write was to live and to enjoy.' Bowen's large output included historical novels, children's books, and short stories, including many tales of horror and the supernatural. Amongst her best-known pieces of supernatural fiction are 'The Avenging of Ann Leete' and 'The Crown Derby Plate'.

10

'In Due Course' by Sir Andrew Caldecott (1884–1951). From *Not Exactly Ghosts* (1947). Caldecott was a career Civil Servant who spent many years in the Malay Service and became governor of Hong Kong, and later Ceylon. His Far Eastern experiences inform several of his stories set in the fictitious colony of Kongea. *Not Exactly Ghosts*, written in his retirement, was followed in 1948 by a second collection of stories, *Fire Burns Blue*.

11

'A Christmas Game' by A[lan] N[oel] L[atimer] Munby (1913–74). From *The Alabaster Hand, and Other Ghost Stories* (1949). Like his mentor in supernatural fiction, M. R. James, 'Tim' Munby was a Fellow of King's College, Cambridge, and a distinguished bibliographer who used his antiquarian knowledge to enrich the background of his stories, which were written whilst Munby was a prisoner of war in Germany from 1942 to 1945.

12

'Florinda' by Shamus Frazer (i.e. James Ian Arbuthnot Frazer, 1912–66). From *The Tandem Book of Ghost Stories* (1965). Oxford educated, Frazer achieved some success during the 1930s and 1940s with novels such as *Acorned Hog* (1933) and *Blow, Blow Your Trumpets* (1945). In 1965, the year before his death, four of his supernatural stories appeared in anthologies; others, intended to be collected as *Where Human Pathways End: Tales of the Dead and the Undead*, remained unpublished.

ACKNOWLEDGEMENTS

The editor and publisher gratefully acknowledge permission to use the following copyright material:

E. F. Benson, 'The Face' from *Spook Stories* (1928). Reproduced by kind permission of A. P. Watt Ltd., London, on behalf of the executors of the estate of K. S. P. McDowell.

Sir A. Caldecott, 'In Due Course' from *Not Exactly Ghosts* (1947). Reprinted by kind permission of the author's family.

W. W. Jacobs, 'The Toll-House' from *Sailors' Knots* (1909). © The Society of Authors as the literary representative of the estate of W. W. Jacobs.

M. R. James, 'Number 13' from *Ghost Stories of an Antiquary* (1904). Reprinted by kind permission of N. J. R. James.

A. N. L. Munby, 'A Christmas Game' from *The Alabaster Hand, and Other Ghost Stories* (1949). Reprinted by kind permission of Mrs Sheila Munby.

OXFORD

MORE OXFORD PAPERBACKS

This book is just one of nearly 1000 Oxford Paperbacks currently in print. If you would like details of other Oxford Paperbacks, including titles in the World's Classics, Oxford Reference, Oxford Books, OPUS, Past Masters, Oxford Authors, and Oxford Shakespeare series, please write to:

UK and Europe: Oxford Paperbacks Publicity Manager, Arts and Reference Publicity Department, Oxford University Press, Walton Street, Oxford OX2 6DP.

Customers in UK and Europe will find Oxford Paperbacks available in all good bookshops. But in case of difficulty please send orders to the Cash-with-Order Department, Oxford University Press Distribution Services, Saxon Way West, Corby, Northants NN18 9ES. Tel: 01536 741519; Fax: 01536 746337. Please send a cheque for the total cost of the books, plus £1.75 postage and packing for orders under £20; £2.75 for orders over £20. Customers outside the UK should add 10% of the cost of the books for postage and packing.

USA: Oxford Paperbacks Marketing Manager, Oxford University Press, Inc., 200 Madison Avenue, New York, N.Y. 10016.

Canada: Trade Department, Oxford University Press, 70 Wynford Drive, Don Mills, Ontario M3C 1J9.

Australia: Trade Marketing Manager, Oxford University Press, G.P.O. Box 2784Y, Melbourne 3001, Victoria.

South Africa: Oxford University Press, P.O. Box 1141, Cape Town 8000.

ILLUSTRATED HISTORIES IN
OXFORD PAPERBACKS

THE OXFORD ILLUSTRATED HISTORY
OF ENGLISH LITERATURE

Edited by Pat Rogers

Britain possesses a literary heritage which is almost unrivalled in the Western world. In this volume, the richness, diversity, and continuity of that tradition are explored by a group of Britain's foremost literary scholars.

Chapter by chapter the authors trace the history of English literature, from its first stirrings in Anglo-Saxon poetry to the present day. At its heart towers the figure of Shakespeare, who is accorded a special chapter to himself. Other major figures such as Chaucer, Milton, Donne, Wordsworth, Dickens, Eliot, and Auden are treated in depth, and the story is brought up to date with discussion of living authors such as Seamus Heaney and Edward Bond.

'[a] lovely volume . . . put in your thumb and pull out plums' Michael Foot

'scholarly and enthusiastic people have written inspiring essays that induce an eagerness in their readers to return to the writers they admire' *Economist*

CLASSICS

Mary Beard and John Henderson

This *Very Short Introduction* to Classics links a haunting temple on a lonely mountainside to the glory of ancient Greece and the grandeur of Rome, and to Classics within modern culture—from Jefferson and Byron to Asterix and Ben-Hur.

'This little book should be in the hands of every student, and every tourist to the lands of the ancient world . . . a splendid piece of work'
Peter Wiseman
Author of *Talking to Virgil*

'an eminently readable and useful guide to many of the modern debates enlivening the field . . . the most up-to-date and accessible introduction available'
Edith Hall
Author of *Inventing the Barbarian*

'lively and up-to-date . . . it shows classics as a living enterprise, not a warehouse of relics'
New Statesman and Society

'nobody could fail to be informed and entertained—the accent of the book is provocative and stimulating'
Times Literary Supplement

POLITICS

Kenneth Minogue

Since politics is both complex and controversial it is easy to miss the wood for the trees. In this Very Short Introduction Kenneth Minogue has brought the many dimensions of politics into a single focus: he discusses both the everyday grind of democracy and the attraction of grand ideals such as freedom and justice.

'Kenneth Minogue is a very lively stylist who does not distort difficult ideas.'
Maurice Cranston

'a dazzling but unpretentious display of great scholarship and humane reflection'
Professor Neil O'Sullivan, University of Hull

'Minogue is an admirable choice for showing us the nuts and bolts of the subject.'
Nicholas Lezard, *Guardian*

'This is a fascinating book which sketches, in a very short space, one view of the nature of politics . . . the reader is challenged, provoked and stimulated by Minogue's trenchant views.'
Talking Politics

ARCHAEOLOGY

Paul Bahn

'Archaeology starts, really, at the point when the first recognizable 'artefacts' appear—on current evidence, that was in East Africa about 2.5 million years ago—and stretches right up to the present day. What you threw in the garbage yesterday, no matter how useless, disgusting, or potentially embarrassing, has now become part of the recent archaeological record.'

This Very Short Introduction reflects the enduring popularity of archaeology—a subject which appeals as a pastime, career, and academic discipline, encompasses the whole globe, and surveys 2.5 million years. From deserts to jungles, from deep caves to mountain-tops, from pebble tools to satellite photographs, from excavation to abstract theory, archaeology interacts with nearly every other discipline in its attempts to reconstruct the past.

'very lively indeed and remarkably perceptive . . . a quite brilliant and level-headed look at the curious world of archaeology'
Professor Barry Cunliffe,
University of Oxford

BUDDHISM

Damien Keown

'Karma can be either good or bad. Buddhists speak of good karma as "merit", and much effort is expended in acquiring it. Some picture it as a kind of spiritual capital—like money in a bank account—whereby credit is built up as the deposit on a heavenly rebirth.'

This Very Short Introduction introduces the reader both to the teachings of the Buddha and to the integration of Buddhism into daily life. What are the distinctive features of Buddhism? Who was the Buddha, and what are his teachings? How has Buddhist thought developed over the centuries, and how can contemporary dilemmas be faced from a Buddhist perspective?

'Damien Keown's book is a readable and wonderfully lucid introduction to one of mankind's most beautiful, profound, and compelling systems of wisdom. The rise of the East makes understanding and learning from Buddhism, a living doctrine, more urgent than ever before. Keown's impressive powers of explanation help us to come to terms with a vital contemporary reality.'
Bryan Appleyard

JUDAISM

Norman Solomon

'Norman Solomon has achieved the near impossible with his enlightened very short introduction to Judaism. Since it is well known that Judaism is almost impossible to summarize, and that there are as many different opinions about Jewish matters as there are Jews, this is a small masterpiece in its success in representing various shades of Jewish opinion, often mutually contradictory. Solomon also manages to keep the reader engaged, never patronizes, assumes little knowledge but a keen mind, and takes us through Jewish life and history with such gusto that one feels enlivened, rather than exhausted, at the end.'
Rabbi Julia Neuberger

'This book will serve a very useful purpose indeed. I'll use it myself to discuss, to teach, agree with, and disagree with, in the Jewish manner!'
Rabbi Lionel Blue

'A magnificent achievement. Dr Solomon's treatment, fresh, very readable, witty and stimulating, will delight everyone interested in religion in the modern world.'
Dr Louis Jacobs, University of London

THE GREAT GAME
ON SECRET SERVICE IN HIGH ASIA

Peter Hopkirk

For nearly a century the two most powerful nations on earth—Victorian Britain and Tsarist Russia—fought a secret war in the lonely passes and deserts of Central Asia. Those engaged in this shadowy struggle called it the 'Great Game', a phrase immortalized in Kipling's *Kim*.

When play first began the two rival empires lay nearly 2,000 miles apart. By the end, some Russian outposts were within 20 miles of India.

This book tells the story of the Great Game through the exploits of the young officers, both British and Russian, who risked their lives playing it. Disguised as holy men or native horse-traders, they mapped secret passes, gathered intelligence, and sought the allegiance of powerful khans. Some never returned.

'A terrific collection of yarns; an invaluable work of imperial history.'
Observer

'brilliant'
Daily Telegraph

'highly entertaining'
Independent on Sunday